Written, Illustrated & Designed in Ukraine
Printed in the United Kingdom

The Black Sea
WHALE

A Beacon in the Sea of Troubles

Editor-in-Chief: Ulana Suprun
Managing Editor: Viktoriia Antonenko

Copy Editor: James Merritt
Production Supervisor: Irina Yurchenko
Stories written by Oleksii Dubrov, Marichka Melnyk, Cadmus,
Oleh Mahdych, Viktoriia Antonenko, Nazar Tokar, Sergej Sumlenny.
Illustrated by Beata Kurkul, Antonina Semenova, Oleh Smal, Olenka Zahorodnyk,
Mykhailo Aleksandrov, Asta Legios, Uliana Balan, Oleksandr Terez.
Titans of translation include Ardis Chrystal and Stefko Bandera.
Cover illustrated by Mykhailo Aleksandrov.
Journal designed by Zakhar Kryvoshyya.
The font Kamenyar is designed by Zakhar Kryvoshyya
and *Humus* is designed by Andrij Shevchenko.
Produced by Marko Suprun.

WWW.BLACKSEAWHALE.COM
The Black Sea Whale is published by Rogue Umbrella, LTD.
ISBN 978-1-7385616-1-2

Please send reprint, corrections, or other inquiries to: story@blackseawhale.com
If you are interested in writing or illustrating for *The Black Sea Whale*,
please send an email to: story@blackseawhale.com
Printed by Park Communications, a Carbon Neutral Company,
on FSC® certified paper.

Business operations with financial
climate contribution
ClimatePartner.com/13766-2411-1004

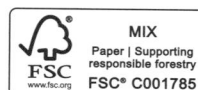

MIX
Paper | Supporting
responsible forestry
FSC® C001785
www.fsc.org

No matter how they spin it, it ends the same:
That torturers ignored the lesson, for shame.
They may shoot the brain where ideas are wrought,
But never can they execute all thoughts.

—VASYL SYMONENKO
(8.01.1935–13.12.1963)

CONTENTS

THE END OF TYRANNY
BEGINS WITH SAVING A WHALE

"We speak for the 70 countries that have begged you: stop whaling!"

Twenty-four metres is about seven storeys and when looking up from the streets of London at a building of that height, it does seem impressive. But standing on an object of similar size, like the deck of a 24-metre-long ship floating in the Pacific Ocean, one can't help but feel Lilliputian-like tiny.

The sides of this particular ship were brightly painted with red, yellow, green, blue, and purple stripes and an image of a sperm whale, and a red-and-white flag with a maple leaf was unfurled on the mast. On the deck, a bearded man with wind-tousled hair dressed in a black shirt with a bright floral print was shouting through a loudspeaker: "These whales belong to all the people of the Earth, not just those proud and mighty, successful nations like yours, which have the machinery to kill them." Ironically, the man's name was Bob Hunter, and he was talking through a megaphone to the sailors who were standing along the railings of the *Dalniy Vostok*,

a massive ship with three decks, 182 metres long and 24 metres wide. The ship's hull was awash with reddish brown stains and bloody detritus.

The *Dalniy Vostok* was a whaling ship, whose name translates as the "Far East," an homage to the remote region that made up one third of the territory of the Soviet Union and now comprises more than 40 per cent of the Russian Federation. In 1963, the ship took its maiden voyage and together with 12 slightly smaller vessels, it formed the Soviet Russian Empire's hunt for whales in the North Pacific. In the summer of 1976, somewhere in the waters between Mexico and Hawaii, a confrontation took place between a handful of scruffy eco-activists from Vancouver and the Soviet whale hunters. Only five years earlier, the activists had created an organisation to raise awareness about the spread of nuclear weapons, global warming, and the genocide of whales, naming it Greenpeace. With only a paltry five years of eco-activism, these rookies were facing more than 40 years of Soviet whaling experience (not counting the whale hunting days of the Russian Empire). Indeed, the then Soviet whale hunters ranked in first place among all other countries of the world, even outdoing Japan, in the killing of whales. The odds of stopping the Soviet Russian slaughter of whales were clearly against the new idealists from Greenpeace. However, never underestimate the power of tenacity.

The tête-à-tête between Greenpeace and the *Dalniy Vostok* was only the organisation's second anti-whaling mission; the first campaign to protect whales happened in the summer of 1975. Then, the activists desperately chased Soviet whaling ships in inflatable motorboats, blocking them from shooting harpoons at their prey. Photos from this confrontation were splashed on the front pages of Western media, forcing the public's attention to the wholesale extermination of the world's largest marine mammals on the brink of extinction.

In a photo dated 1 July 1976, activists Eileen Chivers and Fred Easton approach a floating "whale murder factory" on a tiny Zodiac boat, holding a banner on which one word was written in white letters on a red background: "NYET." Unfortunately, the dead carcasses of whales being dragged by cables behind the ship, leaving a bloody trail in the water and a stench attracting sharks, did not fall in the frame. Yet, even without the gory details, the photo proved to be striking enough to meaningfully change the way people thought about whales.

Ever since the middle of the 19th century, thanks to Herman Melville's novel *Moby-Dick*, most people saw whales as huge, dangerous sea monsters against whom men fought courageously and heroically. The Greenpeace activists showed the world the roles of monster and hero were (and remain) in fact reversed, making them real harbingers of change destroying centuries of axiomatic thinking.

In 1982, the International Whaling Commission (finally) voted to impose a moratorium on commercial whaling beginning in 1986. Although the Soviet Union opposed this decision (because the totalitarian regime was never concerned about its people, why would it suddenly be worried about killing some "fish," even big ones?), the *Dalniy Vostok* took to the seas only a few more times following the confrontation with Greenpeace, and then vanished.

The industrial scale of whale extermination by the USSR eventually would be revealed many years later, after its collapse. When talking with former Soviet whalers, American researcher Ryan Tucker Jones, author of the book *Red Leviathan: The Secret History of Soviet Whaling* (2022), observed how, in their economy, in their politics, and in their culture, Russia's Soviet Union formally institutionalised, bureaucratised, and incentivised genocide: "I shared their fascination with whales. But what I perceived as genocide, they thought of simply as work, and I was amazed at how little their recollections included danger or drama." When pervasive societal indifference to the treatment of others, be it animal or human, becomes the cultural milieu, a job requiring you to kill for your survival becomes pedestrian, as benign as delivering pizza. The absence of compassion for another is the hallmark of success for repressive systems like today's Russian Empire or its Soviet Union.

Politically, this cultural phenomenon has often been expressed as a right to dominate some one, some thing, or some place, making systems of repression possible, and is not unique in the history of ideas. At the opening ceremony of the Baltimore Sanitary Fair on 18 April 1864, standing behind the speaker's podium set in the middle of the spacious hall at the Maryland Institute lavishly decorated with American flags, five-pointed stars, bouquets of fresh flowers, and evergreen garlands, Abraham Lincoln delivered a lecture on liberty. "We all declare for liberty; but in using the same word we do not all mean the same thing," Lincoln said. Almost a year following his address, the American Civil War would come to an end.

Perhaps understanding the festering social ill of slavery would continue to infect the American Republic, Lincoln resorted to allegory to illustrate his point: "The shepherd drives the wolf from the sheep's throat, for which the sheep thanks the shepherd as his liberator, while the wolf denounces him for the same act, as the destroyer of liberty... Plainly, the sheep and the wolf are not agreed upon a definition of the word 'liberty'."

America rejected the "Wolf's Dictionary" definition of liberty with the adoption by Congress of the 13th Amendment to the US Constitution, prohibiting slavery (1865), and the 14th Amendment, emphasising no state can deprive someone of life, liberty, or property without due process (1868). Yet, it would take another 100 years, following the Civil Rights Act, for society to accept a more shared understanding of liberty, thereby establishing a cultural norm. However, only in 2024 has an American President formally apologised to Native Americans. Objectively, more work needs to be done to develop just cultural norms, especially considering the failure of the Equal Rights Amendment in the US and the reified international system of gender apartheid. Will the wolf's liberty prevail and become the dominant culture guiding our politics despite the growing number of advanced and affluent liberal democracies?

Unfortunately, Russia's full-scale invasion of Ukraine (and the response by the United Nations to this naked aggression) has shown the global community's refusal to flatly reject the wolf's liberty as an organizing principle for the world. Instead, the rights of the abuser are weighed equally with the abused. A system of belief suggesting the rights of "whales" and "whalers" are morally equivalent, is rationally absurd. Yet, there remain influential voices demanding Ukraine accept the wolf's liberty.

Shelling the village of Bamut in Chechnya with a rocket launcher bearing the inscription "Peace to your home" in 1996; invading Georgia as part of a "Peace Operation" in 2008; denying the presence of Russian soldiers in Ukraine's Crimean Peninsula and invading Ukraine's Donbas in 2014; the wanton death and destruction of Syrians in 2015; and mocking Washington's warnings of Russia's intent to invade Ukraine in 2022 as "western hysteria," are just a few recent examples of the Kremlin's style of deceit and what life has become under the wolf's liberty.

The language of the wolf's liberty explains the abduction of Ukrainian children from their homes in Ukraine and their enslavement in resettlement camps in the Far East as an "evacuation of orphans." It proselytises a special military operation to denazify and demilitarise a country, asserting the tyranny of occupation is in fact, peace for land. This is not prosaic ambiguity. It is O'Brien torturing Winston into wanting, yearning, and even loving to believe, not simply concede, he is holding up five fingers, not four.

A society in which Lincoln's wolf's liberty becomes canon, whether in its state or its culture, easily normalises delusional disorders. For example: women are witches, people are property, or whales are monsters, and even, Ukrainians are Nazis. Policies built upon these delusions would include burning witches at the stake, creating the African slave trade, writing heroic epics to sanitise – even codify – the killing of whales, and implementing a genocide against Ukraine.

A nation's independent state remains the agency qualified to protect its cultural autonomy and national interest. Life inside a liberal democratic state, even one with flaws, is better than living under the cultural tyranny of the wolf's liberty. Liberal democracies are stronger together.

A not insignificant part of Ukrainian society was always aware of their barbaric neighbour (collective memory is resilient despite the passage of time). It took the beating of students in 2013 by the Berkut special forces of the Interior Ministry troops to awaken the nation. And at dawn on 24 February 2022, the world was awoken when they heard the whistles and explosions of Russian missiles hitting the cities of Lviv, Ternopil, Odesa, Mykolaiv, Kherson, Dnipro, Kharkiv, Sumy, Mariupol, and Kyiv.

Every day Ukrainians choose to fight; and maybe, from afar, it looks hopeless, futile, and far-fetched – not unlike a confrontation between a tiny inflatable rubber boat, "armed" only with banners and cameras, hoping to stop a genocide of whales, pitted against a massive steel-hulled ship equipped with harpoons. But for 11 years since the Russians first invaded Ukraine, someone has at last shown the world how to respond to the wolf's notion of liberty.

The second issue of *The Black Sea Whale* reveals what is hiding behind the mask of hypocrisy, rejects stale euphemisms, and frankly calls things by their real names. This issue is sometimes painful, at other times shockingly beautiful, making it a valuable therapeutic experience.

In 2022, the city of Mariupol was devastated by the Russian army not unlike the Baturyn Tragedy of 1708, when Russia's Peter the Great ordered the city to be razed and his troops to burn and loot what remained. The anguish brought by Russia's wanton destruction of Ukraine's cities has vaccinated Ukrainians against Russophilia. Today's national war for independence is evidence of increasing maturity, insight, and self-esteem among Ukrainians and a chance to end the dystopia of the Russian Empire. Oleksii Dubrov describes how Ukraine is breaking the cycle of violence perpetrated by its ravenous, abusive neighbour in his story "Mature Ukraine."

"The emergence of a totalitarian society in Russia, founded on the principles of mysticism, chauvinism, and the desire for total war, a society fed by resentment and the dream of revanchism, was wildly successful, albeit going unnoticed by almost all observers," writes Sergej Sumlenny in "The Entertainment Industry of Russian Irredentism." Sumlenny offers a warning: "Russia's real enemy is the West, particularly the United States and the United Kingdom." Total war against the whole world has been deeply ingrained into Russian culture and the "intellectual Novichok" has been shown to be no less dangerous and even more deadly than the original toxin.

"What's really interesting is that the hammer and sickle do not evoke as much negative emotion as does the swastika," Cadmus writes from the trenches of Russia's war against Ukraine. Who wins the Olympics of bloodthirstiness – the Nazis or the communists? Have we done enough to condemn the symbols of totalitarianism to prevent new ones from sanitising murder? "The first to fall victim to any utopian belief system is the mind; only later does it spill into the physical world," he explains. Communism never had its Nuremberg. Has that allowed the Zwastika to be imbued with the same deadly power? From the relative safety of a foxhole, Cadmus shares his insight about truth in "Hammer and Sickle = Death and Famine."

Every culture has a mythical being adults frighten children with to get them to behave properly or in a manner convenient for the adult. The Russian "bogeyman" is Smuta. "If you don't listen to the emperor, the Smuta will get you!" Putin says, addressing schoolchildren in Sochi. His threats are persuasive, because whether it is Russian schoolchildren or their parents and grandparents, no one has ever seen the Smuta, yet almost every citizen of the Russian Federation is riddled with a deep-seated fear of encountering it. Oleh Mahdych and Marichka Melnyk uncover that a dynasty of personal fear toward losing the throne has been guiding Russian leaders for centuries, evolving into a national paranoia abused by the dictatorial regime in the Kremlin today in "The Spectre of Smuta."

Western advocates of a "middle ground" find it uncomfortable to acknowledge it was not Putin who personally tortured people in Bucha nor was it Putin's caterer Prigozhin who fired missiles at the city of Dnipro. It was someone and something else. For years, Russian media personalities were gainfully employed and comfortable as propagandists for the Kremlin. Some have fled Russia and today are snugly ensconced in Western media outlets, asserting they are not "those kinds of Russians." They claim responsibility for the war against Ukraine is Putin's alone. Their rhetoric is different, but have they truly changed? "It was these artificially created opinion leaders who for almost

20 years laid the groundwork for the current war in Ukraine," writes Nazar Tokar in "The Adventures of Russian Propagandists." Is their displacement a cry for safety or a creeping Russian occupation of Western media?

The Soviet Union's Constitution guaranteed equal rights for women, but hidden behind this pronouncement of emancipation lay unfettered exploitation. "A Working Woman's Tale" by Marichka Melnyk is the story of a fictional young woman set in historically accurate surroundings: she lives and works as a welder at the *Krasnaya Zvyezda* factory in Kirovohrad in 1952. Melnyk reveals the desperate reality of life for Ukrainian women during the revolving door of occupation by Nazi and Soviet regimes in World War II immersing readers in the repressive, tortuous culture women were subjected to under Soviet rule during the 1950s.

"He's too... freedom-loving? Rebellious? Fearless?" the teachers at Model Boarding School No.1 in the Chinese Occupation Zone of Moscow whispered among themselves as they watched Mrs Mao, the principal and (occasional) math teacher, just about break her paddle on the back of eight-year-old Hector, attempting to beat what she perceived as insolence out of him. His behaviour was completely inappropriate for a true servant of the Republic. When subjected to the absolute domination of a callous authoritarian with no internal boundaries can your true self survive? "The Lost Ones" by Viktoriia Antonenko is the next chapter in the *Deus ex Ucraina* series set in an alternate reality following the Winter Crisis, when the Russian Federation as we know it was erased from the face of the Earth.

We hope you enjoy reading these stories from Ukraine as much as we did creating them.

The Editors
The Black Sea Whale

#ESSAYS

Mature Ukraine

Story by Oleksii Dubrov
Illustrated by Beata Kurkul

Oleh Mahdych, Stanislav Hreshchyshyn, Cadmus, and Marichka Melnyk
contributed to this story.

ONE ICY DECEMBER NIGHT, LONG before there were airports, the devil landed in St. Petersburg, the capital of the Russian Empire. Riding on his back was Vakula, an ordinary blacksmith from the Ukrainian village of Dykanka near Poltava. The blacksmith had braved the long distance from home through a snowstorm to acquire a pair of slippers worn by the *tsaritsa*. Oksana, a girl from his village, refused to marry Vakula unless he brought them to her. Upon arriving at the royal palace, Vakula met some Zaporizhian Cossack envoys, who had come to the capital on their own mission. The blacksmith joined their entourage, managed to get an audience with the tsaritsa, who awarded him her slippers, and as a result, won over the girl — his beloved Oksana.

Every Ukrainian knows this story, "Christmas Eve," written by Ukrainian-born Russian writer Nikolai Gogol and published in 1832 in St. Petersburg. Gogol, then a novice writer, invented a story which appealed to the masses and would go on to be adapted into dozens of operas, theatrical plays, and films. The first silent film version of the story came out in 1913, back when cinematography was still in its infancy as an art form.

At the time the short story was published in 1832, sixty-eight years had passed since Catherine II, also known as Catherine the Great — the very same tsaritsa whose slippers the blacksmith Vakula set his sights on — had issued the decree abolishing the Hetmanate of the Zaporizhian Cossacks, later doing the same to their fortress, the Sich. Gogol didn't explain exactly what the Cossack envoys had asked Catherine, but he did include a whole section where he eloquently recounts in meticulous detail how the Ukrainians admired the luxurious palace and fawned over the tsaritsa, calling her nothing other than "mum." Catherine, for her part, was happy "His Highness [Potemkin] fulfilled his promise to acquaint me today with a people under my dominion, whom I have not yet seen." The Zaporizhian Cossacks, like Vakula, weren't familiar with the customs of the court and appeared somewhat crude, but Catherine admired their simple nature so much she granted at least one request — the slippers. As for the Zaporizhian Sich, we all know what happened there: the tsaritsa destroyed it. Gogol neglected to mention that fact in his story.

Simpleness would be a trait attributed to Ukrainians for the next 200 years. Ukrainians were seen as a kind and hospitable people who could cook, dance, and sing well, and were also pleasant and funny. People with these characteristics do not pose a threat. At least this is how Russians *wanted to* and continue to *want to* see Ukrainians within their empire. Nikolai Gogol, whom Ukrainians so desperately seek to attribute as their own, was adept at creating narratives Russians wanted to hear about Ukrainians. The Zaporizhian Cossacks in "Christmas Eve" look pitiful, like defeated victims grovelling before their abuser, whom they are convinced they truly love. They fawn over their master and in return receive smiles and mercy in the form of slippers... and a destroyed Sich.

In abusive relationships, the aggressor strives to break the victim's inner strength physically and psychologically, to subdue their will. The weaker partner loses faith in their own strength, their self-esteem suffers, and they lose the ability to make independent decisions. Worst of all — the victim believes this is normal and is drawn even closer to the aggressor. Victimhood, so eloquently described by Gogol, was one of the worst consequences of the *russkiy mir* (Russian World) for Ukrainians — the Russians forced upon us the image of what they thought an ideal Ukrainian should be.

In 1503, more than 300 years before the publication of Gogol's "Christmas Eve," the latest of the Moscow-Lithuanian wars ended with the Grand Duchy of Lithuania losing 20 cities and at least a third of its territory, resulting in the Grand Duchy of Moscow reaching the borders of Kyiv. But Lithuania's defeat is not the main point here: it would go on to reconquer most of its territory. In the peace settlement with Lithuanian Grand Duke Alexander, Grand Prince Ivan III of Moscow demanded he be recognised as "Sovereign of all Rus'." Thus, an idea crystallised among the Russian elites, fuelling their ambitions for centuries, irrespective of ideologies, methods, or political systems. Moscow, having plagiarised Byzantium's coat of arms with the double-headed eagle, proclaimed itself the successor of Kyivan Rus' and used every means possible over the coming centuries to *collect* and rule over lands of the former medieval state. Russians, before they were even Russians, were hooked on the idea like a drug, constantly injecting themselves with it, and have been unable to break their addiction to this day.

The Rus' state emerged and flourished in the 10–12th centuries, long before Moscow existed. Its capital was Kyiv. However, by the early 16th century, Kyiv had not been independent for several centuries. The city and region hadn't come close to regaining its status as a centre of influence after its destruction by the Mongol invasion in 1240. Ukrainians, most of whom called themselves Rusyns or People of Rus' at the time (the Muscovites weren't part of the club, nor were they particularly interested in joining it), were the true descendants and

heirs of former Kyivan Rus'. They helped the Lithuanians create the civilised Grand Duchy of Lithuania; they defended themselves against the aggressive Catholic Kingdom of Poland while, at the same time, incorporating themselves into it; they fought against the Crimean Khanate, while occasionally allying with it; and they grew accustomed to the rule of the Moscow Principality. Nobles of Rusyn origin took turns enlisting Muscovites, Lithuanians, and Poles to resolve their personal property disputes and political problems.

For example, in 1508, Mykhailo Hlynsky, a member of one of these noble families, asked the Muscovites to help him in his claim against the Poles, who had taken away the privileges and positions granted to him by the Lithuanians. Having failed in his attempt to return what he had lost, Hlynsky fled to Moscow, where he was given the status of a Russian noble or *boyar*, became the father-in-law of the Prince of Moscow, was later imprisoned, and subsequently released. Upon regaining his freedom, he once again rose through the ranks in the highest circles of power, was jailed a second time, and eventually died in prison.

Among all the elites and nobles of the Eastern European region, only those from Rus' (proto-Ukraine) didn't take any serious steps to amass the "lands of Rus'." It was much easier to join existing systems or states. These systems were, to a greater or lesser extent, foreign to Ukrainians: they had different languages, religions or denominations, cultures, and traditions. Thus, our ancestors, including our elites, were always "foreigners" and treated as second-class citizens. Nevertheless, all the energy of the most active and most influential people of Rus', who were often more educated and advanced than their neighbours, was geared towards effectively incorporating themselves into other states rather than creating their own.

The Zaporizhian Cossacks gathered strength and popularity starting in the mid-16th century, well before they got the chance to become characters in one of Gogol's stories. They were warriors who took up arms to fight for their status and "liberties." Several decades later, the Cossack leader Hetman Petro Sahaidachny had expanded their mission, burning down Crimean fortresses, Ottoman cities, and even part of Moscow. Hetman Bohdan Khmelnytsky used both weapons and diplomacy to create a quasi-independent state. However, at the time, the ambition and military might for full independence was lacking. It would be fair to say the idea of an independent state simply did not exist among the elites nor in the general population. Under the Pereyaslav Agreement signed by Khmelnytsky in 1654, the Hetmanate became a protectorate of Moscow. This was the foundation upon which the gradual transformation of the Zaporizhian Cossacks from skilled warriors into simple-minded literary heroes was built.

In the coming decades, the elites would constantly search for bizarre models of survival where the main goal was to protect their own privileges and status in exchange for some form of dependence.

The positions taken by the Cossack elites also changed depending on the situation. In 1664, Ivan Bohun and Ivan Vyhovsky were killed one month apart in the Chernihiv and Kyiv regions, respectively. The former was killed by the Poles for allegedly being a traitor with ties to the Muscovites; the latter was killed by Cossacks under Pavlo Teteria (then Hetman of Right-Bank Ukraine) for allegedly supporting an anti-Polish uprising. Both knew Bohdan Khmelnytsky well. When the Pereyaslav Agreement was proposed, Bohun strongly opposed the treaty with Moscow and refused to pledge allegiance to the tsar. Vyhovsky, on the other hand, was one of the most ardent supporters of the alliance with the northern neighbour, although he would sign another agreement with the Poles a few years later. Each of the two Cossacks changed their position to the opposite one by the time of their deaths 10 years after the Pereyaslav Agreement. In the coming decades, the elites would constantly search for bizarre models of survival where the main goal was to protect their own privileges and status in exchange for some form of dependence. Although they were much closer culturally to the Catholic Poles and Lithuanians, Ukrainians increasingly gave in to the false narrative about their Muscovite Orthodox "brothers."

While the Cossacks usually fought against the Poles on the battlefield to gain "liberties," these same types of "battles" with the Muscovites were increasingly settled through negotiations, supplication, and humiliation, at the cost of betraying one's own self. As a result, true independence was transformed into autonomy, which over the decades became increasingly restricted. Having entered into an abusive relationship of their own free will, the Cossacks, along with the rest of the population of Ukraine, gradually spiralled downwards into victimhood.

In 1709, Hetman Ivan Mazepa and King Charles XII of Sweden joined forces to challenge Muscovite rule over Ukrainian lands. Although Mazepa's time as Hetman of Left-Bank Ukraine starting in 1687 was a period of

Ukraine became the object of physical, mental, econonomic, and cultural abuse, and Ukrainians knowingly played the game.

cultural and economic growth in the region, it also witnessed a gradual decline of the institution of the Hetmanate. In October 1708, an armed rebellion against Tsar Peter I would

have seemed logical given the military might of the Swedish army, although Mazepa's potential contribution as a military ally was rather modest. After half a century, people across the Hetmanate had grown accustomed to the presence of Muscovite military garrisons. Many Cossack officers maintained ties with the tsar's representatives — Gogol's characters, the Zaporizhian Cossack envoys, didn't just appear from nowhere. The punishment for collaboration with the adventuresome Mazepa was deemed harsher than anything that could happen by remaining loyal to the tsar. The slaughter of the entire civilian population of Baturyn, their torture, persecution, and murder by "Orthodox abusers," was received by the people with an almost tacit acceptance of such a fate. A hundred years earlier, there had been a different, more healthy reaction in the form of armed resistance to similar behaviour by Catholic Poles or Muslim Tatars. After all, the Cossack movement emerged in part as a response to regular attacks against the population by the Crimean Khanate.

The local elites chose to reiterate their allegiance to the tsar, and Ivan Skoropadsky was formally elected as the new hetman in Mazepa's place. At the Battle of Poltava in the summer of 1709, neither the Swedish king nor the Muscovite tsar gave the Cossacks any substantive role in their battle plans. Charles XII had them surround Poltava and defend the military camp, while Peter I stationed them far away from the main positions of his troops. When making the choice between independence and special status as a vassal you choose the latter, you ultimately surrender both. The military might of the Cossacks Europe had once respected became a source of second-rate human capital. For Ukrainians on both sides of the redoubts, the battle was lost before it even started. Over the next 300 years, the main players in the wars on Ukraine's land would be foreign armies, or armies controlled by foreigners.

The evolution from Mazepa's failure to Gogol's story was just a matter of time. Ukraine became the object of physical, mental,

At the time, loving Ukraine as your ancestral territory and homeland, while simultaneously serving the Russians, had become part of everyday culture. Developing the Russian language, preserving their traditions, hating the Poles, and caring about the success of the Russian state project were deeply ingrained in the minds of Ukraine's elites.

Most leaders of Ukrainian society at the turn of the century and the writers from that time whose works were included in Ukrainian academic curricula did not foresee Ukraine nor themselves as being independent. Autonomy within the Austro-Hungarian or Russian Empire was their highest aspiration. The sovereignty of the metropoles wasn't even challenged. Meanwhile, the Finns, Lithuanians, Latvians, and Estonians, whose populations were much smaller, had very different and much greater ambitions. The wave of fascination with socialism in those countries (which also happened in Poland, although the Poles put independence first) didn't distract them from their quest for statehood. Conversely, one group of Ukrainian elites fell for the new fairy tale expounded by their Russian brothers about the need for class struggle against the global bourgeoisie, while others joined in to sing the old song about "one great nation." These Ukrainians saw the Poles or the "bourgeois West" — or even their fellow Ukrainians, the ones who sought independence — as the greatest threat.

In early 1919, Colonel Petro Bolbochan of the Army of the Ukrainian People's Republic, one of the most talented military figures of the Ukrainian national liberation revolution of 1917–1921 and a graduate of the Chuhuyiv Military School in the Kharkiv region, wrote: "You [the political leaders of the Directorate] work especially hard and spend a lot of time thinking about how not to anger and how to please your Bolshevik comrades in Moscow, so as not to appear anti-democratic in their eyes. You don't see by doing this you are cultivating the same kinds of Bolshevik ideals in Ukraine and are leading Ukraine towards a 'single united Russia' through Bolshevism."

economic, and cultural abuse, and Ukrainians knowingly played the game. We can't say for certain what sentiments toward the question of statehood prevailed among Ukrainian peasants in the 19th century, but most likely there were no sentiments at all. Those who had just recently fled to the Sich and taken up arms were forced to accept serfdom — a role uncharacteristic for Ukrainians. Those who were lucky enough to join the elites first and foremost sought to serve.

In 1892, the Ukrainian writer and cultural activist Borys Hrinchenko wrote several letters to his colleague, the economist and philosopher Mykhailo Drahomanov, in which he explained that Ukrainian public figures in the region along the Dnipro River had two souls — Ukrainian and Russian:

"As a member of the intelligentsia in Russia at the time, he [the Ukrainian] was pulled here and there, toward his native land and toward the 'Stanislav on his neck' [The Imperial Order of Saint Stanislav, an honorary medal whose name had been stolen from the Poles by the Russian Empire and was awarded mainly to officials]; they wanted to serve their native land while not angering those giving out the 'Stanislav.' Here, of course, phrases such as 'one all-Russian great people,' and 'our mutual history,' and 'common all-Russian culture,' and 'join in the thunder of victory,' as well as all sorts of other wonderful stories, were used as excuses when a compromise had to be made."

Bolbochan wrote the letter while under arrest on orders of the political leadership of the Directorate of the Ukrainian People's Republic. His groundless arrest was likely the result of their irrational fear he would organise a military coup, since he was the leader of one of the few battle-ready Ukrainian army units at the time: albeit a unit completely subordinate to the Directorate and its only chance to stop the Bolsheviks in early 1919. Bolbochan wrote several such letters, filled with the pain of a man who wanted to build an independent Ukraine and was ready to fight for it, but became hostage to the intrigues of small-minded men in high positions. The letters, like the quote above, were addressed primarily to Symon Petliura, who, like the other leaders of the Directorate Volodymyr Vynnychenko and Mykhailo Hrushevsky, was always more afraid of their own military than of the Russians. Actually, they were more afraid of those who carried the idea of an independent Ukraine than of the bearers of the idea of a global revolution of the proletariat (which brought along with it the restoration of the Russian Empire in a new form).

Held in custody for several months, Bolbochan was released only when the situation became catastrophic. Shortly thereafter, the leaders changed their minds again, and, on 28 June 1919, he was executed as a war criminal. He wanted to and could have resisted the Bolsheviks, but lost the war to his own people — those who were afraid of decisive Ukrainians. People whom he had urged to be Ukrainians first and members of some political camp second. You could safely say his killer was Symon Petliura, whom Ukrainians customarily hail as a hero statesman.

Bolbochan wasn't the only one who died seeking to restore the Ukrainian people's sense of independence. On 4 May 1924, a stocky man was found hanged from a tree in an apple orchard on Zhylianska Street in Kyiv, then the centre of the Kyivan *gubernia* (province). There was a suicide note in his pocket, and he was buried a few days later in an isolated part of the cemetery, next to other people who had taken their own lives. Even during the Bolshevik occupation, these rules were still followed.

Not many people came to the funeral — 11 or 12, according to eyewitnesses. In the early 20th century, the person they buried that day at Baikove Cemetery had been ridiculed by Volodymyr Vynnychenko, pushed off the pulpit by Mykhailo Hrushevsky, and sent by the Russians to the front in the summer of 1917 at the request of Symon Petliura. The most popular version proposed to explain his suicide was the angst he felt because of his supposed inclination to cooperate with the NKVD and having been constantly blackmailed. But Volodymyr Shemet and Mykola Marchenko, two of the man's closest friends, reported he was in a very wretched state by the spring of 1924. His life's purpose had collapsed, and he wasn't keen on becoming part of the Ukrainian political émigré community, considering this demoralising rather than a reasonable alternative to staying in Ukraine.

The piece of paper found in Mykola Mikhnovsky's pocket read: "By my own hand, instead of theirs."

The idea of an independent Ukraine, which Mikhnovsky first started actively promoting at the turn of the 20th century, faced the sharpest and harshest resistance not from Russians or Poles, but from Ukrainians. The same Ukrainians in whose names institutes and main streets of cities throughout Ukraine have been christened. And although researchers cite the cause of Mikhnovsky's misunderstandings with the majority of the Ukrainian elite in the late 19th and early 20th centuries as his propensity for being too emotional, rude, and stubborn, it would be naïve to say the peculiarities of his character were the true origin of this sentiment.

Mikhnovsky's demand for Ukrainian independence hit at the heart of the Ukrainian elites' original sin — Russophilia. Having been in an abusive relationship for more than 200 years, the elites had grown accustomed to Russophilia, with its desire to gain favourable special status and not become persona non grata in St. Petersburg or Moscow. Compromising with evil became a new religion. And refusing to compromise was heresy. The most radical idea this compromise allowed was the quest for autonomy as part of a reformed "good" Russia. And eventually Mikhnovsky also agreed to this compromise, prioritising the unity of the Ukrainian political forces over all else.

By making autonomy a first order priority, our intellectuals doomed the quest for independence to failure. This cultural mutation from the 18–19th centuries fell on fertile soil in the 20th century, flourishing alongside the Ukrainian national communists, the process of Ukrainianization, and the acceptance of the USSR as a state Ukrainians could consider their own creation, not their occupier. And, unlike the Baltic countries, for example, we agreed to go along with this.

The "delicacies" the Bolsheviks fed Ukrainians were meant to make them feel better while luring them in. Although Ukrainians were open to leftist ideas, only 3 per cent of peasant homesteads had joined collective farms by the early 1920s, and by the end of the decade, the process had slowed significantly. The farmers preferred to work their own land, preserving the opportunity to increase earnings and to expand. But the communists decided to break the people's will in the name of a defunct idea. Stalin set out to collectivise the villages as quickly as possible.

Being able to work their own land awakened something which seemed to have fallen asleep inside Ukrainians since the rise of the Cossacks and was only revived after 1917. They began to sense a responsibility for their own lives and started to resist collectivisation. When the law was passed on the nationalisation of cattle, peasants slaughtered the animals rather than give them away. When the authorities terrorised wealthy farmers to try to destroy them, they got hundreds and thousands of acts of rebellion in response. When tens of thousands of mentally unstable Komsomol members and communist loyalists from the interior of Russia were brought to Ukraine armed with weapons to enforce collectivisation, more than 4,000 uprisings by 1.2 million Ukrainian peasants were organised in 1930 alone. Only the man-made famine — the Holodomor — which took the lives of close to four million people and traumatised a whole generation, could break the resistance of the Ukrainian peasantry. By 1937, "good Russians" and their supporters in Ukraine had collectivised nearly all farms, at a terrible cost.

After WWII, Ukrainians were again labelled as simple-minded, somewhat dumb, but pleasant and funny people. However, now their reputation also included being potential traitors... who nonetheless are talented singers and dancers. The folksy Veryovka choir and Virsky dance ensemble in their quaint embroidered peasant costumes, low-brow comedy duo Tarapunka and Shtepsel, and Ukrainian singers winning vocal competitions only confirmed this view. Russian ideologues upheld this image, elevating the prestige of Russophilia for its victim. Although they undoubtedly achieved success, they themselves believed too strongly in this artificially created narrative.

Russophilia was just a smokescreen, a virus the collective immunity would try to attack every now and then. On 20 September 1987, Dynamo Kyiv football club lost to Spartak Moscow 0–1 in the Ukrainian capital. The angry hosts joined with fans of other Ukrainian teams and started a huge brawl in the stadium with the Russian fans, which quickly spilled over into the streets. The Ukrainian attack spread like wildfire, pushing the enemy back to the central railway station and blocking them there. They even cut off the Russians' means of escape: the Kyiv-Moscow train and the bus for the football team's guests were destroyed. It took the *militsiya* (interior ministry troops), who back then were definitely not on the side of the people, to break things up. Sure, football matches sometimes devolve into fights among fans, but in the USSR, only a match between the teams of Kyiv and Moscow could have turned into such an onslaught, with the unconditional surrender of the latter.

Weeding out narratives ingrained in society for decades is a long and painful process. Ukrainians, in general, preferred to avoid conflict and often tried to sit on two chairs at once, even when the chairs were on fire. By early 1991, Lithuania, Estonia, Latvia, Georgia, Moldova, and Armenia had declared their independence or transition to independence. When the all-Union referendum on preserving the USSR was held in March of that year, those countries ignored it. Ukraine took part and voted "yes."

Ukraine would declare independence later in 1991. Not because it wanted to cast off the shackles of its prolonged occupation, but "In view of the mortal danger surrounding Ukraine in connection with the state coup in the USSR on August 19, 1991..." So, the mortal threat wasn't the USSR, the Russian Empire, or enslavement, but a coup in the metropole. Maybe we wouldn't have declared independence, but since you did what you did over there, you left us no choice. The first sentence of the Ukrainian Declaration of Independence contains a reaction to something happening in Moscow, while the desire of the Ukrainians is laid out in a strange

phrase about the "thousand-year tradition of state development" in the subsequent points. Not the "just right to freedom" and the "result of the struggle for independence," but the right to be independent until Moscow figures things out. And what happened when they figured things out in Moscow?

The history of Ukraine is one of alternating opposing narratives: we're either armed to the teeth Cossacks instilling fear in the most powerful empires (like the Ottoman Empire in the 16–17th centuries), or simple-minded Gogol-esque fawners before the tsaritsa. Either we beat the pants off one of the strongest football teams in the world (in the 2013 match against France in the World Cup playoffs), or we run around the field confused by Kazakhstan, a team five notches below us in the FIFA rankings. Today we show strength, and tomorrow we forget we ever had any.

For centuries, the dominant narrative explaining Ukraine's defeats was its unpreparedness, immaturity, and lack of unity. Our elites weren't as good as other countries' elites; our people were in the dark and far from national consciousness; and our geopolitical location was such we stood no chance at all. We don't know how to unite; we conform too easily; we don't trust the state. But what if the truth lies much deeper? What if all the reasons we're used to hearing and giving are just a manifestation of "poor me" syndrome, which we've used to protect ourselves from the fact that for centuries Ukrainians didn't really want to build their own independent state. And not just because of a personal reluctance or objective geopolitical reasons, but because of the serious psychological effects of living next to an abuser-state.

Living with an abuser can make you idealise them and want to obey rather than oppose them, sometimes even emulate them. The victim may hate the "stronger one" deep down, and love them at the same time. For 30 years, the Establishment and the post-communist

elite tried to build our 603,548sq km not into Ukraine, but a smaller version of Russia, even one with a chance of becoming a member of the EU or NATO. We left Soviet medicine in place but thought the Russians reformed it better because they added the word "insurance." When Moscow changed the name of its militsiya to "police," which continued to terrorise society, Kyiv studied their reforms. We didn't change anything in our cultural sphere, instead we went to conferences in St. Petersburg and admired the scanners they used to digitise museum exhibits. We didn't reform or change anything ourselves, but enthusiastically said, "When I was in Russia..." Moscow was the model to emulate, not the more developed Warsaw or London. We liked being a few years behind the metropole. And the metropole liked it even more... until 2014.

The Revolution of Dignity shook society to its core and made it abundantly clear we could fight back against the abuser. Having ousted an idiot president and starting to regain our lost strength, Ukraine received a slap across the face with the annexation of the Crimean Peninsula and the occupation of our Donbas region. The victim tried to hit back, cast off its simple-mindedness, and go on the offensive. There were positive results and it bought time needed to reassess the situation. We didn't win the war then, but we definitely didn't lose the battle.

If you delve into the history of Russian-Ukrainian relations, it becomes clear Ukrainians have never won a war against the Russians. Yes, Prince Ostrozky destroyed the best Russian cavalry in the Battle of Orsha. Sahaidachny burned part of Moscow. Vyhovsky forced the Muscovites to flee Konotop like they would a nuclear bomb. We won individual battles, but we always lost the wars for some reason for another — especially when we stopped building Ukraine and refocused on being "little Russia." How could a little Russia ever defeat a big Russia?

We were often ashamed to build a "big" Ukraine. It seemed snobbish and unrealistic, and the timing was always wrong. It became a cultural problem. Do Ukrainians call those who want more than what we've had in the past which seemingly suited everyone holier-than-thou dreamers or visionary leaders? What do we do when these drivers of change challenge the established canons of societal compromise with evil — do we stand by and watch them be devoured, or do we lend a hand? What do Ukrainians opt to do when positive change requires conflict with the way things have always been or with the mighty? What if the old ways and the "accepted ones" are defended by moral authorities and even former dissidents?

We've been debating whether we should join NATO since independence until the victory of the Revolution of Dignity. The prevailing opinion was we weren't ready; it would anger Russia; and you can't make such a radical choice when choosing sides. Article 5 of NATO's founding treaty states an attack on one member of the alliance is an attack on all. It's like the motto of the Three Musketeers — "All for one, and one for all." Our own politicians scared us into believing NATO would turn a peaceful and sunny Ukraine, with its *chornozem* (fertile black soil) and hospitable people, into a large military base designed to solve problems for the Americans. But instead of simply "acting like doves of peace," with the help of NATO since Russia's invasion in 2014, we were able to sharpen our teeth.

At 4.00am on 24 February 2022, the Russian army crossed the border en masse and began bombing Ukrainian cities all over the country: Kharkiv, Chernihiv, Sumy, Kyiv, Mariupol, Lviv, Odesa, and others. They brought with them three days' worth of expired food rations and dress uniforms for their triumphant victory parade down Kyiv's main street — Khreshchatyk. To this day, blue and yellow flags still fly over most of those cities.

A lot has been said about the Kremlin's miscalculations: they were ill-prepared; they didn't understand Ukrainians. But our strong resistance to the empire came as a surprise to most of us as well, did it not? For almost two centuries, Russians and Ukrainians alike have loved Gogol's "Christmas Eve." They staged it in separate and joint productions. They laughed at how the royal court liked the simple-minded Vakula.

Big data showed and continues to show Ukrainians should have lost in the 2022 full-scale invasion after several days. Western countries were convinced of it and were awaiting the dawn of "a new reality." Ukrainian diplomats recall this in their interviews. But the collective memory of Konotop and Pereyaslav, Mazepa and Baturyn, Bolbochan and the Ukrainian People's Republic, the Holodomor and collectivisation, the Dynamo-Spartak match, and Russian intervention in Ukraine's Crimean Peninsula proved to be stronger than analysts' forecasts. The phrase "Russian warship, go fuck yourself!" resonated in every part of Ukraine because it expressed the purpose and strength Ukrainians always had inside of them but were afraid to show. The same strength the Cossacks had when they fought the Poles for "liberties" and the peasants had when they killed the Komsomol who came to take their land in the 1930s.

Russians are classic abusers: they can dish it out, but they can't take it. The only way to overcome an abuser is to destroy them. If you accept another compromise, they'll come back again and again, taking advantage of the collective trauma they created themselves. The ongoing people's war for independence is our test of maturity. It's a terrible tragedy, but also a chance for our first victory against Russia in all of history. The chance exists, but success isn't guaranteed. And the risk of repeating traditional mistakes after the war remains.

We have the strength to win, and the NATO principles we have been striving for have always been in our blood. The West was taken by surprise because it hasn't had to repel aggression for a long time. International organisations called to help countries during conflict have proven incapable of upholding their own principles and goals. What good is the United Nations, an organisation whose mission is to ensure peace on the planet, if after the first month of war there was just one resolution condemning Russia's aggression? It speaks to the UN's impotence and challenges its very existence. It must be replaced by a different structure, one more decisive, less bureaucratic, and one which can truly ensure peace for those ready to take responsibility to defend their right to exist, as well as for those who are weaker. One in which 200 member states will not be held hostage by one insane country with veto power.

On 18 March 2021, Vladimir Putin, while in Ukraine's illegally annexed Crimean Peninsula, described to one of his propagandists what he sees as the messianic purpose of his presidency: "The main milestone is the *collection*, the restoration of Russia as a single centralised state." Muscovites have been repeatedly talking about "the gathering of lands" since 1503. Five hundred years have passed but the sick imperialist idea under the guise of the double-headed eagle hasn't changed. The *collectors* achieved their goals so long as Ukrainians were ready to compromise, believe in their own simpleness, and forget about their "sharp teeth." The destroyed city of Mariupol must become what ravaged Baturyn did not — the ultimate vaccine against the *russkiy mir* (Russian World). Then it will become a symbol of a rebuilt, strong, and mature Ukraine. **Ш**

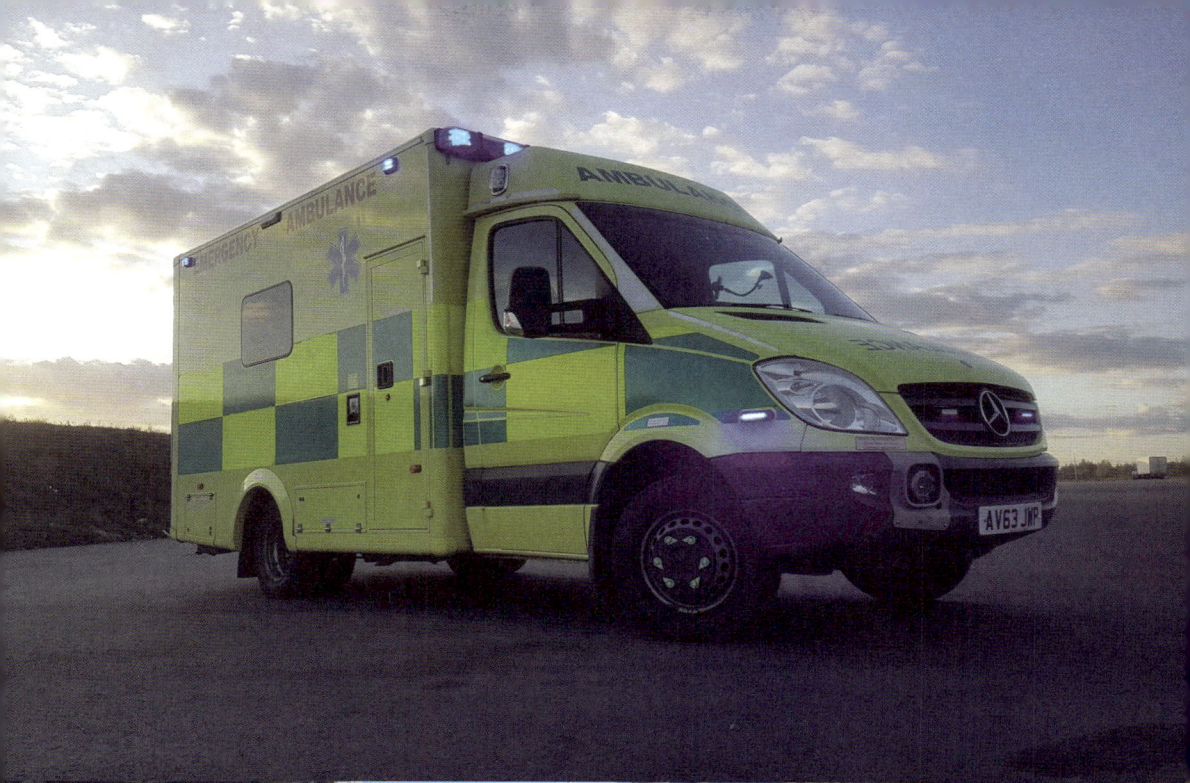

Help Ukraine Operation Palyanytsya

Help Ukraine Operation Palyanytsya (HUOP) was founded in the first days after Russia's full-scale invasion of Ukraine as a rapid response humanitarian project. Since the beginning of our activities, the organization has provided more than $3.9 million in aid, helping approximately 470,000 Ukrainians. HUOP's network of partners consists of 131 organizations located throughout Ukraine. Every project we implement is checked at least thrice for financial compliance, integrity, and safety.

To find out more or make a donation: helpukraine22.org

 Our work

 To help us

The Entertainment Industry of Russian Irredentism

Story by Sergej Sumlenny
Illustrated by Ulana Balan

"War is a natural, everyday event.
There is always a war somewhere.
It has no beginning, no end.
War is life.
War is the beginning of everything."
—White Tiger. Mosfilm, 2012.

"YOU'RE NOT AFRAID?" BOARDING a Pobeda (Victory) Airlines flight headed out of Berlin on a clear, slightly frosty January day in 2021, a blond, blue-eyed man in a green jacket with an ash-coloured scarf wrapped around his neck, half his face hidden behind a blue mask, a small dark grey suitcase in his hands, and a backpack on his shoulder, had as many cameras focused on him as Brad Pitt does when on the red carpet of the Oscars or Golden Globes. As soon as the subject of this frenzy and his wife crossed the threshold of the airplane's cabin, a multilingual cacophony erupted. A continuous barrage of questions in Russian, German, and English engulfed them like an unstoppable deluge. Most of the questions hung in the air unanswered because their recipient could barely insert a "Hello!" in the vocal mayhem.

Trying to push his way through the excited crowd to his seat by the window in the 13th row, "He-Who-Must-Not-Be-Named" initially responded to the greetings and applause of his supporters with restrained hand waves. Eventually, though, he gave in, pausing for a few moments to announce to the entire plane:

"I am very, very happy today!"

The exultant man was Alexei Navalny, Russia's most famous opposition leader, a fierce opponent of Vladimir Putin's dictatorial regime and the hope of many Russians and Westerners for a different, more democratic Russia.

"It was good in Germany, but coming home is always better," he said, storing his belongings with the help of a flight attendant into the overhead luggage compartment. And responding to a question, which had been asked multiple times since he boarded the plane, he asked rhetorically, "What do I have to fear in Russia? What bad things could possibly happen to me in Russia?"

In order to convince the people on the plane and the thousands of his followers on social media Alexei's intentions to return to his homeland were unwavering, Alexei and Yulia Navalny, sitting in their seats and waiting for take-off, recorded a short video and posted it to the politician's Instagram.

"*Malchik* (Boy)!" Yulia said into the camera, without blinking, without even a shadow of a smile on her lips, and with a steely note in her voice. "Bring us some vodka! We're flying home."

The couple was parodying the final scene from the movie *Brother 2*. In the film, the lines Yulia spoke are uttered by sex worker Dasha addressing a male flight attendant on an Aeroflot flight. She is returning home together with the protagonist, her saviour Danila Bagrov, from a decaying, decadent America to an enlightened, spiritual Russia. To reinforce her words, Dasha rips off her black wig, revealing her shaved, bald head to the puzzled flight attendant. Fortunately, Yulia and Alexei limited themselves to only removing their face masks.

17 January 2021, Alexei Navalny's "very happy day," ended with him being taken into police custody as he went through passport control at Moscow's Sheremetyevo Airport. The next day, the Khimki Court approved the detention of the opposition leader for 30 days for not complying with the Federal Penitentiary Service's sentencing provisions. This provoked a wave of protests in Russia and abroad in support of Navalny, but it did not change the situation. At this point, "the gentleman" was placed behind bars and risked being detained for a very long time.

Interestingly, during his imprisonment, Navalny significantly increased his social capital. In May 2021, Amnesty International again granted him the status of a "prisoner of conscience," and in October of the same year he won the Polish Knight of Freedom Award and the Sakharov Prize for Freedom of Thought. He was nominated for the Nobel Peace Prize in 2023 and earned the moniker "the Russian Mandela," and a film about Navalny, documenting his poisoning by Novichok, was awarded the world's most prestigious film awards: the BAFTA and the Oscar for Best Documentary.

"Come on! Poisoned?" In the trailer for the film, the main opponent of Putin's authoritarian regime wrinkles his forehead, spreads his arms wide, then interlocks his fingers on the table in front of him. "Seriously?" he asks, and it is difficult to understand what exactly he means when uttering these words: is it mockery, disdain, or a challenge?

In fact, Navalny was lucky. No matter how much the Kremlin's leader assures the world the Russian government "does not have a custom of killing anyone" and all of Putin's opponents have actually died "at different times of different causes through the actions of different people," it is a great achievement to stay alive when you are such an annoyance for the "tsar of all-Russia" that he does not even refer to you by name.

Russian intelligence services often use chemical weapons against the Kremlin's enemies. Their advantage is in the difficulty of detection. If a forensic examination is not conducted immediately, there may be no detectable traces left behind, so it's likely only the KGB-FSB itself knows for sure the exact number of people who have fallen victim to such special operations. Navalny's poisoning with Novichok, a nerve agent, multiple variations of which have been developed since the 1970s at the State Union Research Institute of Organic Chemistry and Technology as part of the secret *"Foliant"* programme, is now a well-established fact, confirmed by German, French, and Swedish experts at independent laboratories analysing fresh laboratory samples from Navalny. However, while closely following the fate of one famous Russian, the West missed how the Kremlin's political technologists and their henchmen poisoned tens of millions of ordinary Russian citizens with a different type of chemical weapon of mass destruction for decades.

The intellectual variant of Novichok turned out to be no less dangerous, and even more deadly, than the original toxin.

"THE NEAR FUTURE. The civil war in Ukraine has triggered a global catastrophe, changing the map of Europe forever. In an attempt to save the Kyiv Junta from imminent collapse, the West has provoked migrant riots in Russia. Moscow has been burnt to the ground and lay in ruins. Ukraine, ravaged and bloodied by Banderite punishers, has been turned into a wilderness, teeming with gangs who observe only one law: shoot first!

Can the new Makhnoism, which threatens to engulf southern Russia, be stopped? Who will halt the barbaric invasion of the rabid beasts? Who is strong enough to eradicate the Banderite plague, unite the *russkiy mir* (Russian World), and pave the way for the future?" *The Wild Fields 2017. On Ukraine's Ashes* (2014).

The book's cover depicts a fierce battle. An armoured military vehicle sporting the Russian tricolour emerges through flames at breakneck speed and rams a Mercedes SUV emblazoned with an Azov Battalion decal. Thickset men, seasoned thugs, frantically spill out of the SUV. These are Ukrainian nationalists, upon which, at long last, revenge is meted out for the desecration of Moscow and the humiliation of Russians.

This book is just one of thousands like it which have been published in Russia in recent years. All of them openly promote the idea of war, hatred of Russia's neighbours, and a bombastic combination of both inferiority and superiority complexes.

In February 2022, when Russia launched its full-scale attack on Ukraine, the typical Russian soldier was in his early twenties. He was born under Vladimir Putin, went to school under Vladimir Putin, was drafted into the army, killed and raped Ukrainian civilians, and then died or lost his limbs in Ukraine — also under Vladimir Putin.

"The coming war in Ukraine through the eyes of one of its participants... The Kyiv Junta, on orders from its American masters, is unleashing genocide against the Russian population in south-eastern Ukraine. Novorossiya is bleeding to death, but will not surrender. Unable to defeat the militias, the 'Nazi punishers' call for NATO reinforcements. The United States decides to intervene directly in Ukraine. The forces are unevenly matched, and without outside help, Donbas is doomed to destruction. All hope now lies with Russia, the only force which can stop the Banderite genocide..." *Ukraine in Blood. The Banderite Genocide* (2014).

And one more:

"2010. Having provoked massive riots, the 'Orange' Nazis unleash a civil war in Ukraine. With the help of NATO peacekeeping forces and under the cover of American aircraft

The typical Russian solider in his early twenties was born under Vladimir Putin, was drafted into the army, killed and raped Ukrainian civilians, and then died or lost his limbs in Ukraine — also under Vladimir Putin.

His commander, a lieutenant, wasn't much older. In other words, except for maybe a few months, he also lived his entire life under Putin's regime. If they both started reading mass-market paperbacks around the age of 15, which is the standard age for such reading, they were caught in a perfect storm: since the Russian invasion of Ukraine in 2014, Russia has been inundated by an enormous wave of "military science fiction."

This particular genre, inspired by American writers Tom Clancy and Robert Ludlum, has reached new heights in Russia. It progressed from being mass-market bestsellers toying with hypothetical conflicts to a chauvinistic indoctrination propaganda tool to "normalise" the new horrific reality of Russia's global war against a perceived evil in the world.

An advertisement for a book on Russian online bookstores reads:

and armoured vehicles, Western Ukrainian punishers with trident insignias begin to exterminate the Russian-speaking population, wiping out entire cities. Poltava is burnt to the ground, and Dnipropetrovsk is erased from existence. The entire Left Bank [of the Dnipro River], Crimea, and Novorossiya rise up against the invaders. Russia is helping the Resistance fighters with the latest weapons, volunteers, and military advisors... They will crush the damned Banderite trident! They will show the NATO hawks *Kuzhkinu mat* (send them to hell)! The battlefield is Ukraine! This is our final and decisive battle!" *The Battlefield is Ukraine. The Broken Trident* (2014).

Other types of literary Novichok with equally eloquent titles and covers complete the picture, such as *Ukrainian Hell. This is Our War!* (2014), where a Russian soldier captures an American pilot. Another example is

Ukrainian Front. Red Stars over the Maidan (2014), where American planes are destroyed in battle in the skies over the Maidan. Clearly, most of this literature has a similar narrative: Ukraine is the enemy, but actually acts as a puppet of the West, devoid of subjectivity. The United States dreams of destroying Russia, and at first even achieves some success, but the Russians decide to fight back, responding with full-scale war, because they do not fear a battle and are confident in their own strength and fortitude. The climax of their victory is the presence of Russian tanks on downtown Kyiv's Khreshchatyk Street alongside burnt-out American military vehicles, the latter representing the apogee of the "true" triumph over the West.

In the eyes of a Western observer, these books evoke a wide range of emotions, from surprise to disgust. But no one ever thought of perceiving them as a sign of some large-scale dangerous trend. They were simply ignored by the civilised world — apparently as "wildly outrageous" and therefore "not serious" — despite the fact they were printed in vast numbers and, since 2014, when Russia first launched its war against Ukraine, that Russian bookstores have been gradually turning into propaganda distribution centres. In May 2015, Moscow's largest bookstore, Biblio-Globus, located across from the FSB headquarters in Lubyanka, welcomed customers not with displays of books but with exhibits of military paraphernalia: soldier's helmets and all sorts of ammunition. In fact, military genre literature was prominently displayed on its bookshelves and in such substantial numbers, it was hard to believe it made economic sense. More likely, the brightly coloured covers of military alternate history and fantasy books served as ads, promoting radical narratives even to those who did not intend to buy them.

"Did these kinds of books first appear in 2014?" you may ask. "Actually, no," is my answer.

It would be wrong to say the promotion of anti-Ukrainian narratives at the state level in Russia began only in the 2010s. In fact,

these narratives had been present in the entertainment industry at the seemingly spontaneous grassroots level since the early 1990s. In 1992, a young Moscow programmer Vadim Bashurov developed several computer games which were distributed free of charge through pirate sites, the author's only remuneration being fame. One of the games, *Battle on the Black Sea,* was essentially a digital version of *Sea Battle* (Mattel, 1980), where the Russian Fleet opposed the Ukrainian Navy. The game consisted of a sequence of rounds in which players sought to take over individual ports, and the winner was the player who captured all the enemy's ports. Interestingly, the player could only fight on the side of the Russian fleet, and the map of Russia encompassed not only the Russian ports of Novorossiysk and Sochi, but also co-opted the Georgian city of Batumi, identifying it in its Russian language form as "Batum." The level of respect the game developer had for Ukraine was evidenced by the Ukrainian flag hanging upside down, with the yellow stripe on top, dominating the blue.

Battle on the Black Sea was quite popular, if only because it was one of the few games available to play on even very basic computers, and Vadim Bashurov himself made a good career working at Intel's Moscow office. According to his profile on the popular IT portal *habr.ru,* Bashurov currently works at the Sarov Technopark, a Russian military and nuclear research centre. He is proud to have created the first Ukrainomisic computer game and mentions it among his accomplishments.

In 1995, one of Russia's largest IT companies, 1C, joined the movement to create video games normalising war against Ukraine. Today the company is known for its universal bookkeeping programme 1C Accounting, which was developed in accordance with the principles and regulations of financial management in the post-Soviet space. Even in Ukraine, these guidelines were followed until the end of the 2010s. But back in 1995, 1C was interested in Ukraine for a different reason. The computer game it released, a detailed flight simulator for a SU-27 fighter jet, offered players the opportunity to fly a series of missions in the airspace over Ukraine's Crimean Peninsula as part of a simulated war between Russia and Ukraine. Throughout the game, the pilot provides support for "Russian-speaking rebels" opposed to the Ukrainian government, fighting for the secession of Ukraine's Crimean Peninsula, and against the Americans.

In 2008, 1C decided to repeat the success of the SU-27 flight simulator by releasing a KA-50 helicopter simulator. In this game, players flew missions against the Georgian Army and NATO, and the action took place on Georgian territory all the way to Batumi. A leading Russian gaming magazine, *Igromania*, emphasised the need for no moral constraints when completing missions: "There is no 'good vs. evil' here. There

is a clearly defined enemy and an order to destroy the enemy. That is all. What did you think? This is the army. The game does not propose for you to analyse the situation or make a choice."

The geography of these games was expanding with each release, with a focus on the Black Sea. It is hard to say what was the primary driver of this interest: whether the developers felt the war topic was "hot" or whether the Russian authorities saw an opportunity to create and test real maps of potential theatres of war. Whatever the case, the game *KA-50: Black Shark,* which included combat operations in Georgian airspace, was officially released in December 2008, four months after the Russian invasion. Online forums of Russian pilots praised the realism of both the maps of the North Caucasus and the helicopter piloting in this

game. According to the Russian pilots, these simulators were developed in close cooperation with the training centres of the Russian Federation Defence Ministry. Obviously, the gaming company's cooperation with the Russian Ministry of Defence continued: one of the game's top developers, Oleg Tishchenko, was arrested in Georgia in 2018 and extradited to the United States in early 2019 for attempting to smuggle classified documents about American F-16, F-35, F-22, and A-10 aircraft to Russia. That same year, he was tried and convicted of espionage by a Utah court.

Although highly realistic, the flight simulators were not capable of producing a broad propaganda effect. In contrast, the Belarusian-developed online game *World of Tanks* has become a truly effective product of mass military propaganda.

The idea to make a computer game with exceptionally realistic-looking tanks but with a highly simplified interface for the sake of mass use, was born in 2008 in a subculture of Russian amateur historians and military experts who blogged on the *LiveJournal* platform, met periodically for a beer, and frequently visited the Russian Ministry of Defence's Central Museum of Armoured Armament and Equipment in Kubinka near Moscow. The group included a variety of people, ranging from liberal journalist Roman Moguchiy (registered on the portal as *pantherclaw*), whose jobs included working at *Moskovsky Korespondent*, *Snob*, and *Medusa*; TV commentator Sergei Varshavchik *(warsh)*, who had worked for *Moskovsky Korespondent*, state-run news agency *RIA Novosti*, and *Lenta.ru;* moderator of the *ru_politics* community and journalist for the *Moskva 24* TV channel Alexei Baikov *(haeldar)*; top manager of the insurance company MAX Alexei Volodyaev *(hetzer)*; and *Lenta.ru* military columnist Ilya Kramnik *(legatus_minor)*, who later worked for *Izvestia*, where he was fired for criticising Russian Defence Minister Shoigu.

In 2009, the Belarusian company Wargaming, which at the time had developed several other simple games, presented a beta version of *World of Tanks,* an online multiplayer game. Among its beta testers were the aforementioned group of tank history enthusiasts who regularly visited Kubinka. It was this group who convinced the management of the local museum, which preserved historical tanks mainly for the training of cadets at military academies, to allow Wargaming to access the museum exhibits and take detailed photos of the tanks. Thus, the developers achieved the game's unique advantage of having precisely detailed visual representations, indistinguishable from the real tanks. Given that some of these combat vehicles exist in very small numbers, mostly found only in museums, this was extremely exciting for tank history enthusiasts.

In 2010, *World of Tanks* entered the open market. The following year, almost 340,000 people played *World of Tanks* per day on average, and the total number of players reached more than 20 million. In 2013, the game set a Guinness World Record for the number of people playing it simultaneously on the same server — 190,000 players.

> ## "We don't need tankers, we need players from Worldoftanks.ru."
>
> —Russian Deputy Prime Minister
> Dmitry Rogozin

Despite its ostensibly private commercial nature, the *World of Tanks* project apparently enjoyed the support of the governments of two states — Belarus and Russia. Already in 2010 and 2011, the first official *World of Tanks* events were hosted by the Russian national tank museum. In November 2014, six months after Russia's attack on Ukraine, the *World of Tanks* World Championship was opened in Kubinka by Lieutenant General Alexander Shevchenko, the head of the Russian Ministry of Defence's Main Armoured Vehicle Directorate. He confirmed the Russian Ministry of Defence was actively cooperating with Wargaming and anticipated the game would act as a mechanism for recruiting promising tank operators. In 2015, Russian Deputy Prime Minister and former founder of the right-wing radical party Rodina, Dmitry Rogozin, confirmed the same thoughts. "We don't need tankers, we need players from Worldoftanks.ru," he tweeted on the occasion of the upcoming championship. In 2016, the state-owned Belarusian airline Belavia unveiled its new Boeing 737-300 aircraft adorned with *World of Tanks* insignia.

Meanwhile, the most interesting collaboration between the game's developers and the Russian propaganda machine was the release of the movie *White Tiger* in 2012. The film was directed by the ultra-chauvinistic Russian director Karen Shakhnazarov and funded by the state budget. In the story, Soviet tankers are haunted by an unusual and mysterious white German tank. The showdown between the Soviet officer of a T-34 tank and the White Tiger ascends into the mystical realm, where it turns out the latter is the quintessence of European hatred for Russia. Although the T-34 damages the White Tiger, it still escapes. As the protagonist Ivan Naydenov states at the end of the film: "The war will not end until I destroy it [the White Tiger]... It is waiting. It will wait for 20 years, 50, maybe even 100. And it will claw its way back to the surface. It has to be destroyed..."

This was the main message of the film: the German-Soviet war was allegedly a global invasion of Russia by the West and a manifestation of Absolute Evil. The final scenes of the film include a long pseudo-philosophical conversation between Adolf Hitler and the devil in hell, where the German dictator claims he was only fulfilling Europe's collective desire to destroy Russia, which Europeans hate because of its otherness:

"We know each other too well and for too long. Too much binds us together for me to hide my thoughts from you. The war is lost. I know it. It is not just lost — Europe is defeated. But can you imagine what will happen tomorrow? Tragically, poor Germany will be accused of all sorts of mortal sins. The

German people will be blamed for everything. Thousands of books will be written about this. They will find thousands of inconsequential documents. They will invent hundreds of memoirs. And we — Germany and I — will appear before the world as unimaginable monsters of the human race, as the spawns of hell. But in fact, we simply found the courage to realise what Europe dreamed of!

"We proposed to Europe: you are considering doing it, so let's do it! It's like surgery — it hurts at first, but then the body recovers. Did we not fulfil the secret dream of every European citizen? Wasn't that the reason for all our victories? After all, everyone knew what they were afraid to tell even their wives. But we announced it loud and clear, as it should be, for we are a courageous and virile nation.

"They have always disliked Jews. All their lives they were afraid of this dark, strange country in the East, this centaur, wild and alien for Europe — Russia... I said: let's solve both these problems, solve them once and for all... Did we invent something new? No. We simply clarified the issues on which the whole of Europe wanted clarity. That's all.

"As long as the Earth revolves around the Sun, as long as there is cold and heat, storm and sunshine, there will be conflict, including among people and nations. If people stayed in paradise, they would have rotted. Humanity has become what it is because of the struggle! War is a natural, everyday event. There is always a war somewhere. It has no beginning, no end. War is life. War is the beginning of everything."

THE THEME OF THE WEST'S ETERNAL, everlasting hatred of Russia, and thus the need to oppose it, to be prepared for war and, in the ideal scenario, to attack the West yourself when the enemy is weaker than you, has permeated Russian culture. If you distil the mass narratives fed to Russians, they all boil down to either an inferiority complex or megalomania, and in both cases, they contain revanchist sentiments.

Since the 1990s, the fundamental desire of the Kremlin and its disciples has been to restore "Great Russia," which in turn was seen as an opportunity to inflict pain on anyone and everyone, without needing any justification. This explains the renaissance of books united by the theme of whitewashing the Soviet dictator Joseph Stalin. These books appeared en masse on Russian bookshelves at the start of the 2010s. Already in 2009, against the backdrop of the global financial crisis, Stalin was portrayed as an expert on the best prescriptions for escaping the grip of capitalism:

"In the late 1920s and early 1930s, a terrible crisis shook the world. Industrial production fell by 30 to 70 per cent in various countries. Millions of people lost their jobs and were left without means of subsistence. At the same time, the economy of the USSR not only remained unaffected by the crisis, but continued to develop at an accelerated pace. The standard of living of the Soviet population increased several times. According to the University of Houston and the CIA, during the 70 years of Soviet rule, industry in the USSR grew six times faster than in the rest of the world, with the bulk of the growth achieved under Stalin!" *Stalin Against the Crisis* (2009).

Stalin's Repressions: The Big Lie of the 20th Century (2009); *A Stalinist's Handbook* (2010); *Be Proud, Not Sorry! The Truth about the Stalinist Era* (2011); and *Beria: The Best Manager of the 20th Century* (2017) are typical titles of the books spreading Russia's intellectual Novichok. Most of their authors admired Stalin's cruelty, seeing it as the only way to succeed and an inspiration for modern Russia.

"Is it possible to save Russia without taking into account the invaluable experience of Stalin, who once resurrected the country from the ashes and turned the USSR into a superpower? Is it possible to modernise the economy without breaking the shackles of predatory 'liberalism,' without eliminating the 'fifth column' following Beria's example, and without imprisoning swindlers and thieves? Would a true patriot grovel before the 'Washington *Obkom*' [literally the Washington Regional Communist Party Committee, a pejorative term used in the Russian media implying crucial decisions need to be approved by and/or made in the United States] and slander the great Stalinist legacy?" the authors of the 2013 *Kremlin Pygmies Against the Titan Stalin* ask rhetorically in the book's description.

The wave of these flattering and sycophantic books was so precipitous, that in 2011 a grassroots initiative emerged with the slogan "Stop publishing Stalinist books!" However, it was a lone voice crying out in the wilderness. How could it be otherwise? After all, the appearance of testaments to Stalin on the Russian book market, which was under the strict control of the FSB secret police, could not have been an accident. In this context, Russian publishers exhibited no remorse. For example, in response to criticism of the *Stalinist* book series, Exmo Publishing Company CEO Oleg Novikov said he "considers himself obliged to cater to the tastes of his readers, not to censor them," and when asked whether he would publish *Mein Kampf* if his readers were interested in it, he replied he did not see "any commercial potential in this book."

Stalinist literature was an indicator of the demand for a revision of history, sending a very clear signal which was completely missed by the West: Russia harbours a deep resentment towards the world, as well as a seemingly contradictory desire to deny and at the same time repeat the crimes of the past. These feelings are continuing to be strongly fuelled today, in particular through the books by the popular Russian author Valery Shambarov: *Ivan Grozny Against the Fifth Column* (2016); *The Russian Victory March Through Europe* (2016); *The Heroic History of Russia for Children* (2019); *The Great Empires of Ancient Russia* (2021); *Holy Russia Against Barbaric Europe* (2022); *Fascist Europe* (2022); and *Russia — the Land Upon Which Saints Walk* (2023).

Russian attempts to rewrite history are not limited to whitewashing Stalin's crimes — they also advocate punishing former Soviet republics. Each of these books describes the conflict according to the same storyline: an "anti-Russian regime of American puppets" comes to power in a neighbouring country, and Russia can either win or be destroyed in the fight against it. For example, the author of the book *Battlefield Tbilisi* (2010) writes:

"The August 2009 defeat *[sic!]* taught the Tbilisi dictator and his Western patrons nothing. Having quickly rebuilt their military capabilities with the help of NATO, Georgians are launching a new war against South Ossetia. Avalanches of Abrams tanks and T-72s modernised in Ukraine are once again storming Tskhinvali. Air cover is provided by F-16 multi-purpose fighters and Apache attack helicopters. American pilots and Estonian snipers, Banderite militants and unconquered Chechen terrorists, are all fighting on the side of the invaders. What can Russia do to counter these international forces? Is our Army capable of defending its allies and our own military facilities? And will this next war in the Caucasus escalate into World War III?

"The latest MiGs and SUs against Georgian air defence! T-90s against Abrams! Russian special forces against NATO commandos! The Russian bear against the American eagle and Georgian jackal!"

Far from being satisfied with speculating about future regional victories over former colonies — which have been independent states for more than 30 years — the utterly poisoned Russian society has begun to fantasise about supposed past triumphs.

Few countries have the same attitude toward their own history as Russia. Back in the days of the Soviet Union, it was a popular joke that Russia is a "country with an unpredictable past," meaning it was impossible to guess how yesterday's events would be described tomorrow. The importance of history for state propaganda and the degree of its militarisation can be appreciated when noting the president of the Russian Historical Society Sergei Naryshkin is also the head of the Russian Foreign Intelligence Service (SVR), and the president of the Russian Military History Society Vladimir Medinsky also served as the Minister of Culture of the Russian Federation from 2012 to 2020.

It was Medinsky who defined the quintessential Russian understanding of the use of history. Whereas in the early 1830s, the head of the tsarist secret police, General

Alexander Benckendorf, formulated the concept "Russia's past was glorious, its present is indescribably majestic, and as for the future, it is beyond anything the wildest imagination can conjure up," the "minister of the Russian spirit" Medinsky expanded on this idea to assert Russian history was not simply glorious, but glorious to the degree that the West falsified it out of envy.

Even before being appointed minister, Medinsky launched the *Myths about Russia* book series, which released 13 titles (totalling 170,000 copies) in 2010–2011, including: *On Russian Drunkenness, Cruelty, and Laziness; On Russian Slavery, Squalor, and the 'Prison of Nations'; On Russian Democracy, Squalor, and the 'Prison of Nations'; On Russian Thievery, the Unique Path, and Prolonged Suffering; Where Do the Myths Come From and Who Are They Useful To;* and more. In 2015, this series was republished and supplemented with additional "myth debunking."

In his essays, the patriot Medinsky constantly emphasised Russia is a great power whose successes have always been a source of fascination for foreigners. His historical novel *The Wall* (2012), about the siege of Smolensk by the Poles in the 17th century during the Great *Smuta* (Time of Troubles), had a single purpose, as noted by Russian literary critic Roman Arbitman (who was fired for his review, by the way) — to explain to readers the advantages of Muscovy compared to Europe:

"Before he dies a courageous death, Grigory (and the author-narrator, who joins him in death) found the strength to patriotically convey to the reader the triumph of what is 'ours' over what is not. 'Oh, Moscow streets! How wide you are! Twice or even three times wider than those in European capitals.' The Smolensk fortress is 'not only the best in Russia, but also in Europe;' and 'what great spikes those were! Not the toy-like decorous ones on Italian palazzos...the spikes were the strongest anywhere.' Of course, Russian gunners are 'the most skilful in Europe,' 'our caviar is the best in the world,' 'our furs are the world's finest,' 'our peasants are more literate

than theirs,' and 'their taxes are much higher than our levies'."

Moreover, Medinsky frankly admitted facts do not matter, and the most important aspect of history is love for the Homeland:

"Facts by themselves don't mean much. To put it more bluntly, in the case of historical mythology, they mean nothing at all. Facts exist only within a concept. Everything starts not with facts, but with interpretation. If you love your homeland, your people, the history you write will always be positive. Always!" he wrote in his book *War. Myths of the USSR*.

This approach is organic for Moscow historiography. Back in the second half of the 1940s, the Soviet Union officially adopted the concept of "the primacy of Soviet [read: Russian] science," which implied any technological discoveries — even those which undoubtedly occurred in the West — were actually made on Russian soil. Thus, it was believed the bicycle, the steam locomotive, and the radio were invented by Russians, namely Yefim Artamonov, father and son Yefim and Miron Cherepanov, and Alexander Popov, respectively. In 1956, the USSR post office issued a stamp dedicated to another historical falsification: the world's first balloon flight, allegedly made by a Russian man named Kryakutny in 1731 (this stamp can be purchased today for about three euros). In 2018, a monument to this fake story was erected in the Russian city of Ryazan, implying it was historical fact. In Russian mythology, all of these stories are just small pieces of a larger puzzle. Many of those who studied in Russian schools, including the soldier mentioned above who lost his legs in Ukraine, were taught and believe the basic Russian perception of history: a keen sense of stolen global victories and the fundamental injustice the world has directed towards Russia.

There are specific reasons for this. The Russian army has repeatedly entered the capitals of European countries, but rarely remained there. Moreover, quite often Russia's victories were gained thanks to coalitions with others. However, official Russian historiography, at least in elementary school history courses, does not mention this fact. That is why the average Kremlin vassal is convinced the Napoleonic Wars ended with the Russian march on Paris. The fact it was a joint victory in an alliance with Britain, Prussia, and Austria is conveniently forgotten by Russians. More so, many grieve France did not become a Russian colony. Likewise, the Russian-Austrian capture of Berlin in 1760 and Russia's withdrawal from the Seven Years' War in 1762 are remembered as "an unfairly stolen victory," along with many other similar legends.

This focus on "stolen victories" is a long-standing phenomenon, nurtured by tsarist writers. Alexander Pushkin, in a letter to the "mad" Pavel Chaadayev from 19 October 1836, wrote: "It is Russia and its vast expanses which swallowed the Mongol invasion. The Tatars did not dare to cross our western borders and leave us in the rear. They retreated to their deserts, and Christian civilisation was saved... so by our martyrdom, the vigorous development of Catholic Europe was spared from any hindrance." Obviously, the "great" Russian poet of the 19th century fully shared the views of modern, uneducated Russians, proclaiming Europe owes Russia a debt of gratitude in this and many other cases.

The pain of the "stolen victories" does not subside. In 1995, at the peak of the wave of Russian democracy and the most open society in the last 300 years of Russia's existence, the Russian film *Gardes-Marines III* became a cult classic. A sequel to *Gardes-Marines, Charge!* and *Viva, Gardes-Marines*, the films represented an attempt to tell the story of the French Musketeers, but set in Russia. The series is the story of three friends who experience intrigues and conspiracies in the struggle for the glory of their country. Only, unlike the Alexandre Dumas books, the Russian "musketeers" are much more concerned with the fate of their homeland and much less with wine and love. This is especially evident in the final scene of the film, which looks like it was tailored to be used as part of a patriotism course in elementary school.

In the story, the brave Russian officers (three gardes-marines) are convinced they have every chance of winning the Battle of Gros-Jeghersdorf (1757), capturing King Friedrich of Prussia, and thus ending the war triumphantly. But a foolish Russian general, who worships the German king and believes in him more than in his own officers, cannot conceive his idol can be defeated and orders the Russian army to retreat. The heroes try to protest, but one of them is arrested, and... once again the Russians are left without a victory.

The camera pans the muddy battlefield, then angles up to show the blue sky, and the voiceover confirms in a melancholy tone: yes, victory was stolen from the Russians. Moreover, despite taking Berlin three years later in 1760, this new success would also be stolen from them, and Berlin would be returned to Prussia. Russia's rosy dreams of dominating the territory from the Pacific Ocean to the North Sea will not be realised. It is hard to imagine a clearer example of the "stab in the back" theory, a concept of chauvinism the Nazis later used in the 1920s to spread the idea the German army had emerged from World War I not defeated but betrayed by the Communists and Jews.

All it takes is a brave and clever Russian accidental time traveller, who understands the importance of the historical moment, to journey from the present to a key place and time in the past and prevent the theft of victory.

Thus, it is not surprising stories about *popadanstvo* (accidental time travel) have taken root in Russian propagandist books. This technique is one in which readers can contemplate with pleasure how such stolen glories are returned, the historical fabric put in its proper place, and Russia finally takes its rightful role as the ruler of the world — the role snatched from Moscow and St Petersburg by the Americans, the British, and, of course, the Jews. All it takes is a brave and clever Russian accidental time traveller, who understands the importance of the historical moment, to journey from the present to a key place and time in the past and prevent the theft of victory.

In fact, it was not the Russians who invented the literary technique allowing a person to travel back through years or even centuries, inhabit someone else's body or find themselves in an undeveloped society, and dramatically change the course of history or achieve other remarkable results. In 1889, the American author Mark Twain wrote what seems to be the first work of this kind, *A Connecticut Yankee in King Arthur's Court,* but this novel is more of a satirical mockery of a traditional hierarchical society, which was contrasted with the ingenuity and egalitarianism of the United States.

Other authors have used similar contrasts, such as the knowledge and perseverance of the individual versus the ignorance of the many. For example, in 1947, the American science fiction writer Edmond Hamilton wrote the first novel in the eponymous series of stories, *The Star Kings.* It tells the story of an Earth-born military veteran, now a bank clerk in peacetime, who misses the challenges of war. He soon finds himself in the body of a star prince from a distant galaxy and leads his people to victory in a grand war. In 1964, another American science fiction writer, Harry Harrison, published *The Ethical Engineer,* a story about a man who finds himself on a world with artificially restricted technological progress. He tries to advance society to devise a way to escape from the savage planet.

However, in the West, books on "accidental time travel" were not very popular. And these stories were not meant to manipulate national psychological traumas. Meanwhile, the use of this literary technique by Russians has reached an absolutely unprecedented scale, combining *popadantsi* — those who find themselves in other bodies and time dimensions — with the dream of a great and indivisible Russia.

The storylines of these tales are extremely broad. Russian accidental time travellers move into very different bodies. In *The Tsar from the Future* (2013), a young man wakes up in the body of Russian Emperor Nicholas II, prevents the Russian Revolution, defeats Great Britain, and conquers Istanbul with the help of modern weapons. In the book *Rise up, Russia!* (2009), the "involuntary time travellers" find themselves in the bodies of Nicholas II, Alexander III, and a number of Russian merchants:

"Oleg Tarugin, an Afghan war veteran, is spirited into the body of Nicholas II and changes history — in our favour, of course. His friend, engineer Dmitry Politov, who is now in the body of a merchant and industrialist named Rukavishnikov, comes to his aid. Their contemporary friends also want to lend a hand. They decide to join their colleagues and strengthen the team with their knowledge and experience. With their support, the country's industrial sphere makes a leap forward. Cars from Nizhny Novgorod become the epitome of fashion. A machine gun developed there proves to be better than the one designed by Hiram Maxim himself.

"But the team of time travellers faces increasing resistance. Unexpectedly, the Russo-Japanese War threatens to break out 15 years earlier. In addition, Emperor Alexander III and his family are assassinated. Powerful external forces seeking to prevent Russia from developing and becoming stronger are trying to slow down or reverse its rapid development by all and any means, hoping to put history back on track. Will the 'Gentlemen from the Future' succeed in overcoming the inertia of time?"

This description is one of many demonstrating Russian "accidental time travelling" focuses mainly on fantasies of violence. The Russians of today pass on to the Russians of the past modern weapons which have been successfully used against other countries, and this is how Russian dominance in the world is achieved. What is being exported from today's Russia to the Russia of the past are not social progress, human rights, or other principles and approaches to building an effective and open society, but rather conveyance of primitive engineering and military solutions which give Russia an allegedly absolute advantage.

It is not surprising to find the plots of the fantasies written by the authors of these books are very similar. Russia's main enemies are successful world empires: The United States and the United Kingdom, the latter appearing as the enemy more often. In the book *Corporation 'Russian America'* (2018), a Russian finds himself in the 18th century, conquering the American colonies, destroying the British Empire, and "stopping the genocide of the Indians." The cover of the book *London Must Be Destroyed! The Russian Assault on England* (2014) shows Russian special forces with automatic weapons under the command of Admiral Ushakov storming the British *HMS Victory,* Admiral Nelson's ship, in the midst of the Battle of Trafalgar.

The author of *The Vanguard of 'Accidental Time Travelers': Sinking Britain to the Bottom of the Sea!* (2012) describes his book:

"... The boarding of the British Empire's ships by the Vanguard of the involuntary time travellers has begun! Our fast-moving frigates are raging on the shipping lanes of the 'Mistress of the Seas.' British warships, pummelled by rapid-fire gunnery, burn and sink in the English Channel. The Emperor Paul's SMERSH eliminates the best agents of the British secret services. The history of Europe takes a different tack. In this alternate reality, neither the Patriotic War of 1812, nor the Battle of Borodino, nor the great fire in Moscow will come to pass. In this 'glorious past,' Napoleon will become Russia's ally. In this 'brave new world,' the victorious Russian-French forces will push the Brits into the sea and send the British Empire to the seabed of history!"

It is interesting to note SMERSH, Stalin's terrorist intelligence service created during WWII, is actively involved in Russia's victory over Britain. This is another example of focusing on the greatness of the Soviet Union, even though the "accidental time traveller" jumps back in history from the time of the modern Russian Federation. Russia's triumph, curiously, is achieved through an alliance with Napoleonic France against Britain. Indeed, such an alliance did exist for a short time between the two sworn enemies, in particular after the Treaty of Tilsit in 1807, but how did this imaginary Russian-Napoleonic alliance against England come to pass? And, on a similar note, what do these Russian authors think about World War II and the cooperation between another set of sworn enemies/allies, Stalin and Hitler?

> **One of the biggest misunderstandings about Russia in the West is that Western policy makers believe Russia is an anti-German and anti-Nazi country. It is not.**

THE MOST SECRET AND SORDID dreams of Russians are exposed in novels about "accidental time travellers" set during World War II. Nikolai Kulbaka, a researcher of this phenomenon, has estimated that between 2006 and 2022, about 2,500 "accidental time traveller" books, another type of literary Novichok, were published in Russia. Of the 1,300 books he was able to analyse, the largest number (256) relate to being caught in the maelstrom of the Great Patriotic War of 1941–1945 [what Russia calls WWII]. World War I is in second place (33 books), and 1917, the time of the Russian Revolution against the tsar, is in third place (21 books).

In the eyes of the Russians, the Great Patriotic War is the golden key to hacking reality and achieving ultimate victory. Just as the war against Ukraine in 2014–2024 is described in the rhetoric of the Great Patriotic War, the dream of conquering the whole world is based on this historical moment.

One of the biggest misunderstandings about Russia in the West is that Western policy makers believe Russia is an anti-German and anti-Nazi country. It is not. The fact Hitler broke his alliance with Stalin and began destroying the Soviet Union instead of attacking other nations in an alliance with the Soviet Union, deeply and irreparably traumatised Russians. Their ultimate dream consists of changing history where the continuation of the alliance between the two dictators transforms World War II into the struggle Stalin dreamed of — a war against the capitalist Western world.

Some of the books on the shelves of Russian bookstores in this genre include *Comrade Führer. The Triumph of the Blitzkrieg* (2012):

"Our man leads the Third Reich! A Russian 'accidental time traveller' inhabits the body of Adolf Hitler! Will he succeed in defeating England by conducting Operation Sea Lion, the invasion of the British Isles? Will he dare to lead a military coup to remove the Nazi Party from power and destroy the SS? Will 'Comrade Führer' be able to prevent a clash with Stalin, averting Germany's suicidal war against the USSR?"

And here is its sequel, *Comrade Hitler. The Hanging of Churchill* (2013):

"Our 'accidental time traveller,' transferred into the body of Adolf Hitler, changes the history of World War II! What price will have to be paid for the invasion of Britain? Will it be possible to hang the 'warmonger' Churchill for crimes against humanity? Will the Reich form an alliance with Stalin's USSR? Will Comrade Hitler and Comrade Stalin be able to defeat the United States and create an atomic bomb before the Americans?"

It is impossible to imagine such intellectual poison could have appeared in Russia's central bookstores without Kremlin and FSB approval, as even minor deviations by publishers from the state-approved narrative are severely punished. In particular, the publishing house Ultra.Kultura, which endeavoured to publish books with an alternative view of political and social processes, such as on the legalisation of marijuana, was forced to destroy all copies of its books, denied stands at book fairs, and eventually went bankrupt. Moreover, the unsanctioned appearance of Adolf Hitler on the cover of a book, wearing the uniform of Russian paratroopers and burning London together with Stalin, is unrealistic after 2022, when simply mentioning the Molotov-Ribbentrop Pact of 1939 can result in a criminal case for an ordinary person and a 90-day closure of a business.

Similarly, it is impossible to imagine a book titled *Attacking the Future!* (2011) could be in circulation on the free market without the FSB's "blessing." The book cover features two brothers-in-arms, a Russian special forces officer and a Wehrmacht soldier, embracing each other:

"…Germany withdraws from the war and unites with the USSR in the Eurasian Union, which is rapidly gaining strength. Unable to accept its loss of world domination, the Alliance of the Democratic Atlantic starts World War III, and when the American invasion of Europe ends in complete failure, it uses nuclear weapons. Stalin responds with thermonuclear strikes on the enemy fleet and the Los Alamos Atomic Project. The USSR against HELL! The Russian-German brotherhood in arms against the 'star-spangled' plague! The Soviet Army, in alliance with the Wehrmacht, is ATTACKING THE FUTURE! and liberating the entire world!"

Each of these books, and dozens or even hundreds of other unmentioned similar examples of literary Novichok, are the epitome of the Russian dream of revanchism and punishment of anyone and everyone within reach. The only difference between them is in which direction and against which background this revanchism is realised, and what narratives it uses: Soviet ones, more current Russian Federation themes, or a combination of both.

The key to understanding the nuclear cocktail based on Soviet pop culture used by contemporary Russian propaganda is the revanchist song "A Medal for the City of Washington," which has gone through an interesting evolution. In 1945-1946, the Soviet composer Matvey Blanter and the Soviet poet Mikhail Isakovsky wrote the song "The Enemies Burnt My Family's Home," in which they depicted the grief of a soldier returning from the Great Patriotic War ("I've been heading home to you for four years, / I've conquered three countries…"), but there is no one left to welcome him home, and the medal "For the Capture of Budapest" pinned to his chest cannot console the lonely veteran who lost his family and home during the war.

Initially, the song was semi-banned due to its anti-war narrative, but later it became known as "A Medal for the City of Budapest" and was even used at official events when the USSR changed its rhetoric to emphasise its alleged peacefulness. Later, at the grassroots level, its words were rewritten, and since then it has been celebrating the alleged self-destruction of the United States (and almost half the world) as a result of a drunken blunder by an illiterate American president who accidentally presses the nuclear launch button at a party "in honour of Bandera," and the song is now known as "A Medal for the City of Washington." Today, various versions of this song can be found on the Internet, including videos with the ruins of New York and Washington DC, or brazen mockery of Barack and Michelle Obama.

Of course, each of these individual facts was perceived by Western observers as an unfortunately crude joke — a deviation from the norm of Russia's "Great Culture." Even war criminals like the Russian author Zakhar Prilepin, who created his own terrorist battalion and boasted his unit had killed more people in Ukraine than any other military unit, have basked in the warm embrace of German admirers of Russian culture, including Jens Siegert, the long-time director of the Heinrich Böll Foundation in Russia, who considered Prilepin "the most talented Russian writer of his time."

What from a distance looks like exotic characteristics of a mysterious Russia *was*, and *still is*, state propaganda aimed at dehumanisation, which is broadcast through all types of media: movies, books, and computer games, as well as jokes and songs, which poison Russians en masse.

At the dawn of Putin's rule, way back in 2001 (!), a song parodying the popular children's song "Blue Wagon" from the Soviet cartoon *Old Lady Shapoklyak* (1974) was played on Russian television's Channel 5 music program *Ships Called at Our Harbour*. Instead of innocent lyrics about the passage of time, which at first barely crawls forward, then rushes along at full speed like the train carrying Cheburashka, Shapoklyak, and the crocodile Gena to a "bright future," circus performer Olga Rodionova, accompanied by the audience's enthusiastic applause, sang about a nuclear attack on the United States:

Slowly the rocket drifts away,
You can't expect to meet it again.
Though we don't feel pity for America,
China beware, you may be next.

Like a tablecloth, a tablecloth,
the chlorine gas spreads.
The chlorine seeps in through
the gas mask.
Everyone, everyone believes
it will be alright.
I think, I think I've lost my sight.

We may have insulted someone
unintentionally,
By dropping 15 megatons.
We see the charred and burnt earth
Where the Pentagon used to stand.

Eighteen years later, in 2019, on the occasion of "Defender of the Fatherland" Day, the song about the nuclear attack on America was performed in St Isaac's Cathedral — the largest cathedral in St Petersburg. This time, it was sung not by an unknown marginalised karaoke amateur performer, but by the St Petersburg Concert Choir led by "Honoured Artist of Russia" Vladimir Begletsov:

...

In a nuclear-powered submarine
With a dozen bombs
a hundred megatons each,
I crossed the Atlantic
and ordered the gunner:
"Aim it, I say, Petrov,
at the city of Washington!"

Tru-la-la, tru-la-la-la,
I can do it all for three roubles!
...
Sweetly slumbering in Norfolk,
the lights along the shore,
Tired toy soldiers are sleepin',
Negroes are sleepin',
I'm sorry, America, good America,
But it was a big mistake to discover you
five hundred years ago.

These lines were written in the 1980s as a no-holds-barred parody, an anti-systemic joke, but just like the song "A Medal for the City of Washington," they are used today by Russian propagandists to normalise aggressive Russian rhetoric. This propaganda discourse continued in force during Vladimir Putin's 2018 presentation in the Kremlin of an animated video simulating a nuclear strike on Florida.

The myth of the Great Patriotic War is similarly widely used by Russian cinema, as can be seen on the *Kinopoisk* website. Over the course of the 2000s, at least 162 films and TV series on military topics were produced, including feature films dedicated to individual pieces of equipment like *T-34* (2018) or *Kalashnikov* (2020). These films were made in accordance with an order from Minister Vladimir Medinsky, who explained his approach to the Soviet war mythology as follows: "If the Soviet myth about the war is outdated, it must be washed, cleaned, polished, and filled with new content... We absolutely need a positive mythology."

That is why in the more recent films, the Stalinist NKVD (People's Commissariat of Internal Affairs, precursor to the KGB) occasionally reaches an understanding with the Russian Orthodox Church. Sometimes these two institutions even merge in the guise of one person and act for the common cause, as in the Kremlin-funded blockbuster film *Maria. Saving Moscow* (2022): "Winter 1941, the height of the Battle of Moscow. A priest's daughter, who has become a junior lieutenant in the NKVD, goes behind enemy lines to retrieve a miraculous icon. According to legend, it is this holy artefact which is supposed to save the capital."

The union of mysticism with the idea of the absolute value of the state, for the sake of which one should ignore any political discrepancies (this argument is routinely used to ignore the totalitarian nature of the USSR and the crimes committed in the name of the Soviet state), has become a characteristic feature of Russian cinema regarding the Great Patriotic War. And the "accidental time travellers" trope fits perfectly into this narrative.

Russian cinema made extensive use of this storytelling technique. Moreover, Russian filmmakers introduced the topic to the general public even before the book market for "accidental time travellers" flourished. In 2008, Russia's largest state television channel *Rossiya* aired the movie *We Are From the Future*. In the story, four friends with very different personalities and preferences — from a historian who languishes in libraries to a right-wing skinhead with a swastika tattooed on his body — scavenge for ancient weapons and other artefacts in the forests near Leningrad. While searching for their treasure, they offend an elderly woman who lost her son in the war (this anachronistic part of the story is apparently meant to be mystical). The elderly woman punishes the four friends by sending them back in time to the year 1942, where fierce battles with the Wehrmacht are taking place. As a result of this adventure, the four friends change their perception of history becoming "true patriots," rescue the son of the elderly woman who sent them on their journey through time, and eventually return to the present. At the end of the film, the skinhead uses a jagged rock to scratch the swastika tattoo off his skin.

We have this film to thank for the birth of the reverence for the myth of the *Great Patriotic War* created by the Russian state. Since then, referring to the war without the proper amount of religious piety has become a terrible sin punishable by the equivalent of the death penalty: teleportation to the past (specifically, into the past according to Russian "scriptures"), where sinners can be saved only if they fully and sincerely believe in the official Russian historical narrative. In 2010, the plot of the movie *The Fog* was based on this very principle, and in 2012, its sequel, *The Fog 2*, continued the tradition.

Sometimes additional twists and turns were added to this simple concept. For example, the film *We Are From the Future 2* (2010) promoted the narrative of a "neo-Nazi" Ukraine. The film begins with the protagonists, a mix of Russians and Ukrainians, attending a music festival in modern-day Lviv, where they are confronted by Ukrainian "fans" of the Nazi SS. After the entire group is thrown back in time, they are captured by the Ukrainian Insurgent Army. The Ukrainians in the group are transformed, adopting the Russian worldview. One of these Ukrainian *"mankurts"* (originally, unthinking slaves in Chinghiz Aimatov's novel *The Day Lasts More Than a Hundred Years,* in Soviet times the term referred to people who have disavowed their homeland), who repents of the "sin of anti-Russianism," was played by the renown Ukrainian actor Dmytro Stupka.

All of these films, produced by state media companies and financed by the Russian state in the 2000s, were aimed at creating a unified hyper-militarised culture. Russian youth needed to believe the "Great Patriotic War" had never ended. It is continuing today, and the new generation must fight to the end if they want to survive.

Films produced by state media companies and financed by the Russian state in the 2000s, were aimed at creating a unified hyper-militarised culture. Russian youth needed to believe the "Great Patriotic War" had never ended. It is continuing today, and the new generation must fight to the end if they want to survive.

proper amount of religious piety has become a terrible sin punishable by the equivalent of the death penalty: teleportation to the

Russian politicians did not shy away from revanchist statements; revanchist films became blockbusters; revanchist books were widely distributed; and revanchist songs were sung everywhere. Unfortunately, things happening openly attract less attention than they should. Outright disgusting statements, insane storylines, ludicrous and toxic lyrics — in the eyes of a civilised person, all this looked like a bad joke, tasteless and outlandish, and better to simply ignore. But this is exactly what has been happening for years with Russian propaganda, which has permeated all spheres of life and prepared Russians for an all-out war against the world. A war for Russia's dominance, for the return of its "legitimate place" in geopolitics, which was "stolen" by the damned Americans, British, Jews, Ukrainians, and other nations. So, it is not surprising to see comments about the films and books like:

"Russia and the world would be very different if even 25 per cent of what the author fantasises about came true."

"In my humble opinion, Britain should be destroyed by a direct hit from a nuclear bomb."

"We should start awarding medals like this."

NO MOVIE OR BOOK CAN comprehensively reflect a culture, but the Russian film *Brother 2* came close.

The plot of this important artefact of contemporary Russian culture is quite simple. The protagonist, a young man named Danila, with a child-like face and sensual lips, is a veteran of the First Chechen War (1994-1996) who is searching for a foothold in the flourishing (for some) Moscow of the late 1990s. By chance, he learns his army buddy, to whom he owes his life and who now works as a security guard at a bank, has been murdered by his mafia employer. Fulfilling the last promise to his dead friend to help his friend's brother in the United States, Danila travels to Chicago, where he discovers a local criminal group is producing violent pornographic films where Russian girls are raped to entertain American paedophiles.

Ukrainian gangsters and Black pimps are on the side of the local mafia, and Danila is deceived by a caricatured American Jew, but

nothing can stop the Russian hero, who has become newly infused with patriotism and the belief that "Russians don't leave their people behind in a war." In Danila's view, there is indeed a constant war in the world — between Russia, which is powered by truth, and America, which is ruled by money.

The film contains all the markers of contemporary Russian nationalism, including a demonstrative rejection of Western political correctness. While shooting a Black man, the protagonist cheerfully uses the N-word and explains: "That's what they taught me at school. In China there are Chinese, in Germany there are Germans, in Israel there are Jews, and in Africa there are N*ggers."

In the end, all of Russia's enemies are defeated, including the foolish Ukrainian nationalist who is killed by Danila's buddy's brother who proclaims: "You bastards will answer to me for Sevastopol!" The Russian hero's spontaneous ally, an American "redneck" long-haul trucker, receives his reward, and Danila and his girlfriend Dasha board a plane to Russia. That's when the catchphrase Navalny and his wife repeated on their video is spoken by Dasha: "*Malchik,* you don't get it... Bring us some vodka! We're flying home!"

Released in 2000, at the dawn of Putin's rule, *Brother 2* is not simply a blockbuster — it is a film Putin regularly quotes in his public statements. The film's protagonist became part of Putin's 2004 election campaign, when ads with Putin's photo were captioned with the slogan "Putin is our president," and next to him on the ad was Sergei Bodrov's photo, the actor who played Danila, displaying the caption "Danila is our brother."

"Strength in truth," asserts Danila in the movie, while threatening an American with a weapon.

"Strength in truth," proclaimed Alexei Navalny, delivering the defendant's last word in court in February 2021 before his imprisonment.

"Strength in truth," Vladimir Putin declared as he addressed an ecstatic crowd on Red Square during a congratulatory speech on the occasion of Russia's "reunification" with the temporarily occupied Ukrainian territories of Luhansk, Donetsk, Zaporizhia, and Kherson in September 2022.

This phrase was also used by Russian propagandist media to the maximum extent possible during the full-scale invasion of Ukraine, often repeated by *Parlamentskaya Gazeta, TASS, Sputnik, Gazeta.ru,* etc. It turns out dictator Putin and his lackeys, opposition leader Navalny (who supposedly fought against Putin's dictatorship), and ordinary Russians, are united by a single cultural code: the dream of revenge and unlimited, unrestrained violence.

The "Intellectual Novichok" has fulfilled its mission: (nearly) everyone has been intoxicated.

It is difficult to say why the myriad signals of the development of a militaristic chauvinistic society in Russia remained unheeded by the West. In 2019, I visited the Russian Urals, namely occupied Bashkortostan. In the small city of Sibai, I watched hundreds of girls and boys in the main square of the city practising marching in parade formation, goosestepping as professionally as an honour guard. These young people belonged to the paramilitary organisation *Yunarmiya,* which in 2019 reported membership just short of a million schoolboys and schoolgirls (and in 2023, 1.4 million). Obviously, they spent several hundred hours on drill training, and they performed quite skilfully. But I also remember when I tried to convince a high-ranking official at the German embassy in Kyiv of the danger of what I had seen, I was met with profound scepticism.

A dangerous mixture of ignorance, admiration for Russia, laziness, and corruption prevented European think tanks, embassies, and media from connecting the (obvious) dots. Many of the Western experts who worked in Russia had read Tolstoy or Dostoevsky, met with Russian "liberals," and on this basis believed they knew Russia. The warning signs were ignored. They would have spoiled the sweet-sounding idea of economic cooperation and the concept of "*Wandel durch*

Handel" — "change through trade." My warnings were dismissed as "indolent" or "too cynical." They complained my observations were "focused on the exceptions to the rule and did not take into account the global perspective," they were "exaggerated" or even sounded "Russophobic."

Perhaps the very idea that in the 21st century, a country with all possible offers of cooperation — G8, G20, NATO–Russia Council, Partnership for Peace, PACE, and more — could voluntarily and happily choose the path of war was too frightening for many. "What do you want? Do you want us to stop building 'Nord Stream' because a book was published in Russia about a guy who was transported into Hitler's head, and another book claims Nicholas II prevented a revolution by using a grenade launcher?"

The emergence of a totalitarian society in Russia, founded on the principles of mysticism, chauvinism, and the desire for total war, a society fed by resentment and the dream of revanchism, was wildly successful, albeit going unnoticed by almost all observers.

The genocidal war against Ukraine is but the start of the consequences resulting from the cultural poisoning by "Intellectual Novichok," because Russia's real enemy is the West, particularly the United States and the United Kingdom. ⱳ

Hammer + Sickle = Death + Famine

Story by Cadmus
Illustrated by Oleh Smal

MOST PEOPLE BORN IN THE Soviet Union (or those who spent even a short time living there) have heard this poem. In the 1990s, it even appeared in the lyrics of a song by at least one rock band. Quoting it today on social media elicits profound anger in Russians, who then join in a unified chorus of nostalgia.

It turns out this epigram, devoted to the Soviet state's symbols, is not the product of folklore, as one might initially suspect. The sarcastic stanza first appeared in a German agitprop leaflet in 1941 serving as a kind of free pass to be taken into German captivity. The backside of the leaflet calls on the reader to surrender, promising both food and work. Marvellous propaganda! So good, in fact, people can recite these simple four lines more than 80 (!) years after the Nazis first put them into circulation.

There's no better propaganda than the truth. The Stalin-era Soviet Union was obviously not the best place in the world to live. Millions of people died from famine, hundreds of thousands were exiled, hundreds of thousands more were shot. There was no logic to who would be imprisoned or killed. Anyone could be arbitrarily designated a *kurkul* (wealthy farmer), or "enemy of the state," or "foreign fascist spy."

In some cases, these types of accusations ended in a bitter twist of irony. A great example is found in a scene from Ivan Bahrianyi's semi-autobiographical novel *Garden of Gethsemane* (1950). It so happened when night fell over the prison, one of the inmates of the penitentiary on Sovnarkom Street in downtown Kharkiv, the "Armenian *otaman*" Karapetyan, would begin his traditional daily routine of entertaining his fellow brothers-in-misfortune. Packing tobacco into his pipe, he got a light from Engineer N., who was sitting beside him on the prison cell bench. After taking a drag, he looked N. straight in the eye, and said: "You built a nice prison here. Very nice... Thank you, brother..."

When living in a society where a fellow inmate is the man who designed the prison and is now its prisoner, there's nothing left to do but live your life hoping a similar twist of fate will somehow pass you by. You experience a sense of temporary relief when they take your neighbour away, because it wasn't you. At least not this time around. So, it's no surprise this particular poem on a German propaganda leaflet about getting "f*cked" by the state resonated within the souls of Red Army soldiers.

Not all German propaganda was as successful. A leaflet with a picture of General Andrey Vlasov elicited disgust from Soviet soldiers and their commanders. It's understandable, because nobody likes a traitor. Initially, the Germans were in no hurry to send the "Vlasovites" to the frontlines. They did not see active combat duty until 1944, when the Germans thought the example of the ex-Soviet military commander, deserter, and defector would somehow show his former associates the "proper" path to take.

It should come as no surprise a poem making fun of Soviet state symbols was popular during the Stalin era. What's more impressive is the fact it has survived to this day. Nazi Germany was crushed, along with its ability to print leaflets, so the words could no longer be read on paper. However, the poem spread by word of mouth and was quoted everywhere. As luck would have it, the poetic form simplified its commission to memory. And its constant repetition signified solidarity with its meaning. A lot of Soviet citizens genuinely felt the hammer and sickle represented something other than what was officially articulated.

The human mind has amazing capabilities: it can organise unrelated items into a system and see images in what is nothing but a random set of figures. At some point in our lives, we have all seen clouds that look like a cat, bear, boat, etc. In 1976, the Viking-1 spacecraft took pictures of Cydonia, a region in the northern hemisphere of the planet Mars. One of the pictures included an elevated landform with steep sides, which had the appearance of a human face. Scientists immediately explained this was an illusion, the result of the interplay between light and shadow. But there were those who insisted this image was proof of the existence of a heretofore unknown civilisation on Mars. In the end, technological progress provided the opportunity to snap a better picture of the strange Martian mesa. And, as expected, in high-definition images, there is no human face visible.

The propensity to see things not really there is called *pareidolia*: from the Greek *para,* meaning "beside," "near," or "instead of," and *eidolon* meaning "image." Pareidolia of the human face is one of the most common visual illusions we encounter. Scientists have shown the same parts of the brain are used by a person trying to recognise a face as when distinguishing between real and fake ones. Humans inherited this practice from primates, who use it to identify predators. Nature's intention was to make our social interactions easier, to help us distinguish between familiar and unfamiliar people, and to glean information from their appearance.

But the default software nature installed apparently contained a small glitch, and it produced wildly unexpected results. This glitch is what gives most conspiracy theories the opportunity to flourish: human brains can interpret random bits of information as proof of the existence of an organisation or plot hiding some terrible secret. That the earth is flat, for example. Luckily, such behaviour on the part of homo sapiens is most likely a deviation from the norm. On a grand scale, this power of the human brain provides an evolutionary advantage by allowing us to build complex civilisational social systems. It lets people agree the letter "A" symbolises the [a] sound. Reading me right now, you simply need to decode these symbols. By creating a consensus that certain symbols designate certain sounds, we invented phonetical writing. The only people who missed out on this social contract were doctors — nobody can read their handwriting.

Humanity has surrounded its everyday life with numerous symbolic systems only truly understood in their cultural contexts. Sometimes, our symbols can be taken quite literally. A person depicted in a painting symbolises a person, and nothing else. In some cases, a symbol can be completely unrelated to its subject or its meaning. A red traffic light signals the requirement to stop; but, on its own, red is only a colour. And, in some parallel galaxy, red could easily serve as the traffic signal to "go."

But let's leave this droll theorising aside and consider another example. Take the painting "Annunciation" by Italian artist Fra Angelico from the 15th century. Its subject matter is the Archangel Gabriel informing the Virgin Mary she is pregnant. The painting shows a beam of light emanating from the sun (in the top left corner of the canvas) to the young woman seated in the archway of a Renaissance style portico (lower right corner). A conspiracy theory fan and friend of mine claimed this masterpiece is an example of aliens being depicted in classical artwork. When I pointed out this is an image of the Immaculate Conception, he looked at me as if I had been the one trying to convince him aliens exist, and not vice-versa. It would be interesting to see how a conspiracy theorist may have painted this particular biblical story in Fra Angelico's place.

All joking aside, the beam of light as a symbol of the Immaculate Conception or

a white dove representing the Holy Spirit in Renaissance paintings (how else are you supposed to draw a spirit?) are naturally interpreted differently today, 600 years later, than they were by the artist's contemporaries. To truly understand symbols, you must immerse yourself in their context.

The most important aspect of any symbol, in my opinion, is its ability to hold an infinitely large amount of information. The cross, for example, embodies all Christian culture and the entire history of Christianity for millions of faithful. And for millions of atheists as well, for they too see the cross as symbolising something. All the information expressed by the cross (essentially two lines intersecting at a right angle) would not fit on a single computer. Not even on a dozen computers, because it consists of a countless number of pages containing a multitude of different stories sharing a single symbol in common. The human mind's ability to fit a limitless amount of information in a simple symbol is astounding. This is, perhaps, one of the few advantages our minds have over machine intelligence. And one of the main reasons why we're the ones making machines and not the other way around. For now.

From this perspective, a state symbol is a kind of zip file condensing the entirety of a modern people's culture and history into a single image. A country's emblem or flag is a quick way of communicating a lot of information about the country in the shortest possible time. The person viewing the symbol obtains a certain amount of information from it, depending on the cultural context they're seeing it in.

In ridiculing the Soviet's intersecting hammer and sickle, German propaganda attempted to change this symbol's cultural context, which was fairly limited at the time. In fact, its story spanned a single generation: the hammer and sickle image was invented in 1918 from scratch, so to speak, conceptually symbolising the union of proletarians and peasants, which, according to Marxist-Leninist doctrine, were class allies against the bourgeoisie. Communism was supposed to come after the subjugated masses' victory in an international proletarian revolution. Their political ideology, therefore, was directed forward, towards a "bright future." A paradise for the majority was to be built on the backs of a minority group

considered to be "the exploiters." In other words, the communist ideology by default demanded a victim to be sacrificed. And although that victim was supposed to be the bourgeoisie, the peasants, supposedly the closest class allies to the proletariat, were the ones who suffered the most. They died by the millions from artificially created famines.

Nazi propagandists skilfully hit their mark when they came up with the little ditty about the Soviet emblem. But did the Nazis think their own symbol's staying power would only last a few years? Probably not. The swastika was not invented by the Germans. It had existed for thousands of years. The "hooked cross," as the Nazis themselves referred to it, was approved by Adolf Hitler as the symbol of the *Nationalsozialistische Deutsche Arbeiterpartei* (NSDAP, National Socialist German Workers Party) in the 1920s. The party's red, white, and black flag repeated the colour scheme of the flag of the German Empire, which was destroyed in the aftermath of World War I.

The swastika was extraordinarily popular at the time. Its meaning was something along the lines of "Good luck!" and was considered to be a sign of good fortune. It was used by commercial brands like Coca Cola. Still, nobody claimed exclusive rights to it.

"How the world came to love the swastika" was the topic of a BBC article from 23 October 2014. Tracing the symbol's history, the author mentioned a statuette of a bird carved out of a mammoth tusk and supposedly decorated with a pattern made of swastikas. Researchers dated the statue to the end of the Ice Age. The valuable find was made in 1908 during the excavation of the Mezine site in Chernihiv Oblast, and is housed today in the National Museum of History in Kyiv. Referencing this bird statuette, some speculate the oldest known swastika was made on the territory of Ukraine. Numerous tall tales flow from this "claim to fame." In reality, however, the markings on the bird were a pattern called a "meander" or "Greek key," made by carving a single continuous line repeating this motif.

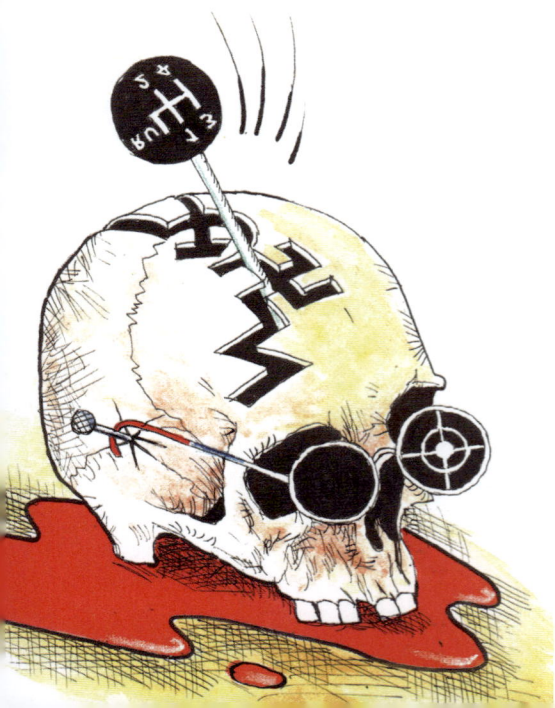

The swastika began gaining popularity among the Germans after Heinrich Schliemann excavated Troy at the end of the 19th century. Three thousand years separate us from this settlement where actual swastikas were found on pieces of broken ceramics. Many took this symbol as a specific sign indicating a higher level of civilisation. Adherents of this perspective reasoned the swastika must have appeared everywhere the Aryans went. And being a higher and more civilised people, the Aryans were, of course, destined to rule the world.

Actually, the swastika's dissemination can be explained in lots of different ways. For example, by the migration of peoples once living in relative proximity to each other to different parts of the world. Another possibility to consider is the trade and sale of ceramics, or anything else which happened to be branded with swastika logos. In the Bronze Age and early Iron Age, nobody demanded compliance to intellectual property laws and copyrights. A design on some dishware found its way to another city, where the locals became fond of the symbol, and began copying it for decorating their own dishes. From there, it could be passed on to more places. These two explanations are interconnected because they are not mutually exclusive. Tribes, whose culture incorporated the swastika, could have migrated and resettled, and started trading their ceramic wares.

There is no evidence the initial use of the swastika had any sacred meaning, or that it was used exclusively by members of a single ethnic group. There is also no indication the population of Troy migrated north, or Trojans originated in the north. And there is absolutely no proof at all Aryans are the only ones allowed to use swastikas, as the theory's adherents profess. They would expect Jews to get struck by lightning if they drew a swastika.

Ignoring these historical inconsistencies and in defiance of common sense, the pseudoscientific theories continued to be spread by occult societies in Austria and Germany whose members included those who later became Hitler's political partners. One of the articles of faith they espoused was the belief in the existence of a country called Thule, located in the Far North and home to the descendants of the original Aryans, who had survived the destruction of Atlantis. A society bearing the name "Thule" devoted its time to searching for antiquities in support of the migration-and-settlement-of-supreme-Aryan-race theories, all seasoned with the spice of Scandinavian mythology and magic. Runes, in particular, were popular among the group members for the sacral and mystical powers they were believed to contain.

Adolf Hitler's irrational personality made him an ideal recipient of pseudoscientific theories: ideal in terms of the impact they had on him, as well as in his efforts to bring these theories to life. (He was no different from those who saw a Martian civilisation behind the human face on Mars.) A German army corporal during WWI, Hitler lamented the German Empire's defeat and pined for revenge. The ideology of Nazism, in contrast to communism, did not seek to build a "bright future," but sought a return to a "bright past." The freshest memory of past greatness which could be restored was the recently defeated Empire. That is why the NSDAP flag is cast in an identical colour scheme with the Empire's flag. The mythical "Aryan state" was a more distant but ultimate ideal. In its quest to make itself great again, Germany needed victims. Instead of the bourgeoisie, which were the sacrificial lambs of the communists, the Nazis targeted Jews, Slavs, and other *untermenschen* (subhumans). Both ideologies prioritised the rights of the majority over those of minorities.

In the end, Nazism was destroyed in 1945. Hitler shot himself, and the swastika became a symbolic synonym for the Holocaust. The hooked cross is banned in some countries. In others, like in the US, where symbols can't be banned because of the First Amendment of the US Constitution's freedom of speech protections, the swastika is only used by extremists. Whoever publicly displays a swastika for reasons other than education is guaranteed to wind up in social exile.

As a political-economic system, communism existed longer than Nazism, finally coming to its demise in 1991. Even though some communist parties are still in power in their countries today, they were forced to accept serious reforms. Party members in countries like China and Vietnam rejected numerous ideological dogmas. Otherwise, they would have been forced to exclude the "enemy" class of successful capitalists from their party's ranks. But what's really interesting is that the hammer and sickle do not evoke as much negative emotion as does the swastika.

In Ukraine, the law condemning totalitarian regimes and prohibition of propaganda of their symbols was only adopted in 2015. Even after the law's adoption, it took eight years and a full-scale invasion by Russia to remove the hammer and sickle from the shield in the raised arm of the *Batkivshchyna-Maty* (Fatherland-Mother), one of Kyiv's most prominent monuments, which towers over the capital city from a hill overlooking the Dnipro River. And to this day the law does not prevent some (thankfully) former members of Ukraine's parliament from showing off these symbols in public. On 31 December 2020, for example, Ilya Kiva posted a photo of himself wearing a Russian fur earflap hat adorned with communist symbols on social media. Despite the (tepid) public outcry, he went unpunished. Contrast this to what happened after the 20 March 2021 protest in defence of pro-Ukrainian activist Serhiy Sternenko on Bankova St. in Kyiv, when a swastika magically appeared on the walls of the Office of the President's Building. This too led to a public outcry, until it was proven the swastika was spray painted after the protest was over. Its appearance was a pure provocation.

Significantly, refugees from the Soviet Union recognised the equivalence between the two totalitarian regimes and their symbols much earlier than the rest of the world did. They initiated the establishment of "Black Ribbon Day" in Canada way back in February 1986. Black ribbons became a symbol of the protest against the Soviet Union and its occupation of all their homelands. This day is now marked annually every 23 August, on the anniversary of the signing of the Molotov-Ribbentrop Pact. In 1987, this initiative was picked up by the Baltic States, and its largest manifestation became the 1989 "Baltic Way" chain of freedom stretching across Lithuania, Latvia, and Estonia.

The Parliamentary Assembly of the Council of Europe (PACE) adopted a resolution in 1996 on "Measures to dismantle the heritage of former communist totalitarian systems." In time, most Eastern European countries encoded the ban on using the hammer and sickle imagery in law, the only exceptions being Belarus and Romania (although the latter banned its Communist Party back on 12 January 1990). An attempt to ban communist symbols was made in the European Parliament in 2005, but the idea of a pan-European prohibition was rejected after the hammer and sickle and five-pointed star were deemed inappropriate for inclusion in a law on racism. So, the issue was left for regulation by the individual member states at the national level.

In 2009, Vaclav Havel and Joachim Gauck initiated the designation by the European Parliament of 23 August as the "European Day of Remembrance for Victims of Stalinism and Nazism." This was a direct legacy of the Black Ribbon movement, which began two decades earlier. Fast forward to 2019, and the European Parliament adopted another resolution, this one called "On the importance of European remembrance for the future of Europe," a document equating, for the first time in history, the victims of the hammer and sickle with those of the swastika. It also expressed deep concern over the "continued use of symbols of totalitarian regimes in the public sphere and for commercial purposes" and Russia's ongoing efforts to whitewash its totalitarian regime's reputation.

The latter could not leave such a slap in the face unanswered. In December 2019, during a meeting of the *Pobyeda* (the Soviet victory in World War II) organising committee, Vladimir Putin called the European resolution "baseless, unjustifiable lies." A few weeks later, in January 2020, the US publication *The National Interest* published Russia's official reaction to the Europeans in an article entitled "The Real Lessons of the 75th Anniversary of World War II." This opus serves as a sort of guidebook to the Russian kingdom of crooked mirrors, whose subjects full-heartedly espouse "the human face" on Mars is real, and where they exhibit no common sense, as they try to recruit new members to their cult. This sect's leader, incidentally, signed a law in July 2021 banning any comparisons of the current Russian political and military leadership's goals and activities to those of either the Soviet Union or Nazi Germany.

Meanwhile, a number of communist parties do continue to operate in Europe. Communists are in parliament in the Czech Republic, for example. There are also fairly

strong communist parties in both Italy and France. Their elected members sit in the European Parliament. However, certain progress has been made even among the ranks of European communists when it comes to their understanding of what the Soviet symbols really mean. The Communist Party of France rejected the hammer and sickle in favour of the five-pointed star, which led to disgruntled rumblings among their supporters. Still, you have to admit, it's inconceivable for there to be a Nazi party in the European Parliament today, or, for that matter, any party with a swastika in its logo.

Communism hasn't had its Nuremberg. Nobody who committed crimes against humanity in its name has been sentenced at trial with the entire world watching. Driven to despair, Hitler ended his life by suicide. Stalin, in comparison, died a natural death

following a stroke. The primary reason for this contrast is the Soviet Union ended up in the victors' circle after the war, allowing it to prolong its existence. And because the greatest number of victims of the Soviet totalitarian system were killed during Stalin's rule, this provided the basis for claiming a specific person, not an entire ideology, was to blame for the crimes. We don't know what Nazism would have looked like without Hitler. Perhaps Jews wouldn't have been targeted for killing, but only for deportation from Europe. By the end of the war, the Nazis agreed to trade Jews for trucks filled with supplies and money. Saving people's lives meant the Allies were inadvertently forced to support the Wehrmacht. In order to save their army from collapse, the Germans had to drop their racist theories. Some Germans even tried to assassinate Hitler. Now that's something no Soviet ever tried to do.

Sometimes a purely mechanical approach is used to compare the evils caused by Nazism and communism. It's obvious what that approach is: comparing the number of victims. The explanatory section of the PACE resolution sets the number of victims of communism at a little under 95 million (95,000,000!) people. One study attempted to propose 100 million victims but was mercilessly criticised for trying too hard to reach a round number. Whether or not this decreases the scope of the catastrophe is a rhetorical question. In the Olympics of Genocide, the Communists beat the Nazis hands down.

The argument that in each particular case it's not communism, but a specific authoritarian leader who is to blame, should be rejected outright. There was mass murder and famine in every country where communist rule was established. To deny this connection means you're either very stupid, or clearly biased. Bloody times followed communism wherever it went, the bloodiest typically occurring during the initial period of rule by its first leaders, who brought their murderous ideology to life with unforeseen zeal. In the Soviet Union, it was Josef Stalin (Vladimir

Lenin was the first, technically speaking, although he only ruled for a very short time). It was Mao Zedong in China, Kim Il-sung in North Korea, and Pol Pot in Cambodia. Every single one of these countries was ravaged by famine. A popular joke during the period of Brezhnev-era stagnation went like this: "Leonid Ilyich [Brezhnev], we're moving towards communism, but there's nothing to eat! Answer: Nobody said meals would be served on the journey." Ironic, isn't it?

After its first leaders were gone, communism did actually tend to soften. The heirs of the bloodthirsty tyrants understood spinning the flywheel of repression no longer made sense. The people's power of resistance was fully broken. When you're hungry, you think about finding food, not toppling the government. And it also made little sense for the rulers to keep killing their own subjects.

Unfortunately, there has never been any substantive trial nor verdict on communist terror and those who caused it. There are numerous reasons for this. The first one is political: conducting any tribunal was made impossible by the fact the Soviet Union enjoyed military might and veto powers in the United Nations. Russia had enjoyed protection from prosecution by the power vested in their control of supplies of natural gas (not as much anymore since February 2022) and their possession of nuclear weapons. And then there's China, the world's second-largest economy, where the Communist Party led by Xi Jinping is currently resurrecting the cult of Mao's personality. While humanity revels in the technological progress it has made, it's turning a blind eye to the suffering of millions in the name of political conjuncture.

In practica! terms, the victims of communism have never received any compensation. This stands in stark contrast to Holocaust victims. Germany and its mega corporations pay cash to those people who suffered from the crimes of Nazism. While it's true no amount of money can bring back millions of lives, it is a palpable expression of the admission of guilt. Words tend to carry a lot more weight when the person uttering them pulls a few coins out of their pocket. Then it becomes more than words: it is direct action.

The lion's share of the victims of communism fall to China (65 million) and the Soviet Union (20 million). And that's only counting the dead, not all of whom have been recognised as victims. The victims are further divided into several categories: those who died from famine, those who were shot, those sent into exile, and those imprisoned in concentration camps. One person suffered during the Stalinist repressions, while another became a prisoner of conscience under Brezhnev. To the east, in China, there were those who were bad at catching sparrows, those who died from famine as their harvest was consumed by insects, and those victims who were beaten to death by the *hongweibings* (Red Guards) for failing to meet certain cultural standards. While individual crimes and tragedies are readily discussed in public, unfortunately, too little time is spent talking about the victims of communism in general, in big picture terms.

There have been instances when communists themselves have admitted to their own "excesses." The Soviet Union took such a step after Stalin's death, with the "rehabilitation" of a limited number of repressed persons. Nikita Khrushchev's speech at the XX Congress of the Communist Party of the Soviet Union in 1956 was the culmination of the process debunking Stalin's cult of personality. The new leader's speech during the closed session shocked some of the older party members. There were even rumours Polish Communist Boleslaw Bierut's heart attack on 12 March 1956 was caused by the emotional trauma he sustained from listening to the speech Khrushchev delivered at the congress. But there was really nothing revolutionary about the speech. All the repressions and purges of the past were blamed on the character flaws of his dead boss. And, despite the hullabaloo, the moustachioed tyrant's embalmed corpse continued being displayed next to Lenin's in the Mausoleum for another five years.

The process of rehabilitation picked up speed after Khrushchev's speech. Somewhat. Case files were dug up from the archives and found their way back onto prosecutors' desks, and, from there, were sent to the Supreme Court for commutation. Most of the commuted sentences were in cases brought forward by the prisoners' own family members. A few of the lucky ones even received a small compensation equivalent to a total of two months of minimum wage. The rank-and-file executors of the repressions went mostly unpunished. Only those at the very top of the security services were shot, primarily those who were a part of "Beria's crew." It is bitterly ironic that the Soviet Rehabilitation Commission was headed by the General Prosecutor of the Soviet Union, Roman Rudenko, the same person who, during the repressions, had the honour of belonging to one of the "special troikas." These were extrajudicial repressive organs with the power to issue and carry out death sentences. The victims of communism were being "rehabilitated" by one of their former executioners.

In 2018, Ukraine's parliament, the *Verkhovna Rada,* passed a new law on the rehabilitation of victims of political repressions. The old law, passed in 1991, did not include members of the Organization of Ukrainian Nationalists and Ukrainian Insurgent Army among the victims, nor any other people or groups who took up arms against the Bolsheviks; for example, the soldiers of the Ukrainian National Republic Army, or the peasants who revolted against collectivisation. In May 2021, Ukraine's Cabinet of Ministers passed the resolution which required finally starting the process of paying out compensation to the victims of repressions. The amount was calculated according to a simple formula: one monthly minimum wage (6,500 UAH in July 2022, equivalent to 175 USD) multiplied by the number of months of imprisonment. This not insignificant amount was welcomed by those few who had survived until then, since their pensions were quite meagre, due to the minimal number of years they had officially accumulated in the workforce.

Meanwhile, those who once sentenced Ukraine's dissidents under the Soviets continue to peacefully collect their judge's pensions from independent Ukraine. Take Hryhoriy Zubets, for example, the former deputy head of the Kyiv City Court, who presided over publicist Valeriy Marchenko's case on 13–14 March 1984. Marchenko stood accused of violating Article 62 of the Ukrainian SSR Criminal Code: "anti-Soviet agitation and propaganda." The defendant was ruled to be a "particularly dangerous recidivist" and sentenced to 10 years in a "special regime colony" followed by five years of exile. Marchenko died on 5 October 1984, in a prison clinic in Leningrad. Zubets, meanwhile, continued building his career: he was promoted to become the head of Kyiv City Court in 1993, then appointed a member of the Higher Qualification Commission of Judges in Ukraine, finally passing his judge's robe on to his son as his legacy. President Petro Poroshenko awarded Zubets with the Order of Prince Yaroslav the Wise on 6 October 2017 for his *"substantial personal contribution to the development of a rule of law-based state, for providing the defence of citizens' constitutional rights and freedoms, for many years of seminal work, and for a high level of professionalism."*

Contrast that to the example provided by Poland in the late 1990s, when it demanded the extradition of Helena Wolinska-Brus from Great Britain. She was a military prosecutor in the communist Polish People's Republic. Poland's Institute of National Memory determined she had participated in one-sided investigations and unfair trials of members of the anti-communist Polish resistance during the 1950s. In 2006, she was stripped of her prosecutor's pension along with her other state awards, and in 2007, the Military District Court of Warsaw issued a European warrant for Wolinska's arrest. Only her death spared her a trial.

Ukrainians are gradually learning how to respect the victims of totalitarian regimes, but, unlike the Poles, Ukrainians continue to reward their executioners.

Humanity, unfortunately, has failed to offer the victims of communism anything more than the opportunity to legally clear their good names. The victims of Soviet repressions (at least some of them) stopped being treated like felony criminals. But this was all they got. Compared to the victims of Nazism, the victims of communism find themselves in a "lesser" category of victimhood. No retribution, no remorse, nothing but members of European Parliament sporting hammers and sickles on their party logos.

Why is that? Why can't we condemn communism with the same fury and disdain with which we condemn Nazism? It has to do with the magnitude of victims. There were well over 100 million victims of communism, because those who believed in that ideology were also its victims. They were fooled by their own elites and, as might be expected, by their own short-sightedness. The first to fall victim to any utopian belief system is the mind; only later does it spill into the physical world.

If we're incapable of conducting a Nuremberg for communism, then can we at least not tolerate its symbols, which represent the murder of millions of people? Nazism promised a return to the "bright past" on the backs of supposedly racially inferior minorities. Communism was unsentimental about the past, because it was marching towards a "bright future" on the corpses of the hostile bourgeoisie and the supposedly allied peasant class. We need to remember this for the future: any political ideology promising a "bright future" for one part of society dependent on the sacrifice of another, regardless of its size, is no different, in essence, from either Nazism or communism. Promises of paradise for a majority at the price of a minority will always end up creating hell in the here and now.

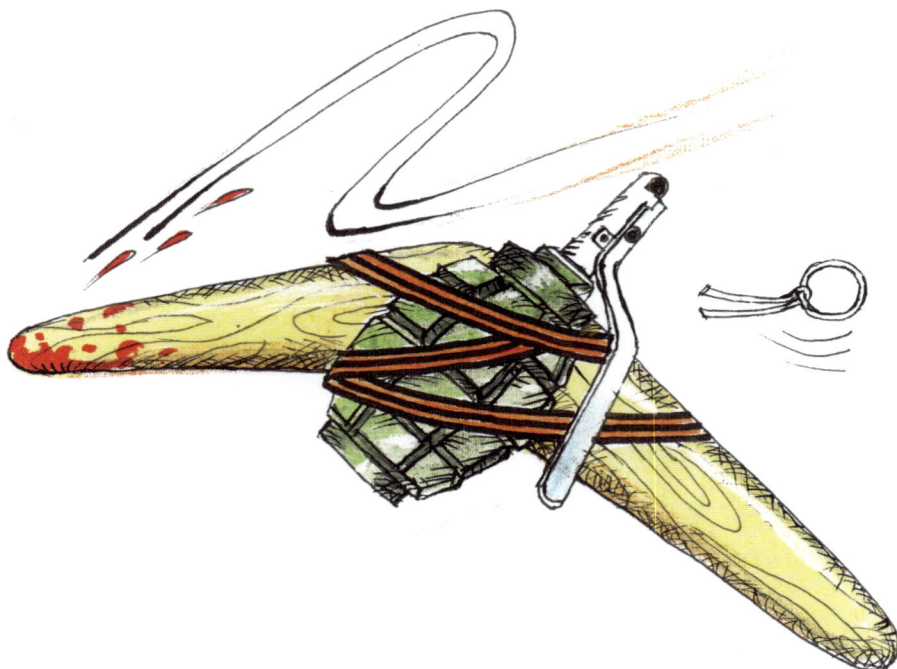

Never again...

As the Kremlin scaled up its war against Ukraine, a new symbol spread like wildfire: the Latin letter "Z" also called a *"zetka."* Russian state media has devoted significant resources to promoting what was initially a military marking. And, judging from the photos of various emblazoned cars, flash mobs, and Z merchandise, this newfound symbol struck a fairly resonant chord within Russian society. The Kremlin's goal in promoting the new symbol is understandable: it's trying to rally its citizens for the war against us.

The symbolic provocation proved successful because the Western media began obsessing over it. The major media players vied to outdo each other in their televised reports and published articles delving into this new Russian symbol of aggression. News agencies around the world reported on the one Russian athlete, who, during the gymnastics competition "Apparatus World Cup" held in Doha, Qatar, in March 2022, accepted his award while wearing a *zetka* on his shirt. That same month, they also reported how children being treated for cancer in a hospice

in Kazan were assembled in the hospital yard to form the letter Z with their bodies while lying on the ground.

The major preoccupation in the reporting on the new Russian symbol was: "What does it mean?" Most would agree, initially, it was simply one of the symbols used to mark military equipment, and was used alongside other letters, like "V" and "O," to prevent Russian soldiers from shooting one another. Foreign journalists' interest into the hidden or obvious meaning of the letter Z was fuelled by Russia. First, their Ministry of Defence explained it stands for *Za pobyedu* (for victory). Then it took on new meanings: *Za Putina* (for Putin), *Za nashykh* (for our guys), etc. These "Za whatevers" are well-suited to the Russian mentality, because they sound like a typical toast one might utter when raising a glass around the table.

The international media's interest in Z's "real," "true," or "initial" meaning only added fuel to the Kremlin propagandists' fires, who, in turn, kept interest in the new symbol going. This technique of political technology is both simple and ingenious: keep promoting the letter Z while everyone else ponders its deep (or not so deep) meaning.

The essence of this new symbol was very accurately captured when it was christened the "Zwastika." This name works well because the visual similarity between the two is striking: the Z looks like a Nazi swastika with its horizonal line missing. This is a good demonstration of how our brains interact with symbolic systems. A person is capable of recognising even partially erased symbols. People can also recycle old forms into new ones, while modernising and improving them in the process.

But let's get back to the questions that need to be raised about this new Russian symbol. One of the most obvious is: why did they decide on this Latin, very "Western" and very un-Russian, letter Z? Clearly, Russian society required consolidation around the war. But why did the war require the introduction of a new symbol, when the Kremlin's imperial arsenal already had so many to choose from? Take your pick: a two-headed eagle, the hammer and sickle, a red five-pointed star, or the *georgiyevskaya lenta* (St. George ribbon), whose colour scheme was copied from baroque and classical art and goes well with any modern colour palette. But the Putin regime, for some reason, felt the need for, or even the demand for, a new symbol.

The superficial explanation is in the symbol's form. More precisely, in the simplicity of copying the symbol. Any idiot can draw a Z, which makes it very similar to the swastika. But the deep underlying reason has to do with infusing the Z with meaning. We understand symbols from their context, but symbols are also capable of creating the context in which they are understood.

For Russia (which declares the war is directed outward, that is, to push a hostile enemy back from its borders, such as the entire NATO bloc of countries, or Nazism, as they claim), the war against Ukraine serves an enormous purpose domestically. The Kremlin started this war in order to transform the Russian state down to its very core. The thing is, after the capture of Ukraine's Crimean Peninsula, the Russian Federation found itself sitting on two chairs at once:

on one, the Kremlin bosses had quenched some of its society's imperial thirst; on the other, in view of the West's weak response and the limited resistance on Ukraine's part, the Russians continued to remain part of the globalised world, even though they had themselves opened the exit door. After eight years, the feeling of satisfaction from the annexation of Ukraine's Crimean Peninsula had worn off, but grabbing any more land meant walking through the opened exit door once and for all, and slamming it as loudly as possible on the way out. It's likely Putin wasn't completely confident about how much Russian society would support the strategic move his state had made. For the globalised world offers a great many advantages in terms of life's comforts: from the ability to travel and eat *jamón*, to furnishing your apartment with items from Ikea.

The decision was ultimately made in February 2022. The Kremlin's final hesitation is laid bare in the turgid euphemism "special military operation," which Russians are required to use in lieu of the word "war." As for the claim average Russians supposedly feared a war between Russia and Ukraine, the Levada Centre reported the results of their annual survey of societal trends for 2021 where 43 per cent of respondents felt Russia should "join the armed conflict on the side of the Donetsk and Luhansk People's Republics (DNR/LNR)" and 65 per cent supported making these territories part of Russia. Seizing Ukrainian lands ranks high in our northern neighbour's hierarchy of needs, apparently higher than repairing roads in Karelia, buying a new iPhone, or eating a burger at McDonald's. All of this gives the Kremlin colossal carte blanche for reconfiguring its authoritarian regime into a totalitarian one. And the letter Z, which was initially used for combat identification purposes, came to be heartily accepted by Russian society, and so became a symbol of this transition.

The world was shocked when terminally ill children in Kazan were forced to lie on the ground in their hospice yard to form a giant letter Z. But few if any discussed what, precisely, was so frightening about that particular flash mob. It horrifies us because the sick children's fragile bodies are being exploited for propaganda purposes.

Questions like "What did the *zetka* (Z) mean in the first place?" or "Why did they pick a letter from the Latin alphabet and not their own Cyrillic?" are definitely secondary. We are witnessing a new totalitarian symbol growing in power right before our eyes. It already represents thousands of deaths and a variety of war crimes, from the plundering of toilets to torture, executions, and raping of civilians. Symbols may only be images, but behind their façade they can conceal stories of unspeakable suffering.

Behind every totalitarian symbol stands its victim. Sometimes, as in the case with the hammer and sickle, its target is an abstract group of people, like "the bourgeoisie." Sometimes, as in the case of the swastika, and the analogous Z symbol, the targets are specific national groups — Jews and Ukrainians. So, the most important question we ought to be asking ourselves is: have we done enough to condemn the totalitarian symbols of the past and ensured new totalitarian symbols do not become lethally powerful in the present? **W**

Deus ex Ucraina: The Fire
Voices in the Ukrainian Wilderness
The Memory Candle and the Light of Mace
Life, Death, and Survivor's Blush

The Black Sea
WHALE

A Beacon in the Sea of Troubles

Nº3

Coming Soon!
Visit BlackSeaWhale.com

IDEAS & STORIES FROM UKRAINE

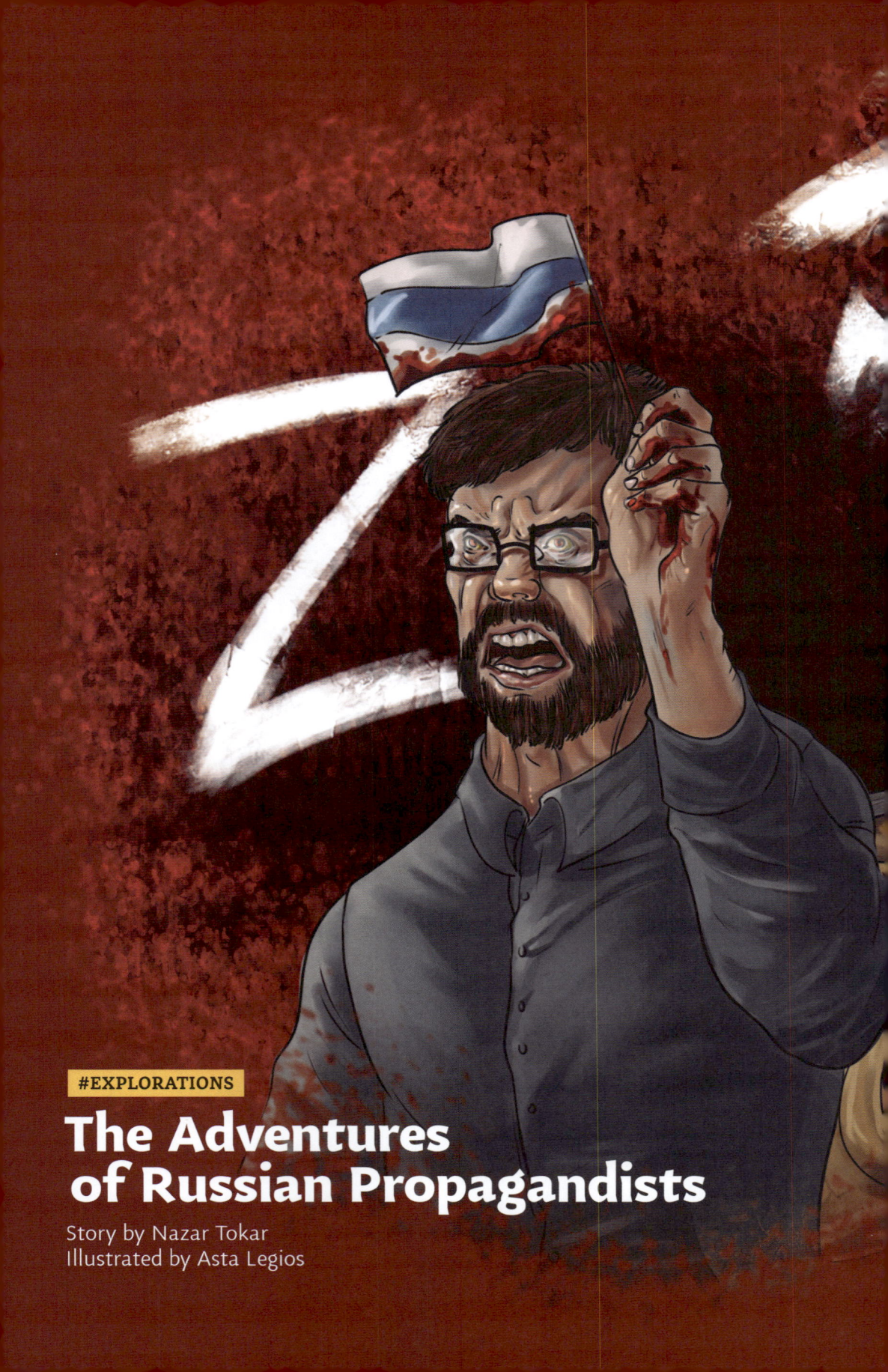

#EXPLORATIONS

The Adventures of Russian Propagandists

Story by Nazar Tokar
Illustrated by Asta Legios

THE WHITE CEILING OF THE OVAL-shaped hall is decorated with bas-reliefs and massive frescoes. Hanging in the centre, a spherical copper chandelier cradles hundreds of light bulbs shining so brightly your eyes hurt. Endless lists of names cover the walls, and if you get close enough, you can discern some of the individual names of those who died in World War II. The crown jewel of this setting is a four-metre-tall bronze statue of a soldier wearing a cloak, his left hand extended upwards, reaching for the sun. In his right hand — an inverted helmet and a wreath, which together, apparently symbolise Stalin's defeat of Hitler.

The Museum of the Great Patriotic War, built in Moscow on *Poklonnaya* (Genuflection) Hill, is crowded on this particular day. Russian flags are hanging everywhere and clean-shaven young men in uniform are standing at attention, holding polished assault rifles to their chests, and straightening their backs to the sound of the Russian national anthem. It is December 2014. Russia has occupied Ukraine's Crimean Peninsula and launched the war against Ukraine's Donbas region less than a year ago. The empire must grow in order not to die, and therefore requires new victories. Just like their grandfathers who once fought in the "Great Patriotic War," these young men would not mind conquering Berlin and building the "dream" empire from Lisbon to Vladivostok.

The museum was built in dedication to Russia's victory in the Great Patriotic War, which is what Russians call World War II. Construction began a year before the Chornobyl tragedy, when, amid the setbacks in the war in Afghanistan and the decrease in world oil prices, the level of Soviet welfare had fallen so low, no slogans of "sausage for two roubles" could keep the Soviet empire together. Construction lasted 10 years, and it was completed in 1995, on the 50th anniversary of the end of the war. It happened at just the right moment, when the collapse of the USSR, inflation, unemployment, corruption, ration cards, and rampant criminality in the former union republics, as well as in Russia itself, did not engender much patriotism. Not to mention having caused another wave of emigration.

On this day in December 2014, soldiers from the 154th Separate Command Regiment are taking their oath. They are part of the army elite, and thus are unlikely to become cannon fodder. Units such as these are sent to the front as a last resort when the leadership becomes desperate, having depleted the stockpile of non-Russians from remote corners of the pseudo-federation to throw at the enemy. Which is why the mothers of these new soldiers aren't particularly worried as they use handkerchiefs to wipe tears of joy rolling down their garishly made-up faces. "The soldiers, transformed forever, march out of the hall carrying their battle flag to the sound of the regimental anthem, which has not changed since Peter the Great," proclaims journalist Dmitry Kozhurin, who works for the *Zvezda* (Star) television channel, solemnly reporting from the museum on this great occasion.

Zvezda is a propaganda "patriotic" TV channel operated by the Ministry of Defence of the Russian Federation. The stories produced by its journalists raise many questions, even among people who are convinced politics doesn't affect them. For example, they have produced and published materials covering themes such as:

- Zombie soldiers are fighting in the Ukrainian army;
- The local population in the west of Ukraine planted kisses on Red Army tanks in 1939 (allegedly welcoming the Russian occupation);
- Schismatics illegally seized the last church of the Ukrainian Orthodox Church (UOC) of the Moscow Patriarchy in the Ivano-Frankivsk region (in reality, churches from the Russian Orthodox Church in Ukraine were voluntarily transitioning over to the Kyiv Patriarchy of the Orthodox Church of Ukraine);
- Ukrainian nationalists have resumed shelling Donetsk city (when the Russian military was actually doing the bombing);
- Czechoslovakia should be grateful to the Soviet Union for the events of 1968;
- The Finnish military, not the Russians, actually started the Winter War of 1939, and many more.

Not a lot of information can be found about the journalist Dmitry Kozhurin, but he definitely worked for the Russian Ministry of Defence channel Zvezda from at least 2014 to 2017. He is listed on their website as an in-house correspondent during those years.

In August 2014, in the first year of the Russian-Ukrainian war, Kozhurin travelled to the Russian border with Ukraine's Donetsk region, which was already occupied by Russian troops, to report the Ukrainian side was blocking Russian humanitarian aid from crossing the border and providing relief for the local population. To quote from Kozhurin himself: "It seems as though the Ukrainian authorities are not willing to speed up the movement of the convoy and do not want to help the people of their own country." That same month, the tragic battle of Ilovaisk took place, with Russian troops surrounding Ukrainian Armed Forces units, killing more than 350 and wounding more than 400 Ukrainian soldiers.

It's worth noting these Russian convoys had a different purpose than was alleged by the Russians: they were delivering food, weapons, military ammunition, fuel and motor oil, and other supplies to the Russian military and pro-Russian proxy forces under the guise of humanitarian aid. These were the "humanitarian items" Ukrainian border guards detected when they were able to gain access to inspect the Russian trucks. The Ministry of Foreign Affairs of Ukraine repeatedly demanded Russia stop supplying weapons under the guise of humanitarian aid, but to no avail.

In the 27 June 2014 episode of the programme *Here's What's Happening* on the Zvezda TV channel, Kozhurin reported Ukrainian refugees were fleeing from Ukraine to Russia. He described how the local administration in the Rostov region of Russia was welcoming refugees, providing them with access to the internet and television, and how much better their lives had become. The journalist pleasantly nodded along as a psychologist assured him the children would easily endure the evacuation and the war.

A few years after these reports, Kozhurin underwent an interesting metamorphosis — he quit the propaganda TV channel, moved to Spain, and, in 2022, started working for the Russian-language channel *Nastayashchee Vremya* (Current Time), where he broadcasts live almost daily about the war in Ukraine from a completely different perspective.

Nastayashchee Vremya is a Russian-language TV channel with a Prague-based editorial office, created by Radio Liberty/Radio Free Europe and Voice of America. It is funded by the US Congress and administered by the US Agency for Global Media. The channel aims to promote democratic values, in particular uncensored news, and a responsible exchange of opinions. Voice of America broadcasts in 48 languages, and this Russian-language service was one of the first channels they established.

Voice of America has a Ukrainian-language radio programme (with extremely meagre funding compared to Nastayashchee Vremya), but it has not created a Ukrainian-language TV channel which could broadcast for at least a few hours a day. As a result, many Ukrainians watch Nastayashchee Vremya instead of the monopolistic and rather primitive television "marathon" shown on all of Ukraine's TV channels since 24 February 2022. The Russian-language Nastayashchee Vremya is popular, with more than three million subscribers on YouTube and, according to the site's statistics, is watched by about the same number of viewers from Ukraine and Russia, the vast majority of which are under the age of 40.

Having watched several of Dmitry Kozhurin's recent programmes, it is hard to find anything wrong with them. Since 2022, he has been saying all the right things and, unlike many other Russians, he allows himself to call the war a war and Putin the aggressor. Kozhurin has become such a "good Russian" he was invited to appear on the Ukrainian state-run TV channel Freedom. At the time he was interviewed, the channel was still broadcasting in Russian. From that time forward, Kozhurin has been considered a liberal journalist not limiting himself to making critical comments about the Russian regime only on an American sponsored channel. The question of whether Dmitry has truly realised the error of his ways and left the dark side, or whether he has simply decided to find a warmer and safer place to live, is rhetorical. I wrote to Dmitry inviting him to comment on his previous work, but at the time of writing this article, I have not yet received a response.

Kozhurin turned out to be just the tip of the iceberg. I decided to find out more about the Russian-language TV channel on Voice of America — Nastayashchee Vremya — and inquire whether he was an exception among the other staff members. Spoiler alert: he was not.

In the autumn of 2022, Russian journalist Harry Knyagnitsky started working in the office of the Russian-language service of Voice of America. Prior to that, he had worked for the Russian propaganda TV channel NTV, where he reported the Ukrainian military allegedly guided artillery by targeting civilian cell phone signals. In the same story from 2014, he claimed residents of the occupied territories were "ready to take up arms," referring to their willingness to participate in the so-called "Donbas militia." Knyagnitsky never once mentioned it was the regular army of the Russian Federation, supplemented by a handful of collaborators, who occupied Ukraine's Crimean Peninsula and parts of the Donbas region.

In another story near the end of 2014, Knyagnitsky reported Russian militants allegedly "had to return fire" otherwise a Ukrainian tank would have destroyed a residential area. At the time, he called the Russian-Ukrainian war in the east of Ukraine a genocide by Ukraine against the "people of Donbas," and the journalist's reporting falsely identified Ukrainian children kidnapped by Russians as war refugees. He is also the author of a story about the detention of the so-called "terrorist group" whose members included Ukrainian filmmaker Oleg Sentsov. Following his detention, Oleg spent five years in captivity, in a Russian prison.

None of Knyagnitsky's reporting at the time mentioned Russian aggression, and he consistently referred to Russian proxies as "militias" or "Donbas self-defence units." Interestingly, the "self-defence" narrative was even picked up by some Ukrainian media outlets. In 2017, Knyagnitsky quit NTV, moved to the United States, claiming in an interview he was no longer willing to "toe the party line." In 2018, he got a job at the Russian-language TV channel RTVi in New York. From 2012 to 2019, this TV channel was owned by Russian businessman Ruslan Sokolov, the former director of the previously mentioned Russian propaganda Zvezda TV channel.

In 2021, in a story titled, "A Year Without George Floyd: How the United States Has Changed and What *Black Lives Matter* Activists Have Achieved," about the protests after the murder of African American George Floyd by a white police officer, Knyagnitsky wrote: "Wherever there are black people, there is crime. That's what the Russians who left South and East Harlem say. A year ago, it was safe there, but after Floyd's death and the protests, it became dangerous. Today it's politically incorrect to associate this with African Americans." In any sane, moreover, mainstream American media, a journalist would have been immediately fired for making such statements, but not in this case. The article had no effect on Knyagnitsky's career.

After leaving NTV, he neglected to change his rhetoric, and in 2019, while still working at RTVi, when Russia seized Ukrainian ships in the Kerch Strait, he claimed Ukraine had allegedly provoked Russia and it was not really clear who was to blame. But soon after switching to the Russian-language Voice of America in 2022, Knyagnitsky did change his tune a little: he began to criticise Russia and even allowed himself to call the war a war.

In 2020, Knyagnitsky cautiously criticised NTV in an interview: "The management forbade me to do live broadcasts with Ukrainians who spoke about Russian shelling and killings. RTVi allowed me to tell the truth about the war." So, it turns out, he had wanted to tell the truth, but the evil managers of NTV forbade him from so doing. Shifting responsibility onto others has always been very popular, in particular at the Nuremberg trials, where Nazis justified committing the bloodiest crimes against humanity as simply obeying orders "that could not be disobeyed."

The year 2016 marked a change in RTVi policy and the channel started expanding its broadcasting network. Well-known Russian journalists began moving to the "rebranded" channel en masse. A significant number of the new employees had previously worked for NTV. In addition to Knyagnitsky, Leonid Parfyonov, Anton Khrekov, Vladislav Andreev,

Dmitry Novikov, Konstantin Goldenzweig, Natalia Metlina, Svetlana Cheban, Marianna Minker, Elsa Gazetdinova, Konstantin Rozhkov, Sergei Mitrofanov, Tikhon Dzyadko, and others joined RTVi. Some of these journalists then proceeded to quietly switch from RTVi to the Russian-language Voice of America. Dzyadko, who served as deputy editor-in-chief of RTVi for almost two years, became editor-in-chief of the "opposition" TV channel *Dozhd* (TV Rain) in 2019. Dozhd caused a scandal in the autumn of 2022 by raising money to buy supplies for the Russian occupation forces in Ukraine. Latvia, Lithuania, and Estonia did not take long to ban the broadcast of this propaganda channel in their countries and did so in December 2022. Another propagandist, Daria Davydova, who had previously worked for Russian state television, where she justified Russia's occupation of Ukraine's Crimean Peninsula, has also been working for Voice of America since the autumn of 2022.

The staff of RTVi paradoxically combines both seemingly opposition journalists and journalists loyal to the Kremlin authorities, some of whom continue to pave the way for their colleagues to find jobs at Voice of America. For example, in 2020, one of RTVi's producers was Sergei Shnurov, the leader of the Russian band Leningrad, which performed frequently for the Kremlin. Shnurov had been co-hosting the programme *About Love* on Channel One Russia since 2016 and in 2019 was appointed to the Public Oversight Council for the State Duma Committee on Culture in the Federal Assembly of the Russian Federation. In this capacity, he has acted as a "release valve" dissipating the anger of Kremlin critics. His songs gently ridiculed the corruption and gaudy lifestyles of officials, but Shnurov eventually wound up alongside those he sang about. From August 2022 to March 2023, RTVi hired another producer, Konstantin Obukhov, a *KVN* performer (KVN is a Russian and former Soviet comedy television show) and one-time producer of entertainment projects on the Russian TV channel TNT, owned by state-run Gazprom.

In March 2023, another former RTVi journalist, Ilya Klishin, also joined Nastayashchee Vremya, having served as editor-in-chief of the Dozhd channel's website in 2013–2016 and having worked previously at RIA Novosti, one of Russia's largest state media agencies. In 2014, he published an article "How Russia can keep Crimea after Putin," reflecting on the legalisation of the occupied Ukrainian peninsula. Since 2022, he has been living in Vilnius and tweeting about anti-war rallies and Russia's problems. After the news about Klishin became public, management of the channel announced he would not be heading up the internet team behind Nastayashchee Vremya.

According to an investigation published in 2023 by Alexei Navalny's team, from 2019 through 2021 RTVi received 1.3 billion roubles from Moscow City Hall in payment for advertising campaigns and as transfers through "shell companies." These payments made up 60 per cent of the channel's budget, which directly points to the Kremlin's funding of the alleged opposition American-based TV media.

But Russian propagandists are not only going to the US. On 14 March 2022, Marina Ovsyannikova erupted onto a live evening broadcast of the Vremya (News) programme on Channel One Russia with a handwritten anti-war poster and shouted several times, "Stop the war! No to war!" At the time, news anchor Yekaterina Andreeva was calmly reporting that Russian Prime Minister Mikhail Mishustin was calling on the Belarusian prime minister to cooperate with Russia to circumvent sanctions. A video of a different story abruptly interrupted the anchor in mid-sentence, and the channel's management subsequently announced an internal investigation. What Ovsyannikova did not write on her poster was there are no live broadcasts on central Russian television, and any "live" broadcasts are aired with a 15-second delay to avoid exactly these kinds of situations.

Ovsyannikova was born in Odesa and had the surname Tkachuk before her marriage. Since 2003, she has been working at Channel One, the job she had long dreamed of. Marina claims someone let the air out of the tyres of her car in the parking lot near the Ostankino television tower as well as that she had been detained for several days by the police as the only consequences of her performance with the poster. Supposedly, over the 19 years she worked at Channel One, she was fine with everything she was doing, but the full-scale invasion of Ukraine by Russian troops on 24 February 2022 affected her so profoundly, she could neither eat nor sleep for several days. The journalist wrote a letter of resignation four days later, paid a fine of thirty thousand roubles ($250), and left the country without any difficulties at the border. In an interview, Ovsyannikova stated she did not support the government but didn't take part in street protests because… she was "too busy."

Having become a hero overnight, Ovsyannikova's name was trending on Twitter, and her lavishly made-up face became a frequent sight on TV and the internet with a host of interviews on Western and liberal Russian media. She started writing protest posts on Facebook and announced she was working on a book. At the same time, in late March and early April 2022, Western media were covering stories about Russian occupation forces' tanks firing on evacuation convoys, Ukrainian and foreign journalists were reporting on the massacres in Bucha and Irpin by Russians, war crimes unheard of since World War II, and the exodus of people trying to leave Ukraine.

But the damage was done. The world's attention shifted for several days from the war crimes of the Russian army to a woman who resolved to say "No!" to the propaganda she herself had been creating for 19 years. Ovsyannikova quickly changed her comfortable existence in Moscow for an equally comfortable one in Berlin. As early as April 2022, she became a journalist for the German media Die Welt, and in June she even returned to her "native" Odesa, causing a flurry of criticism and questions for the Security Service of Ukraine about how she managed to cross the border.

The editor-in-chief of Die Welt, Ulf Poschardt, said Ovsyannikova's protest "upheld the most important journalistic ethics," while Ovsyannikova herself complained about the Ukrainian "haters" who had written in to protest her being given a job at the German media. In May, she was awarded the Václav Havel Prize for her creative protest. This raises the question: can propaganda be considered journalistic work? If not, then hiring Ovsyannikova to work for Die Welt is baffling, since she has no experience in journalism.

In July 2022, Ovsyannikova astonished the public again by unexpectedly returning to Russia. After a single one-woman protest in Moscow, she was re-detained by police and placed under house arrest, where she began writing her autobiography. In the autumn of 2022, her ex-husband said she and her daughter had escaped from arrest, after which she was put on a wanted list, which somehow did not prevent her from leaving the country unhindered, again. In February 2023, Marina presented her German-language book *Zwischen Gut und Böse (Between Good and Evil. How I finally Opposed the Kremlin's Propaganda)* in Paris, which can be bought for €20. The book has already been translated into several languages.

Another example of a propagandist who took root in the West is the Soviet-Russian journalist Nikolai Gorshkov, whose father was a naval intelligence officer in the USSR. In the 1970s, Nikolai studied the United States and Canada at one of the institutes of the

Academy of Sciences of the Soviet Union, and in the 1980s he worked for the World Service of Moscow Radio, whose transmitters operated in the Soviet Union, Eastern Europe, and Cuba. The radio station broadcasted in 70 languages and was one of the main tools of Soviet propaganda aimed at the West. It was later used as the foundation for the Sputnik propaganda media platform.

Gorshkov was a loyal supporter of the Kremlin and frequently accused the West of trying to undermine the Soviet Union. In May 1984, in a programme for Austrian listeners discussing the topic of "The West's Psychological Warfare Against the Soviet Bloc," Gorshkov claimed the USSR was attempting to fix the damage to international relations caused by the West's lies and slander. More than 40 years later, in 2017, he commented on his work as the head of Sputnik in Britain as follows: "In the three years I have been working here, I have never received a call from Moscow telling me what I can and can't say. We are accused of being biased, but sometimes I wonder if there is a bias against us." Gorshkov did not clarify whether he had received calls from any other cities telling him what to say, and the gist of his rhetoric has not changed at all in more than half a century.

Finding a foreign-language journalist from the Soviet Union who is not a member of the state secret services is like finding a live unicorn. In a BBC story dated 21 March 2011, Gorshkov himself recalled his work at Moscow Radio as follows: "It was not just the country's broadcast, it was the broadcast of the CPSU (Communist Party of the Soviet Union). Our bosses worked in the International Department of the Central Committee of the CPSU. They told us, via our managers at the World Service, what we should say, what we should talk about, how we should talk."

None of this stopped him from working in Western media. From 1993 to 2013, Gorshkov was a journalist at the BBC, where he helped set up the Moscow office of the Russian service. It was he who came up with the domain name *bbcrussian.com*, and this format later became the standard for BBC local services. At different times, he lived in London and Moscow, and in 2008–2013, he was the head of the BBC office in Kyiv, responsible for Russia, Belarus, Moldova, Ukraine, and the Western Balkans.

One of Gorshkov's responsibilities was running the BBC Monitoring service, which provided Western media with expertise on various countries. According to Gorshkov, he turned it into a "valuable source of stories" for the BBC, particularly about Ukraine. Researching what kind of expertise the experts provided under Gorshkov's guidance, I came across a 2015 article titled "Ukrainian TV's partisan coverage of conflict belies its bold new journalism." The author of the article is Andriy Kondratyev, a Kyiv resident who worked in President Viktor Yushchenko's press office in 2005–2007. In the article, Kondratyev accused Ukrainian TV channels of calling Russia "the aggressor" too often, and of incorrectly naming "Kremlin-backed rebels" (sic!) as terrorists or bandits. Kondratyev also accused Ukrainian channels of coordinating their messaging and being one-sided, claiming the military operations were presented only from the Ukrainian government's point of view.

Under Gorshkov's leadership, the Ukrainian-language service of BBC Radio held its last live radio broadcast on 29 April 2011, and the following year the *bbc.ua* website launched a Russian-language news section. He could hardly be called interested in developing a Ukrainian news service; instead, Gorshkov was building a branch of the Russian BBC office in the former colony. In March 2014, in an article titled "Will the Ukrainian conflict turn hot?" for the Russian government-funded website *Russia Beyond*, Gorshkov wrote that Luhansk and Donetsk were Russian provinces until they were annexed to Ukraine in 1918. He also mentioned the classic Russian propaganda theme claiming ethnic Russians and Russian-speaking Ukrainians in east Ukraine are unhappy with nationalist and anti-Russian statements made by Kyiv and by those living in Ukraine's western regions.

In 2014, Gorshkov returned to the UK, where until March 2022 he ran the local branch of the Sputnik propaganda news agency, whose editor-in-chief is the infamous Margarita Simonyan.

One of Gorshkov's colleagues, Oksana Brazhnik, the head of Sputnik's Edinburgh office, had previously worked as a political adviser to Vyacheslav Volodin. Volodin was the deputy chief of staff in Putin's presidential administration and is currently the chairman of the State *Duma* (Russia's lower house of Parliament). In April 2022, he demanded to recognise Ukraine as a "terrorist state."

For years, these and many other journalists have been creating and popularising Russian propaganda to promote the phenomenon of the *russkiy mir* (Russian world), which has nothing in common with peace [the Russian word for world is *mir*, which is also the Russian word for peace — *author's note*]. We have already discovered the media they worked for are sponsored by the Kremlin, which means they have the financing to invest in drawing a large audience. This could also have attracted those who did not fully share Putin's or his team's views, but who, seeking a larger audience, were unable or unwilling to look for alternative sources of income. Over time, the Kremlin's policies became more and more aggressive, and eventually, journalists who remained loyal to the imperial government found themselves increasingly isolated. This happened to the most famous of them: Vladimir Solovyov, Yekaterina Andreeva, Margarita Simonyan, and other top journalists in the country. Their property and bank accounts in Europe and the United States have been at least partially seized, and their entry into the European Union and the United States has been hampered or banned, making it very difficult or impossible for them to take a break from their blood-soaked daily routine by luxuriating in a lake house on the shores of Lake Como or in a chalet in the Austrian Alps.

The most famous Russian propagandists are trapped within the borders of their empire and its underdeveloped satellites, from which they will not escape, as the collective West has imposed numerous sanctions on them. However, the same practice should be extended to smaller-scale propagandists. Are the Knyagnitskys, Ovsyannikovas, and Kozhurins really any different from the conventional Solovyovs and Andreevs? If so, then how? And if not, why are some under sanctions while others are successfully building careers in the American media? These are questions which need to be answered.

With a dark cloud on the horizon, the propagandists began to change their tunes, look for escape routes, and attempt to move to the other side of the barricades, at least partially. And even if today most of these people speak in half-truths or even tell the truth, it was these artificially created opinion leaders who for almost 20 years laid the groundwork for the current war in Ukraine, justified the annexation of Georgian territories, the war in Syria, the Central African Republic, and other hot spots, and distorted the memory of both Chechen wars. It was these propagandists who helped the Russian regime to zombify its own people, as well as a part of the population of Ukraine, and even

those in Western countries. These journalists promoted and sometimes still promote the idea not all Russians are bad, some are "good and democratic liberals," while also pushing the narrative Putin is the only one to blame, and all other Russians do not want war. Sanctions, they say, should be lifted, and "Russophobia" is completely unnecessary.

The search for a better life only partially explains the phenomenon of journalists leaving Russia for Western channels. It can also be explained by the development of the FSB's agent network abroad. Over time, we will see many exposés about these agents. *Remember this tweet.

Western lovers of finding a middle ground feel uncomfortable being reminded it was not Putin who personally tortured people in Bucha and it was not Prigozhin who manually guided the missiles fired at Dnipro in January 2023 and Kharkiv in February 2022. It is unlikely Shoigu himself stole toilets and destroyed the Skovoroda Museum in Kharkiv. The likelihood Kadyrov personally drove an APC to capture Kyiv in three days is also negligible. All of this is the work of ordinary Russians, whom their liberals like to call "our boys." By the way, the term "Russian liberal" is way off mark, because what kind of liberalism can there be in a totalitarian system? A "Russian liberal" is an oxymoron, like dry water, because many of them simply want to "reform" their empire, for it to become "more democratic," to have a strong army, and to fight corruption. Ukrainians want the empire to disintegrate.

So, when the second ranked army of the third world failed to take Kyiv, instead managing to lose more manpower and equipment in six months than in 10 years of war in Afghanistan, many journalists started bailing. Those who have something to lose did not want to be responsible for the consequences of their actions. And they don't want to be put in prison alongside their bosses either.

It's important to understand, to be a real journalist in Russia is truly difficult. A real journalist who wants to write the truth has three options: to die, to go to prison on false

charges, or to leave the country. But if, before fleeing Russia, a journalist goes to Ukraine's Crimean Peninsula to report on the "happy" Crimeans living under occupation, or to Rostov to find the "smiles" of children saved by the occupiers, or to the Russian-occupied Donbas region to write stories about the fictitious civil war conjured up by the Kremlin, the so-called journalist is dealing in propaganda and disinformation, not journalism. And he or she should have to answer for their actions, rather than answering questions on an application for a work visa at the US Embassy.

After the backgrounds of the propagandists became known, 15 employees of the Russian-language service of Voice of America sent a non-public request to management in November 2022 demanding the propagandists be fired and in February 2023, the letter was made public. Nevertheless, on 23 February 2023, managers of the Russian-language Voice of America spoke out in support of the propagandists, stating no violations had been found in their work in the newsroom nor at their previous jobs. During the investigation, Davydova and Knyagnitsky were temporarily suspended from work but were never fired.

Voice of America's management is turning a blind eye to open violations of journalistic standards and the use of propaganda. There is an unexpectedly simple explanation for this. The Russian-language service of Voice of America is headed by Irina van Dusen. While she was on long-term leave, one of her managers, Arkadz Charapanski, a former counsellor at the Belarusian Embassy in the United States, ran the service. He applied for political asylum in 2000 and subsequently built a successful American career.

One of the heads of Voice of America's Russian-language service in New York is Mikhail Gutkin, a former employee of the Russian channel NTV. Predictably, he does not see a problem with his former propagandist colleagues working for the US taxpayer funded media. He is, of course, happy with their work, since they continue to have the same approach to their jobs as journalists which also satisfied him when he was part of NTV's management. The propagandists have simply changed their place of employment. Along with Gutkin, Victoria Kupchinetskaya, a former editor of the NTV programme *Today in America,* works for the Russian-language Voice of America. Anonymous sources at Voice of America explained that Kupchinetskaya is Gutkin's common-law wife and is also involved in decision-making.

According to these same anonymous sources at Voice of America, the problem of Russian propagandists was discussed at an internal meeting. However, the main focus of the meeting was not the issue of having propagandists in the ranks of the American media, but how to mitigate public discontent. Therefore, these pseudo-journalists still continue to work for the service and receive a not insignificant salary at the expense of American taxpayers. It is worth noting professional journalists who have never spread propaganda also work in the Ukrainian and Russian-language services of Voice of America, but their propagandist colleagues are destroying the reputation of the entire multilingual news service which these honest journalists have been building for decades.

Developed democracies are now facing a difficult task: to revise their belief of Russia as a monolithic state which had emerged after the collapse of the USSR. What had been the main axiom of "restructuring" at the end of the 20th century turned out to be a false premise, and the variables in this equation have been significantly transformed over the past 30 years. Several Forums of Free Peoples of Post-Russia have already been held, bringing together representatives of at least a dozen nations colonized by the empire. The forums were attended by representatives of governments in exile, civil society organisations, and activists who aim to establish the independence of their states from Russian occupation. The main goal of the meetings is a peaceful and controlled withdrawal of independent democratic states or their unions based on both ethnic and political nations from the so-called "Russian Federation."

Voice of America and Nastayashchee Vremya (the Russian-language Voice of America), where former employees of Russian propaganda outlets work, paid virtually no attention to the Forums of Free Peoples of Post-Russia, instead publishing news stories stating the Prosecutor General's Office of the Russian Federation had called the Forum "undesirable." Ukraine's (Russian-language) service of Radio Donbas *Realii* casually mentioned the Forum in one of its February podcasts, and in August 2022, the Russian-language Radio Liberty published material by Moscow political scientist Alexander Kinev, in which he described the proposed borders of future states as follows: "Its [the Forum — *author's note]* little-known participants, mostly unknown to the general public... published several funny maps of many 'states'." Instead of what he called the "chaos of disintegration," he proposed to revise the structure of the Russian Federation on a democratic basis and de facto preserve the imperial conquests by slightly reformatting the facade of the empire and replacing the current tsar with another.

At the time I wrote this story, Russian-language sites associated with Radio Liberty had made virtually no mention of this initiative. The only exception was *Idel.Realii,* a media project of the Tatar-Bashkir service of Radio Liberty in the Volga region, which has posted materials about each of the Forums on its website.

It's possible I'm not very good at googling and Russian journalists in the United States did write about the Forum of Free Peoples in compliance with industry standards. So, I did my due diligence and contacted Oleg Magaletsky, a co-organiser of the Forum, who confirmed none of the representatives of the American offices of the above-mentioned outlets had asked him for comment. Additional meetings of the Forum took place in Washington, Philadelphia, New York, Tokyo, London, and Paris. The fact that Russian journalists ignore the fate of the subjugated peoples of the Russian Federation is another indication of their bias against the truth.

In Russia, a country with a poor population and a rich government, journalists are used to working for media outlets having power and money, and to do so, they need to learn how to censor their own materials. After Putin came to power, a whole generation of propagandists was raised on a worldview clearly matching the Kremlin's interests, and whose seemingly critical materials still correlate with the ruling party's line. Even if some of these journalists have left for Latvia, the Czech Republic, Britain, or the United States long ago in order to "not toe the party line."

The Russian Federation continues to demonstrate its inability to act as an independent state, and Russian propaganda has failed to understand what freedom of speech means. After all, these propagandists practice neither freedom nor journalism. 𐤔

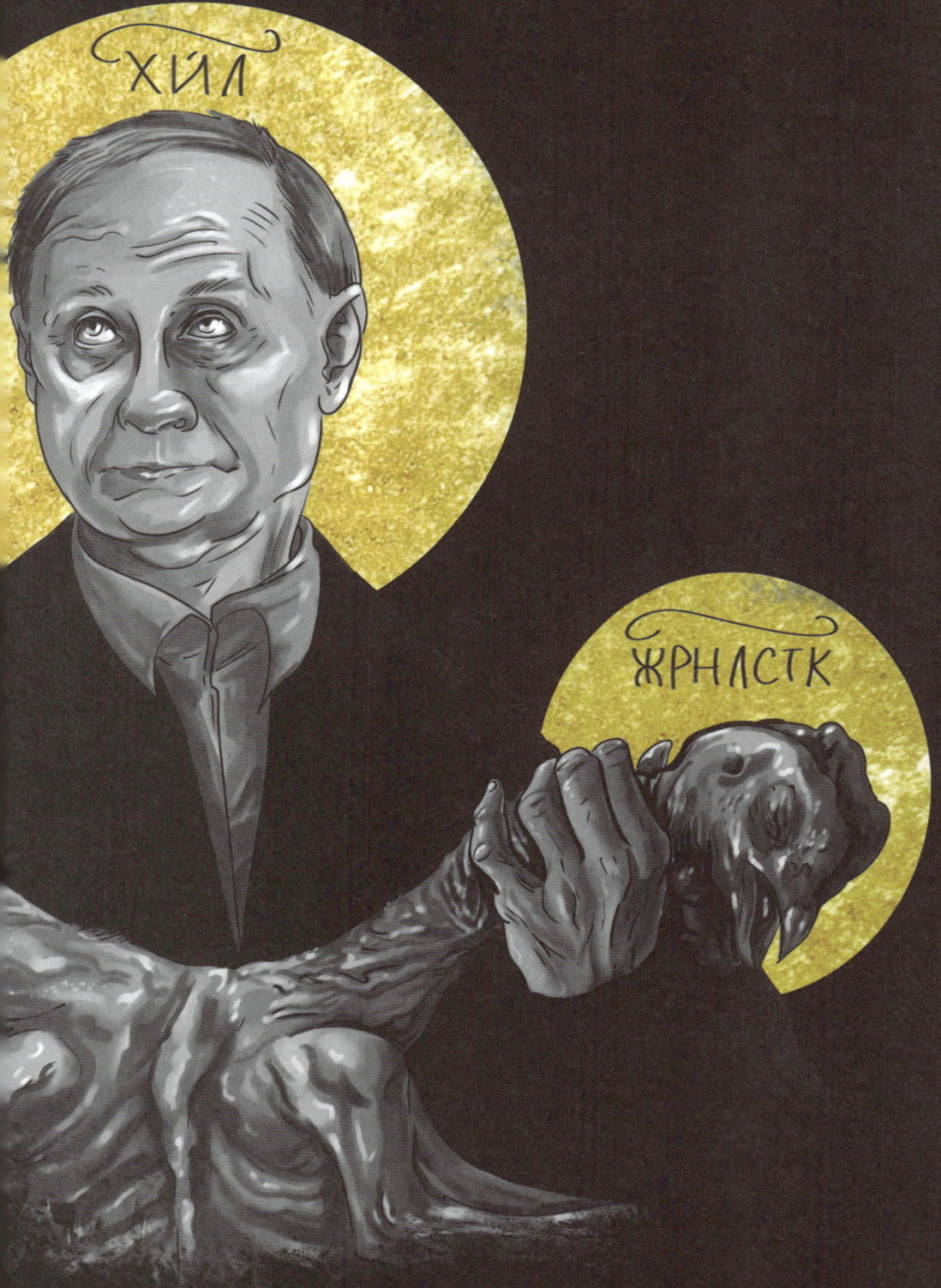

The Spectre of Smuta

Story by Oleh Mahdych and Marichka Me...

Illustrated by Olenka Zahorodnyk

*"There are great smutas starting.
For God's sake,
let us hope no damage is wrought
to this holy place."*

—From a letter written in Church-Slavonic by the monk Symeon Polotsky
of the Trinity Lavra of St. Sergius to chronicler Avraamy Palitsyn,
26 November 1608.

THE FINAL MINUTES OF VLADIMIR Putin's workday were winding down. The Emperor of All Russia was sitting at his writing desk, his gaze drawn to the antique clock hanging above the door leading into his office. He caught the movement of the minute hand striking XII while the hour hand pointed to IX. Three deep "Bongs!" echoed from the corner of the room to the left of the entrance where the century-old wooden floor clock, decorated with exquisite carvings and a dial and pendulum made from precious metal, announced the coming of the ninth hour.

At that exact moment, outside the window, the even older chimes of the *Spasky* or Saviour Tower played the "Glory" chorus from Mikhail Glinka's opera — the official melody performed during the coronation of the Russian emperors. "Glory, glory to our Russian Tsar!" rang the bells. No, this melody never gets old for Putin, although he's heard it at the same exact time every day throughout his 18-year reign.

After straightening the receiver in the cradle of the *vertushka*, the special government phone system which guaranteed a secure and direct line to the Kremlin, Putin decided to stretch his legs a bit. Rising from the plush floral upholstered chair, he stepped over to the window on his left, sandwiched between two large bookcases filled with dictionaries, tomes of laws, and historical opuses, and pushed aside the heavy opaque white curtain which let light in but blocked out the view.

The sun reminded him of a giant *Kolobok*, the character from a Russian fairy tale who was shaped like a little round bun, slowly rolling its way down to dip beneath the horizon. It cast its last rays on the red brick walls crisscrossed with white mortar encompassing the perimeter of the Kremlin, erected in the late 15th to early 16th centuries. Five-pointed ruby glass stars blazed on the towers above the entrance gates. They had been installed relatively recently — in the latter half of the 1930s — by imported workers from the nations colonised by the empire. Their colour was even richer during the sunset, as if they had been sprinkled with fresh blood. Glittering in the light of the evening, the golden two-headed eagles atop the towers of the State Historical Museum, a few steps outside the wall, looked no less predatory nor bloodthirsty as they guarded the great Russian past.

He could have continued basking forever in his beloved view; however, Putin had one more important matter requiring his attention, a task he needed to complete before going home to Rublyovka, the elite suburb of Moscow. Passing by the bookcase on the way back to his desk, he sat down in his chair. Lying next to a desk set made of expensive malachite were six sheets of printed text and a sharpened red pencil. The computer in this office wasn't turned on very often because its owner preferred to work "old school," with paper.

Putin picked up the document he needed to review, maybe even edit, because who knows what the press service had written. Like the Russian proverb says: "Trust, but verify." Though in his suspicious mind, it sounds more like: "Suspect the worst and verify." What if a liberal oppositionist has infiltrated your media and public relations staff and is waiting to screw you? You never know who you may be working with and when to expect their malice to surface.

The text was particularly important to get just right because it had to do with the past, and Putin was not only the top doyen of Russian history, he was also its Creator, its Executor. At least that's the way he saw himself for some time now and nobody around him was going to argue. On occasion he liked to fantasise what the school textbooks would write about his reign; whether he would be mentioned or not wasn't even questioned. He had most certainly solidified a spot for himself in the annals of history and truly believed he would be mentioned alongside Peter the Great, Nicholas I, or Alexander II — emperors whose marble busts he admired every day when he passed them in the corridors of the Senate Palace on the way to his office.

He didn't have any major objections to what had been written. Fortunately, the speechwriters had mastered his style. Putin marked in red pencil the parts he wanted to emphasise. He inherited this habit from another one of his idols who had ruled in the Kremlin, though not as long ago as the ones whose marble busts he sees every day. Like Stalin's, Putin's speeches were printed on a typewriter and not written with a fountain pen and ink on scrolls embossed with a crest as they had been in the time of the tsars.

The emperor underlined several sentences twice. His arm jerked involuntarily, though, and the lines came out a little crooked.

When he was done, the minute hand on the clock across from his desk had passed VI. Now he could finally head home and go to bed with a clear conscience. Tomorrow, he has a flight to Sochi to visit the Sirius Educational Centre for Gifted Children, which, roughly speaking, was to become a breeding ground for the new Russian elite. This was one of those projects Putin was monitoring personally, so he couldn't miss the annual Knowledge Day celebration being held there for the first time since the Centre opened in December 2014.

On 1 September 2015, the Sirius auditorium, designed to fit around 200 people, was jam-packed with teachers, selected students, and parents who had been lucky enough to pass the security checks of the Federal Protective Service and Federal Security Service (FSB). A film crew from the TV channel Russia-24 had arrived to broadcast the emperor's speech live.

There was tension in the air. The Centre's management had prepared for Putin's visit in advance, but nobody is completely immune to surprises.

"OK, children. Only those prepped in advance ask questions. And none of your improvisations. Today, Vladimir Vladimirovich himself will address you and talk about our magnificent past and future." A 40-ish year-old woman, with short blond hair and wearing a knee-length severe black dress, issued her final orders to the students. She scurried up and down the aisles, all the while fondling a silver pen with the "Talent and Success Foundation" logo in her right hand.

At long last, Putin appeared on stage, dressed in a light grey Brioni suit (his favourite brand) probably costing 10 times the average Russian teacher's monthly salary of 35,000 roubles ($522 in September 2015).

The audience welcomed the emperor with a standing ovation.

Equipped with state-of-the-art projectors, the auditorium transformed into the infinite cosmos, with planets, comets, stars, and other celestial bodies displayed on the walls, ceiling, and floor. Putin, standing at the lectern in the centre, appeared as though he was speaking from a galaxy far, far away.

After the traditional welcoming remarks, he moved on to his speech — a history lesson. After all, this was the reason he had travelled the more than 1,500 kilometres spanning the distance from Moscow to the eastern coast of the Black Sea. His speech marked with red pencil was resting on the lectern before him.

"In the history of our country, we have always relied on people who weren't afraid to take responsibility. Many among them were young, bold, independent. Such was Peter I, and the like-minded people with whom he set a new vector of development for Russia."

Putting his hands on both sides of the papers, barely looking down at the words, the emperor started talking about his great (not just great, but majestic!) predecessors. It is important to guide the children properly, so they know whom they should choose as their idols.

Describing the Great Russian Empire's advancements in education and the robust flourishing of science in the Soviet Union, Putin continued to refer to renown individuals — naming Russian ones as well as those appropriated from conquered territories. His posture, voice, and facial expressions all conveyed Putin's utter enjoyment of this moment in another of his roles — that of the Great Teacher and "best friend of Russian children."

The schoolchildren he was trying so hard to impress were unsuccessfully attempting to wipe the looks of boredom from their faces and stifle their yawns (smartphones weren't allowed). They weren't hearing anything new, so showing interest, let alone feigning enthusiasm, was difficult. Only those who had been privileged to sit on the big orange

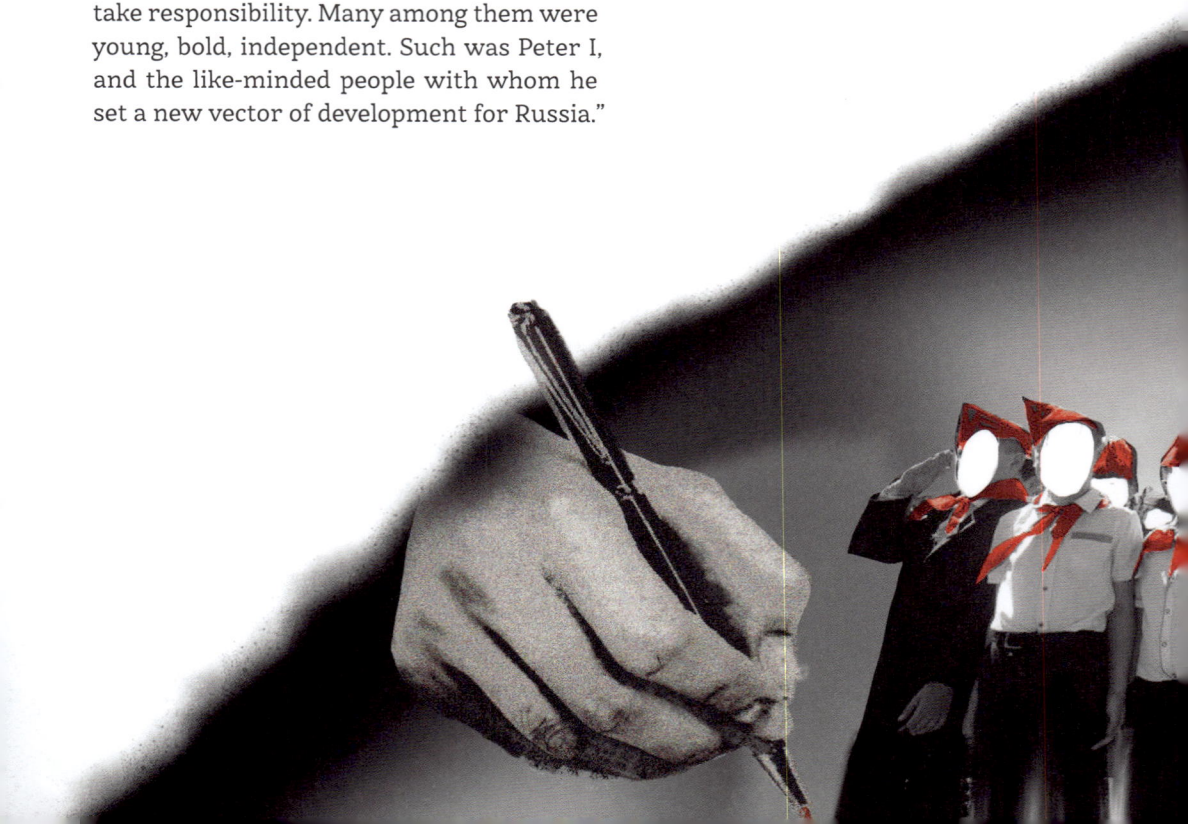

beanbags in front of the stage managed to bravely hold their composure, knowing the TV cameras were focused on them.

Suddenly, Putin's face clouded over and for a split-second, pain and fear flashed in his eyes. He had finally gotten to the part of his speech underlined twice in red.

"Yes, there were also tragic pages in our country's history," he asserted. Although the emperor had taken control of his facial expression, his voice continued to reflect his unease. After all, he was speaking publicly about his greatest fear, about the grave danger threatening his and Russia's well-being... well, primarily his.

"The lessons of *Smutas* [pronounced *smootuhs*], revolutions, civil war, warn us of how dangerous any division is for Russia. Only unity of the people and public consensus can lead to success, ensure the independence of the state, help oppose any powerful and treacherous enemy," he said as he continued his erudite lecture.

Putin's warnings against "division" and calls for "unity" were spoken in a steely tone and bordered on intimidation. One might think he had accidentally gone too far. In reality, he had not — this was his goal.

He wanted to scare the children.

Putin is a sadist. He wanted the kids to experience the pain and fear he personally feels and can't find a way to shake — the pain and fear of *Smuta*, or Time of Troubles. He wanted this still young Russian elite to tremble from the very mention of Smuta. So Smuta becomes their wound, bleeding constantly and never healing. So that as adults

these children would never dare oppose the emperor's policies by taking part in "dubious" political activities or in any other way. Because if they do, they shall summon the Smuta.

Many cultures have mythical creatures used by adults to scare children into behaving or doing what they want the children to do. Some depict the creature as a shapeless spirit, some as a hairy monster with sharp teeth and claws, others as an old man with a cane and raggedy bag going from house to house in search of naughty children. In the English-speaking world this creature is called "the Boogeyman." In Spain, Portugal, and some Latin American countries he's *El Coco*. The equivalent in Slavic folklore is the *Babay*.

"If you don't want to sleep / eat your oatmeal / share your toys, the Babay will come get you!" Parents would use this rhyme to threaten their children. Putin was trying to do the same: "If you don't listen to the emperor, the Smuta will get you!" And consequently, this spectre haunts Russians every day. It's never been seen nor heard; yet everyone carries a subconscious fear of encountering it.

WHAT EXACTLY IS THIS FRIGHTful Smuta causing Putin and his subjects so much angst?

The term "smuta" was first mentioned in Russia's historical chronicles; it was the name given to the battle for the prince's throne.

Power struggles between contenders for the throne were common because there was no clear law on succession. Instead, there were two traditions: the *Lestvitsa* and *Salic* systems, which caused discord when applied simultaneously.

Lestvitsa, according to the Old Slavonic language, was a ladder or staircase, and was mimicked in the pattern of succession, passing the right to rule from brother to brother based on seniority. Whereas under the Salic tradition, the throne passed from father to eldest son. This principle was first recorded in law by the medieval Franks.

Failure to implement a single principle for the line of succession almost always resulted in quarrels. Relatives would start fighting for power before the deceased prince was even buried. Uncles fought nephews and vice versa.

Chroniclers referred to each of these conflicts as smuta, because for them these feuds were seen as troubling times of uncertainty. Today one prince sits on the throne, tomorrow another, and the day after they've switched places again. How do you keep track? Whom do you praise, whom do you criticise? You swear an oath to the brother of a late prince and tomorrow his son's soldiers break into your monastery. And prepare yourself to be forced to rewrite the chronicle (best-case scenario, although very time-consuming) otherwise you'll simply hang from the nearest branch (absolute worst-case scenario).

One notable smuta occurred in Moscow in the mid-15th century. After the death of Prince Vasily I, his brother Yuri and the prince's own son, also named Vasily, fought for the throne. Their feud resulted in the destruction of entire cities, whose inhabitants were slaughtered by supporters of one or the other of the men. Both sides, by the way, didn't shy away from recruiting Tatar mercenaries.

During the 30-year conflict, Yuri died (his son Dmitry inherited the struggle) and Vasily (the son) went blind from torture, ultimately being named the victor. "We've seen it all before," the common folk shrugged. They figured, since this prince is fighting another one, let them have at it, as long as they don't bother us.

Three Great Smutas

Russians single out three Great Smutas, according to their ideological interpretation of history. The first, after which the qualifier "Great" was added to its name, started in 1605 and ended in 1613.

Even though this (typical) struggle for power in Moscow lasted a relatively short time, historians find it extremely difficult to recreate the events clearly and accurately.

Tsar Fyodor Ivanovich died in 1598. Under Salic tradition, which they tried to follow in the state of Muscovy, his son should have inherited the throne. However, Fyodor Ivanovich didn't have any living heirs — neither male nor female. Succession through the Lestvitsa tradition was also impossible, since Dmitry, Fyodor's brother, had died under suspicious circumstances in 1591. So, the logical question arose: Who rules?

A rather unexpected decision followed: the deceased's wife, Irina, was declared *tsaritsa.* Granted, this required turning a blind eye to the fact women didn't have the right to rule and could only be regents for their underage sons — the legal heirs to the throne. However, the tsaritsa didn't appreciate the "emancipation" granted to her by the Russian nobles, known as *boyars,* and abdicated on the ninth day after her husband's death. Fyodor would thus be the last of the Rurik dynasty to rule Moscow.

The boyars convened a *Zemsky Sobor* — an assembly of representatives of all estates and lands tasked with electing a new ruler.

The main contender was Boris Godunov, brother of the short-lived ruler Tsaritsa Irina and de facto head of government. His election campaign was brilliant! Though he was disliked by the *Boyar Duma,* the advisory body of the Muscovite tsar, he was able to reach an agreement with key boyars by bribing some and pressuring others. He also had the Church on his side. Its leader, Patriarch Iov, was Boris' protégé. So, despite the challenges he faced from several notable competitors, Godunov was unanimously elected the next tsar. Modestly refusing the crown for a month after the election, he magnanimously agreed only when a crowd of Muscovites flocked to the monastery where he was staying and tearfully pleaded with him to change his mind.

Meanwhile, the Muscovite state continued licking the wounds caused by the constant wars and repressions of Tsar Ivan Grozny (Ivan the Terrible) — the father of recently deceased Tsar Fyodor, brother-in-law to Boris Godunov. Vast swaths of the country hadn't recovered from the devastation and the mistrust within society continued to grow.

Godunov was a decent manager and used rational measures to overcome the crisis, attempting to improve the deplorable conditions under which ordinary people lived. For example, during the famine in 1601–1603 caused by poor harvests, he ordered the government to organise cost-free distribution of grain from the state reserves. He also introduced a vast construction project to build churches and fortifications to create paid jobs for the population.

Yet, despite all this, public perception of Godunov deteriorated. People with wild imaginations and a penchant for gossip spun incredible tales we would call conspiracy theories today.

It was no secret the new ruler wasn't of royal blood; he wouldn't have assumed the throne had the Rurik dynasty not been extinguished. There were no questions about Fyodor's death — it was natural. The story of his underage brother, Dmitry, found with a knife in his throat, though, seemed quite odd. Nobody believed his death was an accident. It was said he died falling on his blade during an epileptic attack. The rumour mongers began to raise suspicions and even openly accused Boris of being involved in Dmitry's death. They claimed he had been looking out for his own self-interest and supposedly had sent people to eight-year-old Dmitry to "help" him impale himself on his own knife. Without any other heirs, power was granted to Boris' sister, Irina. As planned, she refused the throne, and the cunning and corrupt boyars promptly organised the Zemsky Sobor naming Boris tsar.

Hunger added fuel to the fire, resulting in any remaining common sense still preserved in the minds of Muscovites to go up in smoke. At first people whispered among themselves, subsequently escalating to public pronouncements, claiming all their troubles were nothing more than God's punishment for an illegitimate tsar. Meanwhile, rumours were spreading that Dmitry (Fyodor's younger brother) was still alive and should ascend the throne instead of the usurper Godunov. People started calling him "Tsarevich Dmitry" to reinforce his rightful status.

Then, out of nowhere, men started surfacing claiming to be the "real" Dmitry.

Critical thinking and informational hygiene have never been strong points for Russians, especially in the distant 17th century, when fact-checking was impossible. The illiterate residents of the Muscovite state could not read. Struggling for survival in destitution — they did not travel. Mindlessly pious, they blindly followed the biblical word as interpreted by any Orthodox priest they could find. Abandoned by their tsars, who seldom thought about the commoners, they did not trust official information. Instead, they devoured the most fantastic rumours spreading at lightning speed through the main media channels of the time — markets and fairs.

The conspiracy theory about Dmitry being alive fell on fertile soil. The amazing story became exceedingly popular, describing how in 1591 at Uglich, the residence of the widow

of Ivan the Terrible (his sixth wife Tsaritsa Maria Nagaya) north of Moscow, a boy resembling Dmitry, not the real Dmitry, died from a knife wound to the throat and the two switched identities.

Twelve years after Dmitry's death, in 1603, in the small town of Bragin, then part of the Polish-Lithuanian Commonwealth, one of Prince Adam Wiśniowiecki's servants came down with a serious illness. Thinking he would die, the boy asked to give confession. During his frank conversation with the priest, the servant admitted he was actually Tsarevich Dmitry and showed the priest a gold cross allegedly given to him by his mother, Tsaritsa Maria Nagaya. This young man survived the illness and his claim about his royal origin was confirmed by another of Wiśniowiecki's servants. The stars aligned in the boy's favour when it was revealed the servant just happened to have been born in Uglich.

Fully recovered, this False Dmitry I openly declared his claim to the throne. He was supported by the Polish, Lithuanian, and Rus' nobility, for whom the claim was a way to gain military glory, new lands, and other rewards from the future tsar. Defectors from Moscow, particularly soldiers, also began joining the self-proclaimed tsar's camp.

The Muscovite government insisted this false tsarevich from Bragin was in

fact a monk named Grigory Otrepyev, who for some time served as a secretary in the Boyar Duma and was close to the boyar Fyodor Romanov. Romanov had run against Godunov in the election for the tsar's throne. Afterwards, in 1602, to eliminate his opponent, the newly elected Tsar Godunov had Romanov sent to a monastery. Shortly thereafter, the henchman Grigory Otrepyev disappeared from Moscow without a trace. And now, he appeared out of the clear blue sky, pretending to be the late Dmitry.

Unfortunately, officially exposing Otrepyev as a fraud didn't stop the rumours about Dmitry's miraculous survival from spreading.

In October 1604, False Dmitry I crossed the western border of the Muscovite state with an army recruited in the Polish-Lithuanian Commonwealth. Several border garrisons also joined his side. Godunov sent his own army against the pretender. After some initial victories, the invader was eventually defeated and retreated with his troops to the town of Kromy. The Muscovites encircled them, but failed to capture their commander, who fled with a handful of warriors to Putyvl and lay low for a while.

False Dmitry I, the pretender, was lured out of hiding by the sudden death of Tsar Boris Godunov following a stroke in late April 1605. According to Salic tradition, the next tsar would be Godunov's 16-year-old son Fyodor. He was a smart boy who spoke several languages, but he didn't have any experience in running a state. Weighing the chances of an inexperienced "green" lad being able to handle the crisis now fully under way in the country, the boyars placed their bets on the stronger of the two candidates, in their opinion, and sided with the imposter. The army followed suit and joined the camp of False Dmitry I. A revolt broke out in Moscow. Fyodor, the late Boris Godunov's son, was arrested and removed from power, and soon afterwards he and his mother were executed.

False Dmitry I couldn't contain his joy. His rose-coloured dream of ascending the throne was finally coming true. The only hitch was confirming his royal origin. For that, he needed Maria Nagaya — the mother of the real Dmitry. After face-to-face negotiations in Moscow, where most likely the new tsar intimidated and threatened the elderly woman, she identified him as her son. Dmitry was miraculously alive!

The now crowned pretender saw himself as a change-maker. He spoke about opening a university in Moscow. He declared he would allow his subjects to leave the country at will. He promised people would be free to practice any religion. In the minds of his dark retinue, all these potential innovations bordered on heresy. The boyars, however, were even more vexed by the behaviour of False Dmitry I. He communicated freely with foreigners, didn't observe Orthodox customs, and tried to rule independently without seeking the advice of the Duma. The last point especially riled them.

Rumours began to spread that the throne was occupied by a False Dmitry I.

Less than a year had passed when the deadly silence of the Kremlin corridors was again disturbed by the clanging of swords and sounds of gunshots. On the morning of 17 May 1606, False Dmitry I was killed. His body was cremated, and, for greater fanfare, the ashes were mixed with gunpowder and shot from a cannon towards the western border. "Let the damned cheat go back to where he came from," the boyars must have thought. In his place, Vasily Shuysky was declared the new tsar of the Muscovite state.

If the boyars thought this creative farewell to False Dmitry I would put an end to the claims of fraudulent pretenders to the throne, they were mistaken. From the ashes of one dead bogus tsarevich rose 16 live ones — the alleged sons of Ivan Grozny, Fyodor Ivanovich, and Boris Godunov. The tension in Muscovy was mounting.

The next year, 1607, in the border town of Starodub, at the time part of the Muscovite state, a man suddenly appeared — again without a family or clan — and alleged he was Tsarevich Dmitry. During the interrogation, the imposter told an incredible tale about how during the uprising in the Kremlin the year before, it was not he who had died from the rioters' bullets, but a man looking very much like him. Dmitry, it would seem, was miraculously saved. Twice.

True to form, the people were hoodwinked again. Dissatisfied with Vasily's rule, the boyars, nobles, and military were happy to back False Dmitry II, and his camp of supporters gradually grew larger. The impostor managed to gather an army and set out for Moscow. After he failed to take the capital, he retreated and set up camp in the nearby village of Tushino. There he began to form parallel government structures: his own Boyar Duma, his own *prikazy* (ministries), his own church with a loyal patriarch, and so forth.

Vasily turned to Sweden for help and ceded a section of the Baltic Sea in exchange for a military alliance. The allied army had every chance of soundly defeating False Dmitry II until troops of the Polish-Lithuanian Commonwealth came to the second imposter's aid.

In 1610, after the victory of the Poles over the Muscovite army at Klushino, the boyars staged another coup. The dethroned Tsar Vasily was tonsured and forced to become a monk. The boyars invited Prince Władysław IV — son of King Sigismund III of the Polish-Lithuanian Commonwealth — to rule instead, on the condition he convert from Catholicism to Orthodoxy.

While the negotiations continued, the Muscovite state was ruled by the *Semiboyarschina,* a council of seven boyars, while a Polish-Lithuanian garrison was stationed in the historical heart of the city encompassing the triad of the Kremlin, Kitay-Gorod, and Bely Gorod. The False Dmitry II disappeared amid all these vicissitudes as suddenly as he had appeared.

Not everyone in Moscow approved of the candidacy of the Polish tsarevich Władysław IV. The dissenters began to protest. There was a sizable uprising and parallel government structures separate from those of the boyars were formed. The revolt was led by Kuzma Minin and Prince Dmitry Pozharsky. After two years of fighting, their army expelled the foreign garrison from the city. In 1613, a Zemsky Sobor was convened for the first time in a long while to elect the new tsar. Among the numerous candidates, they chose the youngest one: 16-year-old Mikhail Romanov.

At the start of the 17th century, the residents of the Muscovite state — those who participated and witnessed the events of the time — were dazed and confused.

Who is the tsar today? Whom do we bow to? Is he legitimate or not? Is he really, definitely legitimate? Because there are 16 more on the reserve bench vying for the throne. Whom do we fight for? To whom do we pay taxes? The old barometer an ordinary person had used to guide them through life was broken.

Not everyone fell into frustration and lost the ability to make sense of the lightning-fast changing reality. There were those who took advantage of the situation to advance their own careers, people with a knack for politics. For example, Prince Fyodor Mstislavsky backed four different pretenders during the feuds. First, he served Godunov, then he switched camps to False Dmitry I, next he supported Vasily Shuysky, later he headed the Semiboyarschina, and in 1613 he led the Zemsky Sobor.

Nevertheless, the first Great Smuta was quelled with the ascension to the throne of Mikhail Romanov. Although the fear of something like this happening again in the country didn't disappear. On the contrary, it lurked in the corridors of the Kremlin palaces and became a spectre for all the representatives of the Romanov dynasty. That's why each one of them did everything they could to strengthen the tsar's power and prevent any possibility for deep reform of the Russian Empire. This strategy was sustained for a protracted 300 years. Sooner or later, though, it had to come crashing down.

THE SECOND GREAT SMUTA HIT Russia in 1917–1921. Its harbinger was World War I, which caused a deep economic and political crisis in the Russian Empire led at the time by Tsar Nicholas II, a descendant of the Romanovs.

The obsolescence of the autocratic system of governance had been evident for a long time, becoming particularly acute starting in 1914. The economy proved unable to meet the country's wartime needs swiftly and effectively. Although production capacity had been modernised over the past 30 years, management remained inept. The war also reopened the empire's old wounds. Dissent was spreading among those who had grown tired of tolerating their national humiliation by the titular nation; among those who were dissatisfied with the low standard of living and refused to continue to turn a blind eye to the uneven distribution of wealth; and among those who called for a change in the system of government and criticised the weak development of public institutions.

In March 1917, strikes broke out in Petrograd, the capital of the Russian Empire, over food shortages. Hundreds of thousands of people took to the streets, and the hungry crowd's economic demands soon grew to include political ones. The people demanded the resignation of the current government and formation of a new one. The authorities

responded by banning rallies and ordering everyone to return to work, otherwise force would be used. The most stubborn protesters were sent to the front. When this didn't stop the protests, the emperor gave the order to shoot. This caused some of the military to join the side of the protesters. Strikes demanding more food and against the political elite transformed into a mass demonstration calling for Nicholas II's abdication. Indeed, he signed the abdication manifesto on 15 March while in Pskov.

A provisional government was formed, consisting of deputies of the Duma, businessmen, and public activists, and took over the leadership of the state. The new ministers wanted to implement democratic changes in the country, which obviously couldn't happen instantaneously and required a great amount of effort. Russian society wasn't willing to wait. Any attempts at civilised discussion turned into irreconcilable disputes. Russians on the front didn't want to fight. Russians in the rear demanded immediate solutions to agricultural and social problems. Non-Russian peoples wanted independence, or at least cultural autonomy. The various groups constantly disagreed with one another.

Against the backdrop of this social discord, political forces advocating for strong leadership began to gain more support. In November 1917, they seized control of the country, removed the Provisional Government by force, and started building a dictatorship of the proletariat. Their aim was a state where all power would, supposedly, belong to workers and peasants, while the rights of non-working-class groups — their former exploiters — would be restricted. To ensure a point of no return, on the night of 16–17 July 1918, the Bolsheviks ordered the execution of the entire Romanov royal family.

This policy was certain to meet resistance. Opposing the Bolsheviks, who were known as the "Reds" because of the colour of their flag, were a number of political forces called the "Whites." The latter were mostly monarchists who sought the return of imperial rule.

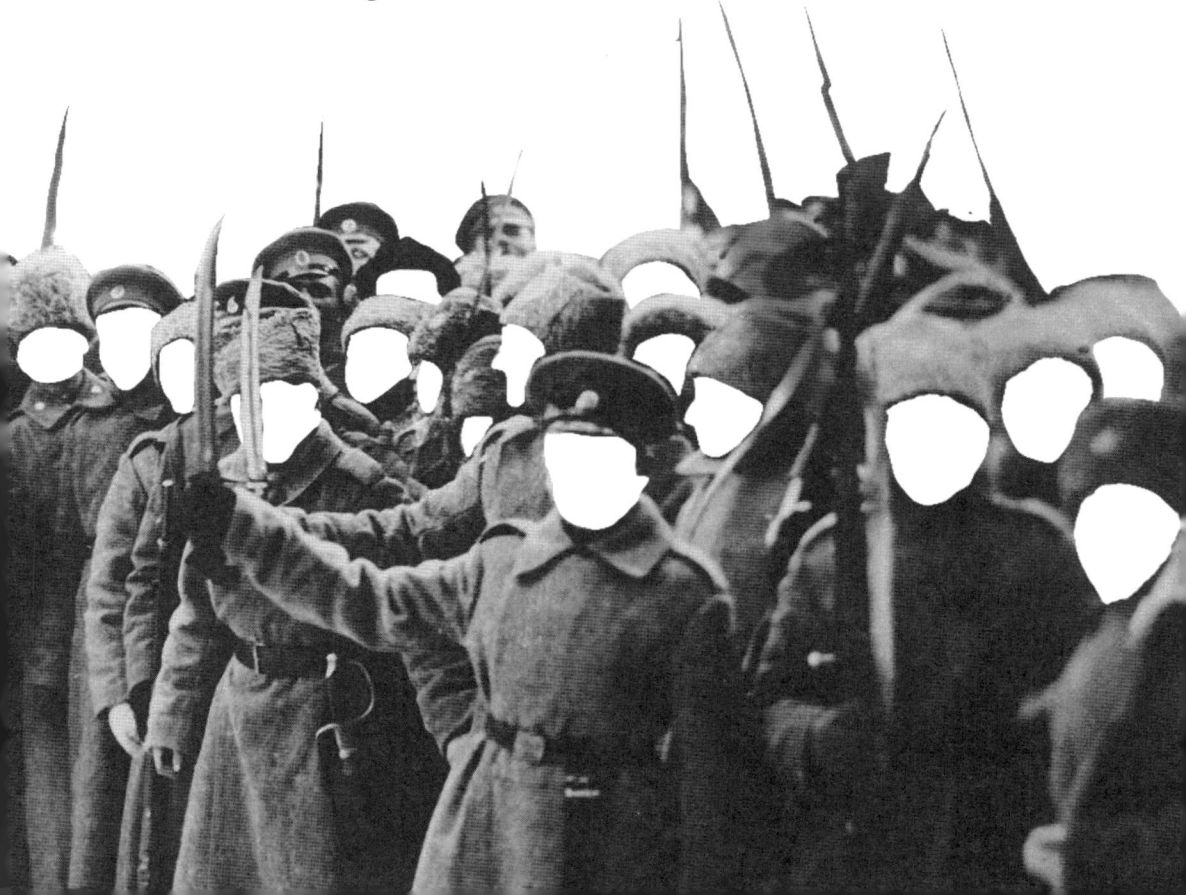

A fierce battle erupted between these two camps, eventually leading to widespread civil war where everyone fought everyone else. As soon as the Reds unleashed mass terror, slaughtering representatives of "enemy classes" regardless of guilt, the Whites would respond with equal violence.

"In the bloody fog of the Russian smuta, people are dying, and the true boundaries of historical events are being blurred," said one of the leaders of the Whites, General Anton Denikin. Incidentally, his book about those times is called *Ocherki Russkoy Smuty* or *Essays on the Russian Smuta.*

Just yesterday, the great empire had "instilled awe." Today, the same empire was rapidly and irreversibly disintegrating. Contributing to its collapse were national independence movements emboldened by foreign armies coming to their aid. Meanwhile, more and more people in the country were starving. By and large, they didn't care who would win, the Reds or the Whites, as long as they didn't experiment with democracy and restored order quickly. The economy had completely ceased to function.

The Great Smuta observed the consequences of its work from a bird's eye view. The spectre grinned widely and rubbed its hands together in satisfaction with the turn of events.

The Smuta retreated only when the victor of the latest Russian feud was more or less evident. It would be the Bolsheviks, who were more brutal and voiced slogans the illiterate population grasped more readily. Afterwards, for a long 70 years, the Red *vozhdy,* the Communist "bosses," managed to maintain the exact same Russian empire, albeit without the Poles, Finns, Latvians, Lithuanians, and Estonians, who managed to break free of the double-headed eagle's sharp claws in 1918–1920. Tragically, during World War II, the Baltic countries once again lost their independence and were occupied by Russia.

This Russian empire had a different name, the Union of Soviet Socialist Republics. And a different coat of arms, with a hammer and sickle, symbolising the unity of workers and peasants. Above them shined a red star. As the Great Soviet Encyclopaedia explains: "...the red five-pointed star is a symbol of the ultimate triumph of the ideas of communism on the five continents of the globe..."

The Bolsheviks' Napoleonic plans, like their communist ideas, weren't realistic nor achievable from the very beginning, and therefore, were destined to fail. The unity of the new state was achieved, in fact, with fire and sword, executions and concentration camps, and not because of a solidarity among the working classes. It was impossible for a contrived unity to last.

The Spectre of the Great Smuta was simply waiting for the right opportunity to rear its head again, for the third time.

THE SPECTRE'S GOLDEN HOUR BEGAN when Mikhail Gorbachev came to power in 1985. It was obvious to everyone the Soviet Empire was in a dangerous crisis; in fact, it was having its last fatal convulsions and was about to be buried in its grave.

At the time, the USSR was addicted to the profits from the sale of oil — it had become the largest supplier of oil and gas to Europe. However, the huge flow of money from abroad did a disservice to the state. Those responsible for improving the economy's functioning stopped worrying about its shortfalls and errors. Why should they, when you can buy anything with petrodollars?

The political system was more dead than alive. Nobody, not even the top party cadres, believed in communist ideals. They mostly tried to maintain a good face, in case their subjects suddenly started wondering what happened to the promise of a society with equality and grace. Indeed, this new society was supposed to magically appear in 1980, because it was designated as such by the Third Program of the Communist Party of the Soviet Union during their XXII Congress on 31 October 1961. The 1980s arrived, albeit without a communist paradise.

Gorbachev declared the start of *Perestroika* — the "restructuring of Soviet society." The policy included various political, economic, and social reforms. However, neither the new General Secretary of the Central Committee of the Communist Party of the Soviet Union nor his closest associates had a clear plan of what to change and how to do it, and most importantly, what was to be the end result of this project.

Ultimately, the reconstruction of the country resembled a failed building renovation. The renovators thought it would be enough to replace the old, faded wallpaper — then realised the wall underneath was covered in mould. Once they started removing the mould, they found the roof was leaking and the internal partitions were half-rotten. When they started replacing the walls and roof, it became clear the foundation had been improperly laid.

It was the same in the Soviet Union. The system's inability to maintain itself and function properly was manifested in every aspect of life. Simple cosmetic repairs wouldn't help. Attempts to partly fix something only revealed much deeper problems. The residents of the building — the national republics — didn't want to continue living in a dangerously unsafe structure threatening to bury them under its rubble. Ukraine, like the other republics, had just started moving out and changing its residency registration, when the building began to crack at the seams and by late December 1991 had collapsed completely.

Russia became a separate country. This seemed like a change for the better, a wonderful chance to finally build a comfortable new home with a proper foundation, new walls, and a sturdy roof. And a good opportunity to forge civilised relations with neighbours and former tenants.

Nevertheless, for many Russians, the collapse of the USSR was a tragedy, a time of smuta. They stopped feeling like they were part of a big empire, a country nearly the whole world feared, one having the power to dictate terms to almost anyone and poke its nose into anyone's affairs, even when unwanted.

The sense of their insignificance was fuelled by the economic difficulties associated with the transition from a planned to a market economy and the tangible drop in living standards.

Many businesses closed. Social benefits were delayed for months or even years. Organised crime gained a solid footing, sometimes so entangled with the law enforcement system, the two were indistinguishable. Corruption and the theft of state property en masse, which had started before Perestroika, reached its apogee. The oft repeated phrase *Perestroika/perekachka/perestrelka,* or Restructure/siphon-off/shoot-to-kill, was an apropos play on words. People were at the brink of survival. When lamenting about how they "lived in poverty before, but are now destitute," they never forgot to add, "however, yesterday the whole world feared us, and now nobody does."

The longing for their great imperial past particularly intensified after the defeat in the first Russo-Chechen War of 1994–1996. Russian society couldn't get over the shock and humiliation. How did Chechen fighters, who yesterday were simple shepherds, manage to force the "valiant Russian army" to retreat? What the Russians didn't understand was these "shepherds" were skilled warriors who were fighting for their own independent state. And this was the key to their victory.

Putin set out to raise Russia from its knees and cast away the Great Smuta. Although at times his own hands shook from fear of this spectre.

RUSSIAN HISTORY — WITH ITS FEUD-
ing princes, revolutions, civil wars,
and collapse of a multinational state —
isn't unique.

In the latter half of the 15th century, the
battle for the royal throne between the House
of York and the House of Lancaster divided
English society in half for 30 years. The conflict, known as the War of the Roses, put
an end to many noble families and took the
lives of nearly a quarter of the country's
population.

In the 17th century, the Polish-Lithuanian
Commonwealth was shaken twice by
a *rokosz* — a rebellion of the nobles against
the king deemed legal if the rights and freedoms of the nobles were encroached. The
Zebrzydowski Rokosz and the Lubomirski
Rokosz were directed against the grab
for absolute power by Sigismund III and
John II Casimir, respectively. These rebel-
lions forced tens of thousands of citizens to
take up swords and meet on the battlefield.

Revolution broke out in France in the late
18th century. The bourgeoisie, workers, arti-
sans, merchants, students, and free peasants gathered on street barricades and at
the walls of the Bastille. With the approval
of some of the clergy and nobility from the
Estates-General, they formed a united front
against the tyranny of Louis XVI. Mass protests led to the removal of the king and his
subsequent execution. The state was declared
a republic, although political stability was
still far off. Military interventions by Austria,
Prussia, Britain, Spain, and others in support
of the monarchy, confrontations between
radical and moderate political forces, constant changes of government — all this kept
France off-balance until Napoleon came to
power through a coup.

Germany's defeat in WWI resulted in
a complex economic and political crisis. The
military mutiny grew into a national uprising forcing Kaiser Wilhelm II to abdicate the
throne and flee the country in November
1918. The struggle between politicians in
favour of a parliamentary democracy with
gradual reforms and those who agitated for

История Великой Российской Империи

Мы ни с кем не хотим воевать, Россия никогда ни на кого не нападала. Это удивительно, когда ни на кого не нападала великая и могучая страна, она только не нападала, защищала свои рубежи.

Напоминаем, что Россия на протяжении всей своей истории никогда ни на кого не нападала. И Россия, которая пережила столько это последняя, которая в Европе, даже хочет

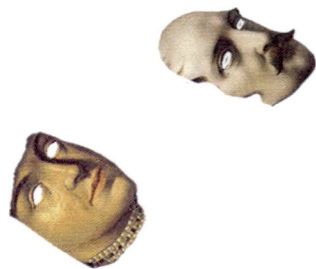

Soviet rule put German society on the brink of civil war.

In the late 20th century, a bloody drama unfolded in the Balkans. Economic, political, and social difficulties were eroding Yugoslavia from within. When the central government rejected the appeals by the Croats, Slovenes, Bosnians, and Macedonians to declare their own independent states, the ensuing wars brought widespread destruction of property, enormous human casualties, and a relentless flow of refugees.

The list of foreign "smutas" can go on and on. There probably isn't a country in the world that hasn't at least once in its history been torn apart by internal strife. While most nations have managed to leave them in the past and move on, the Russians cannot. They are fixated on their own feuds, which happened who knows when and continue to carry this unnecessary fear-inducing baggage of the past into the future, effectively annulling any chance at their own development.

The Russian historical experience isn't unique. What is unique is the Russian reaction to it: an overwhelming, long-lasting fear bordering on paranoia. After all, 999 out of 1,000 times, there are no legitimate grounds for their fear.

What does this fear haunting the more than 140 million residents of Russia stem from and why has it existed for centuries? Its origin is rooted primarily in Russian rulers and their worst personal nightmare — losing the throne. None of them, be it in the distant 15th or current 21st century, has managed to overcome this fear (or at least asked themselves: Do I really need this throne?). Though they have learned to contain the fear, even control it. How? Easily — by building the Russian Empire. The biggest guarantee of preserving power is strengthening the empire, at least in this corner of the world, where nobody considers caring for the people's welfare as a recipe for long-lasting rule.

Starting in the 1480s, Muscovite rulers, having arbitrarily renamed themselves the "sovereigns and grand princes of all Rus'," began to annex the lands of the former Rus' principalities — as if the territories were their legal fiefdoms. And they used any means possible: if they couldn't capture a territory with military force, they used bribery; if money didn't work, they negotiated dynastic marriages; if marriage negotiations broke down, they again gave the command to "Charge!"

To convince Europeans to start accepting the Muscovites as equals, and not savages from the North having recently crawled out of the swamps or emerged from the surrounding forests, the "political technologists" of the time were put on the ruler's payroll. One of them, the monk Filofey of the Spaso-Yelizarov Monastery in Pskov, created a new image for the tsars as holy saviours who were the heirs of "true Christianity." Moscow was declared the "Third Rome" — "two Romes [Rome and Constantinople] have fallen, the third stands, and there will be no fourth." To prove the point, a huge stone fortress containing palaces and churches was built in central Moscow within the walls of the Kremlin, emerging from among the otherwise wooden structures. It would become the face of a new, "civilised" Russia.

Meanwhile, the internal power vertical was being reinforced and any form of self-government or democracy was gradually liquidated. For example, in the mid-17th century, the Zemsky Sobors (an assembly of the nobility), which had elected tsars and passed laws in the past, were stripped of their power, and only retained the right to approve tsarist decisions. As the end of the century approached, the sobors were no longer convened.

Absolute power in the Russian Empire was achieved by Peter I, known as Peter the Great. He issued all the laws, appointed all high-ranking government officials and regional governors from the *dvoryanstvo* or society elites, approved all court sentences, and even appointed the head or *Ober-Procurator,* as well as all the members, of the Synod, which was the highest governing body of the Russian Orthodox Church.

Any plans to limit the emperor's power were suppressed as soon as they became known. In 1730, when Peter the Great's niece Anna Ioanovna assumed the throne, the members of the recently created Supreme Privy Council — the highest governing body — wanted to forbid Empress Anna from unilaterally declaring war, giving away state lands, assigning military ranks, and increasing budget expenditures. Having the backing of the army and the nobles, she rejected these proposals. The council was abolished, its councillors fired from their positions, and arrested soon after.

All the while, the Russian rulers continued to absorb new territories: Siberia, East Ukraine on the left bank of the Dnipro River, and the Baltic lands. By the 18th century, the Russian Empire was one of the largest countries in the world. However, this didn't suffice. The empire continued to acquire lands: in the partition of the Polish-Lithuanian Commonwealth, by capturing the Caucasus, adding Alaska to its reign, and colonising Central Asia.

The three foundations "without which Russia cannot prosper, thrive, or live" — Orthodoxy, Autocracy, Nationality — fully crystallised in the 19th century. Compared to the French motto *"Liberté, Égalité, Fraternité,"* the Russian triad sounded particularly archaic. This didn't stop it from becoming the dominant ideological doctrine of an empire whose "death certificate" was supposedly issued during the 1917 Revolution. The current imperialists dismiss the aforementioned "death" as nothing more than a technicality.

It would seem the mass protests demanding the abdication of Nicholas II, his forced resignation, and subsequent execution, would have clearly shown you can't rule a state in times of social progress without having a constitution in place, providing for the development of political parties, and permitting public debate, and by continuing to neglect the rights of other nationalities.

But when the Bolsheviks seized power in Russia during the civil war, they showed you can do just that. You can strangle social progress and continue to build an empire if you just disguise it a little bit.

Power was concentrated again, except not in the hands of a tsar or emperor. Instead, it was held in the hands of the communist party *vozhd,* the "dear leader," who also happened to rule until his death. The Russians had never had a constitution before; however, over 70 years, the Soviets gave their subjects four: in 1918, 1924, 1936, and 1977. Only these were works of fiction — simply window dressing — especially when it came to civil rights or the self-governance of the national republics.

No alternative opinions were allowed in this "Russian Empire 2.0." Everyone had to do what the only legal all-powerful ruling party said. You couldn't run your own business. Everyone had to work where they were assigned, and you couldn't change jobs. Proving a person's guilt wasn't necessary for someone to be imprisoned, executed, sent to a concentration camp, or have their property confiscated.

On paper, the new empire was a federation of equal republics having the right to secede from the USSR. In reality, Lenin, Stalin, Khrushchev, Brezhnev, and Gorbachev didn't care about the rights of colonies. The degree of their concern may have differed between them: some cared more, others less, but, generally speaking, this was a fact. Governance was centralised and Moscow decided everything. The nationalities were deprived of the right to manage their own lives.

Putin, who came to power at the turn of the 21st century, didn't try to abandon the imperial legacy and build something new, fresh, or democratic.

"Dear Russians, dear countrymen! Today I have been entrusted with the responsibilities of Head of State. In three months, we will hold elections to choose the president of Russia. Let me emphasise there will not be even one minute of a power vacuum in this country. There has not been and there will not be," he said in his first New Year's address as acting president following Boris Yeltsin's resignation.

Since then, the situation with human rights and the governance of territories included in the Russian Federation hasn't changed. Even the slightest hint of criticism of the government in the media can get one branded a "foreign agent," and social media posts with "extremist material" can get you sent to prison for a year. Not only are national political parties and NGOs banned, but there are severe restrictions in schools on the use of the languages of the ethnic groups in the national republics.

Meanwhile, *Tsargrad*, a Russian TV and internet channel, is flourishing. Its founder and chief editor, Konstantin Malofeev, openly boasts: "Empire is our past and future. We can't not be an empire. An empire is who we are." He obviously understands these words are music to Putin's ears, a person who, for the sake of tradition, continues to rule the state from the Kremlin, although today the stone fortress in the centre of Moscow is a symbol of Russia's savagery and archaism. A person who, in pursuit of absolute control, regards with suspicion every word in every speech written for him. A person who is mentally stuck in a bygone era and always checks the time on three clocks simultaneously.

STRONG IMPERIAL POWER HAS lasted so long and been so successful in Russia because its rulers have for centuries nurtured obedient, submissive subjects. They've skimped on carrots while generously beating them with sticks. Their motivation is obvious: if there are no rebels, there is no smuta — their biggest personal nightmare. Smuta, which causes them to be deprived of power and, occasionally, their lives.

Every ruler has tried to avoid this unenviable situation as best they could. Obviously, there was no tolerance for people who posed a threat. In the empire under Nicholas II, for example, the Criminal Code had a separate section on responsibility for sowing smuta. This included unsanctioned rallies, public statements against the authorities, pretending to be a member of the imperial family, and so forth. All these crimes would have easily fit into the adjacent sections of the Criminal Code — "On state change" immediately prior to the one "On smuta," or the one after — "On disobedience of power." Putting it in a separate section was a matter of principle. The convicted "smuta-maker," depending on the severity of the crime, could face 15 days in jail or indefinite exile to Siberia.

In the Soviet Empire, people who "incited smuta" were sentenced under Article 58 of the Penal Code: Counter-Revolutionary Activities. The paranoid Bolshevik vozhds expanded it to 14 sub-articles, the most "popular" of which was the 10th: "Propaganda and agitation calling for overturning, dismantling, or undermining the Soviet regime." The standard punishment for this was 10 years in the GULAG and five years of limitation of rights. During WWII, people convicted under this article were even executed.

Alongside meting out punishment for sowing smuta, Russian emperors also took preventive measures in their battle against it. The rulers instilled in their subjects the idea if the emperor was to suddenly disappear, everyone would suffer. "Any division is deadly for Russia…" There will be disorder, chaos, and instability, just like in the years 1605 to 1613. Or again from 1917 to 1921. Or the mid-1980s to early-1990s. These evil geniuses and virtuoso manipulators made a whole country fear their own worst personal nightmares. They protected themselves from smuta by terrorising everyone else with the threat of the Great Smuta.

The technique for inciting fear among the population hasn't changed much. Just like in the 17th century, the 21st century spectre was and is continuing to be created by a very specific group of specialists. Back then they were called court chroniclers; today they are the political technologists on Putin's payroll.

For example, in February 2022, right before the full-scale invasion of Russian forces into Ukraine, Russian social media channels on Telegram started spreading disinformation about a plan by Ukraine's Special Operation Forces to destabilise Russia. It was called "Smuta," and the outcome was to be a real nightmare — "loss of control, economic upheaval, change in Russia's position in the world arena."

Obviously, the Ukrainians had no such plan. Putin simply needed an excuse to reinstate Russian control over one of its largest former colonies (the loss of which bruised his imperial ego), and to get the population to unconditionally support his policies. He succeeded with the latter. In April 2022, results of a Levada Centre survey revealed 74 per cent of Russians who participated in the poll approved of the war against Ukraine.

THE SUN ON THE NORTHERN COAST of the Black Sea had almost reached its zenith when a man wearing a baseball cap, mud-coloured camouflage, and a bullet-proof vest adorned with a Zwastika and St. George's ribbon, looking completely out of place in this environment, went for a walk on the central square of a Ukrainian city temporarily occupied by Russia. Another man, also in uniform, with a balaclava covering his face and a Kalashnikov assault rifle slung over his shoulder, walked silently two steps behind him.

The outsider was of above average height, with a strong build and dark blond hair. He had a wide forehead with a crimson scar on the left side, drooping eyebrows, light grey-blue eyes with enormous bags under them, and a bulbous "potato" nose. At first glance he looked to be in his forties, but who knows — war always leaves its mark on a man's face. And for the third month since the start of the "special operation," the damned *Banderovtsi,* the name given to Ukrainians who were fighting against the occupation, were resisting so fiercely, even an 18-year-old boy could pass for a grey-haired old man.

The man with the scar stopped for a second and looked around the square.

"Now that's the way it should be!" he mumbled to himself after seeing the Russian tricolour on the flagpole in front of the city council building.

About 50 metres ahead, he spotted a small open space surrounded by spruces, white cedars, and birches. He could hear children's voices echoing from there. As he got closer, the man was stunned by what he saw. A group of nine 13-year-old boys and girls were skateboarding and performing tricks on their bikes and scooters on the smooth pavement.

"You gotta be kidding me!" he thought. Who did these kids think they were, fearlessly enjoying life in the open instead of quietly cowering in the four walls of their apartments? He was going to give these obnoxious kids a good talking to and chase them out of there. Along the way to confront them, though, he changed his mind. No, he wouldn't send them home immediately; first, he'd teach them how to properly love and respect their "new Homeland." He'd give them a *likbez,* a crash course in the new rules, so to speak.

"Hey, kids!" the man with the scar shouted at them. "Get over here, now!"

To make the invitation more convincing, the bodyguard, who was closely following on the heels of the man with the scar the entire time, waved his weapon at the kids. The boys and girls looked at each other, dropped their bikes and scooters, and approached the soldiers.

Having found no better option, the wannabe Putin perched himself atop a nearby concrete bin filled with trash. The guard positioned himself next to the bin. The kids surrounded the two of them in a semicircle.

From his imaginary throne, completely oblivious to how ridiculous he looked, the man with the scar began interrogating the teenagers.

"When did the Great Patriotic War begin?" he asked.

"In 1939," a child's voice rang out, answering without hesitation.

"There it is..." the man said in disappointment, shaking his head, expecting to hear 1941. The boy's answer assured him the youngsters could do with a history lesson.

"Tell me, who is Stepan Bandera... to you?" he asked the brave young boy who dared speak to him.

For a split second there was silence. The man with the scar was proud of himself. He couldn't have come up with a better Babay than the most terrible "smuta-maker" in the history of the Soviet Empire. However, three short words from the boy's mouth forced the occupier to shiver, as an eerie chill ran up his spine.

"He's our father..." ש

MY CAT BLANKIE HAS A SECRET

Olenka Zahorodnyk

Early one morning, a little girl named Olenka noticed her best friend the fluffy feline Blankie wasn't in the kitchen eating his breakfast. This had never happened before and the curious little girl was worried, so she asked her mum and dad a lot of questions, but nothing they said made sense. Her search for answers leads her to Xavier the Rabbit, who knows everything about the way things work. Mustering all the courage she has, Olenka joins Xavier on a journey around the city of Lviv to discover Blankie's secret.

"My Cat Blankie Has a Secret" is a book for both children and adults to read together, encouraging an open and frank discussion about the often difficult, emotionally charged subjects of death, loss, and separation, helping anyone facing the confusion, worry, fear, and anxiety that may result from losing someone they love.

AVAILABLE AT:

#VISIONS

A Working Woman's Tale

Story by Marichka Melnyk
Illustrated by Antonina Semenova

EVEN AS A LITTLE GIRL, SHE COULDN'T UNDERSTAND WHY ALL THE adults around her insisted on calling Stalin the "best friend of Soviet children." Nor could she understand for what exactly he deserved her gratitude.

That, thanks to him, she was orphaned at age nine? That since then the place she called home was more like a prison? Or that in an instant she lost not only her father and mother but also her older brother? She last saw him in 1938, at the Kharkiv Juvenile Registration and Distribution Centre, where the fate of "homeless" children like them was decided. It's then they were split up: she was sent to an orphanage in Chernihiv, and he went to a labour colony in some place called Cheboksary. (Does anyone even know where that is?)

She picked up some very valuable skills at her new home — the Kominterna Orphanage, where the Soviets placed some 500 children of the "repressed." For example, to quickly eat everything you're given, because the older and stronger kids could take your lunch and who knows if there will be any dinner. To sleep two per bed, because there isn't enough space for everyone and it's easier to stay warm that way when the temperature in the common bedroom is only a couple of degrees higher than the temperature outside. She also learnt it's better to listen more and speak less, because every attempt to ask something about her mother or brother led to yelling and threats... and not infrequently a good smack upside the head. She didn't dare mention her father because then she'd be black and blue all over; *Batya* — the director Mykytchyk — would make sure of it. And she had nobody to complain to because she was the daughter of an "enemy of the people."

The only thing left to do was to share her troubles with the "best friend of the children," whose portrait hung in nearly every room in their orphanage. However, he limited himself to watching silently and not getting involved, despite having no qualms about accepting bouquets of flowers and unfounded gratitude for "a happy childhood."

On days when the insults really got to her, she tried in vain to understand what was wrong with her family and what she personally had done to hurt Stalin. Even if her dad had been accused and convicted of counterrevolutionary activities, what did the rest of her family have to do with it? Why was she separated from her mother and brother? Why were they sent to remote corners of the country? They're always talking about the family being the "main unit of society" and "the son is not responsible for the sins of the father," but it turned out this wasn't true. Or was there something about her family she didn't know?

С КАЖДИМ ДНЬОМ ВСЬО РАДОСТНЄЄ ЖИТЬ !

IN A COUNTRY WHERE YOU'RE ONLY ALLOWED TO SPEAK IN PARTY slogans, it's best to keep your mouth shut. This was Olya's number one rule — or rather "Comrade Kukharenko's," as they named her. The plump young woman with blond hair, blue eyes, and a natural pink blush to her cheeks, which highlighted her dimples when she smiled, worked as an electric welder at the *Krasnaya Zvyezda* (Red Star) Factory. If her colleagues or friends asked about her family, Olya would instantly become dejected and say she's an orphan and doesn't remember her parents. She wouldn't give any other details. You could bet that's what everyone who had the words "family member of a traitor to the Motherland" branded on their forehead did.

Brushing off the annoying questions from her roommate at the factory dormitory or colleagues at the workshop was easy. But despite her best efforts to run away from her unfortunate past, it always caught up with her. You can't get a job without first confessing everything in the personnel questionnaire:

1. Name: <u>Olga Andreevna Kukharenko</u>
2. Year, Month, Place of Birth: <u>1929, June, Kharkiv</u>
   …
5. Nationality: <u>Ukrainian</u>

Next came Olya's favourite questions, truthful answers to which would forever ruin her future, including any chance of a promotion, prevent her from membership in the *Komsomol* (the Soviet communist youth group), or the Communist Party, and deny her acceptance to study at the university… Her honesty would even deny her the right to vote, despite there being no actual choices in the elections.

14. Closest relatives: <u>father, Andrei Aleksandrovich Kukharenko,</u>
    <u>b. 1903, convicted; mother, Maria Nikolaevna Kukharenko,</u>
    <u>b. 1905, convicted; brother, Ivan Andreevich Kukharenko, b.</u>
    <u>1925, last seen in 1938 at the Kharkiv Juvenile Distribution</u>
    <u>Centre, fate unknown</u>
    …
18. Have you or your relatives been convicted of a crime, when,
    and what crime? <u>father sentenced in 1938 under Articles 54-6,</u>
    <u>54-10 of the Criminal Code of the USSR by the Troika of the</u>
    <u>NKVD [precursor to the KGB] in the Kharkiv Oblast to 10 years</u>
    <u>without the right to correspondence; mother sentenced in 1938</u>
    <u>by a decision of the Special Council of the NKVD to five years</u>
    <u>in exile as a a family member of a traitor to the Motherland</u>

20. Have you ever been denied the right to vote, when, and why?
     <u>deprived of voting rights in 1946 in accordance with the</u>
     <u>decision of the Central Executive Committee of the USSR of</u>
     <u>8 June 1934 as a family member of a traitor to the Motherland</u>

                                            Date questionnaire completed:
                                                  <u>17 September 1946</u>

Olya didn't dare lie in the questionnaire. It was too risky. If you were caught lying, there was only one option: being sent to the camps like your parents and brother. She was convinced this job was going to be her lifeline. It was a one in a million chance to survive and be rehabilitated, to prove to the authorities, plant management, colleagues, and neighbours she's normal like everyone else. Wasn't this what the Communist Party needed?

She got lucky. Because so many men died in the war there was nobody else to rebuild the economy. There was nobody to work at the factories and fulfil the "five-year plan in four years." This is how women turners, pressers, and fitters appeared in the Ukrainian SSR and the Soviet Union as a whole. Women machinists, motorists, grinders, millers, woodworkers, builders. And women electric welders like herself. At the time there were almost 2.5 times more able-bodied women than men. Even now, in 1952 — eight years after the liberation of Kirovograd — almost half the workers in some of the Krasnaya Zvyezda Factory workshops were women.

These were women who didn't just start working a job at a functioning factory, ready and waiting for them. They rebuilt destroyed facilities with their own hands or introduced new production capabilities for the plants. Being part of this battalion and by no means trying to belittle their achievements, Olya, nevertheless, couldn't let it pass when she heard how everything these days was distorted and exaggerated. She would hear the Communist Party organisers zealously saying at every meeting that the "Hitlerites" destroyed more than 80 per cent of their production capacity and the Soviets heroically rebuilt it in a few years. All she could think then was: *"How convenient there was a war, so now you can blame everything bad that happened on the 'Nazi bastards' while pinning undeserved medals to your own chests."*

The locals who lived through the Nazi occupation told a completely different story, albeit in a whisper. The factory's main buildings were in fact blown up by Soviet sappers in 1941 as the Red Army retreated to the east, but the rest of the facility remained intact. Moreover, the Nazis built new workshops on the ruins of the destroyed ones, and in the summer of 1942 began production of armoured vehicles and other equipment needed for the war. More than 500 workers and engineers from the Krasnaya Zvyezda Factory signed up to work at the Kirovograd Plow and Foundry Plant as it was called then. Today, to speak openly about their fate is spurned, but everyone knows most of the workers were later repressed by the NKVD. This isn't the most pleasant page in the factory's history, and one the current management is trying to forget.

The Hitlerites planned to blow up the factory when they were retreating from the city in November 1943 but ran out of time. Two buildings were slightly damaged in airstrikes during the aerial offensive by the Red Army. Luckily, the factory remained mostly intact, allowing production to restart quickly. In August 1944, there were already 11 functioning workshops, and by early 1950 the Krasnaya Zvyezda Factory had nearly reached pre-war production levels.

Today, in 1952, agricultural machinery continues to be made here as it was in the past. The factory survived two world wars, and except for those times, always stuck to its profile. From the moment it was founded by English entrepreneurs and brothers Robert and Thomas Elworthy, it manufactured mainly seeders, and continued to do so after it was nationalised by the Bolsheviks in 1919. It grew from a small workshop with 12 workers in 1874 to a large factory employing 12,000 by the late 1930s. Before the war started, it produced 10 per cent of all the agricultural machinery in the Soviet Union. In addition to seeders, the Krasnaya Zvyezda Factory also made parts for combines, tractors, mechanised mills, and other machinery — everything Ukrainian collective farms desperately needed to send thousands of tonnes of grain to Moscow every month.

Comrade Kukharenko's job involved the production of seeder frames — a special component made of welded metal pipes, upon which the seeding system is later hung. It was not easy work as you had to drag a heavy welding machine around, albeit on wheels. But the worst thing about this particular job was the heat. The uniforms issued by the factory were basically ordinary dark blue coveralls which failed to protect you from feeling suffocated, even though they're supposed to be heat resistant. You ended up taking a lot of breaks to prevent yourself from fainting, and the more breaks you took, the longer it took to get the work done.

If she failed to meet her quota, or the station or workshop fell behind its targets in the socialist emulation (the officially sanctioned competition between factories) with the Krasnaya Zvyezda's designated and main rival, the Kharkiv *Serp i Molot* (Hammer and Sickle) Factory, then her workday turned from the official seven hours, into eight, nine, or even 10. And this was life, seven days a week.

"During the times of the Elworthy exploiters, people toiled like slaves 12 hours a day. Even on holidays! They worked in completely different conditions than you — in dark, cramped, hot rooms. You should know in the first half of 1907 alone, there were

173 accidents because of the failure to adhere to safety standards," the supervisors of the third mechanical assembly shop where Olya worked would say to encourage the workers. But to her these words were a slap in the face. *"Thank you for eternally freeing us from slavery,"* she would think sarcastically when she couldn't take it anymore. *"Good thing we don't have 16-hour shifts like under the Hitlerites."*

It often felt like the protective mask and gloves would melt and fuse with her skin. But Olya didn't complain. At least not out loud. Even when she really wanted to. She would calm herself by counting to 100 to contain the hurricane of emotions inside and repeat her mantra: *"I got lucky."*

Indeed, she got lucky in autumn 1946 when the people responsible for the mobilisation of the labour reserves turned a blind eye to her "untrustworthiness." That's how she found herself taking factory production training courses and soon afterwards landing a job at the Krasnaya Zvyezda.

She remembers clearly her first day at work. It was a Wednesday, 2 October 1946. On that morning during the daily political information briefing, the workers listened as an article on the front page of *Pravda* was read aloud describing the end of the Nuremburg Trials, announcing the sentences handed down to the Nazi war criminals:

"The biggest trial in history has ended. For the first time, a just punishment has fallen on the heads of the organisers and leaders, the instigators and executors of the criminal plans of the war of aggression..."

The thunderous applause with which her colleagues greeted these words still rings in her ears.

Olya really did get lucky, because the factory directors, when putting in their requests for workers, were increasingly asking for men, preferably unmarried ones. And her current director, Oleksandr Matviyovych Merkulov, was no exception. Currently, she wouldn't have been hired at the factory and would most likely have continued to waste away in Verkhotomsk (a God-forsaken village in the Kemerovo Oblast near Mongolia), where she and the other kids from the Chernihiv orphanage were evacuated in August 1941. Even then she got lucky, because not everyone was relocated away from the Nazi bombings. She overheard the caretakers gossiping about how many of those incarcerated in the Chernihiv prisons were simply shot instead of being evacuated. And for the Soviets there was no fundamental difference between the children of "enemies of the people" and criminals...

IT WAS JUST STARTING TO GET LIGHT OUT WHEN OLYA, DRESSED IN a not-so-new but still attractive light grey double-breasted coat, descended the creaky polished stairs from the second floor of the women's dormitory — a long wooden building, which, if it hadn't been plastered and painted white, would have looked more like a cattle barn than housing for people.

"Good morning, *Myshka* (Little Mouse)!" The pleasant greeting echoed from the watchwoman, a petite but solidly built blue-eyed blond in her forties, sitting at her post to the right of the door. Perched on a platform, the podium and stool she sat on allowed the *vakhterka* (female security guard and custodian) to keep watch on the activities in the women's dormitory. "Running off somewhere again?"

The workers' housing on Nekrasivska Street where Olya lived was about 2.5km from the factory — just over a 30-minute walk. But she always tried to complete the trek faster. She still couldn't get used to the fact she was slumbering on graves and treading over someone's bones every day.

The Soviets encountered a housing problem in Kirovograd when the need for more workers grew. They had run out of space at the workers' quarters on Novomykolayivska Street (built long ago by the Elworthy brothers), so they decided to construct new housing for factory workers on the territory of the old cemeteries in the north-eastern part of Elizabethgrad, which was what the city was called before it was renamed in honour of Sergei Kirov, the First Secretary of the Leningrad Regional Committee of the All-Union Communist Party (Bolsheviks) and organiser of Soviet repressions.

The first shacks appeared on the new location in the 1920s, and the area where the cemeteries were located got its current name, Nekrasovska, after the "great Russian poet" Nikolai Nekrasov, whose centenary was celebrated in 1921. But the district didn't begin to expand actively until after the war, when the current director Merkulov was appointed.

Right before Olya's eyes, 18 new one-storey homes were built in parallel rows on Nekrasovska Street. They were designed for two families, each getting a two-room 54sq m apartment with unheard of amenities at the time, such as running water, electricity, a sidewalk and even trees planted on both sides of each building. A community centre, grocery store, bathhouse, occupational health and safety office, and other service buildings were also built for the workers.

Among the lucky ones to get keys to their own homes on 1 January 1949 were the top performing workers: Vladyslav Kniatkovsky, Kostiantyn Didenko, Serhiy Kryvoruchko, Mykola Kvinker, and others. There was no way Olya could not know the names of these Krasnaya Zvyezda Factory superstars. Their photos loomed before her eyes every day at the factory's main entrance, plastered on the board honouring the best employees, almost never being replaced by anyone else's photos.

She remembers what a sensation the newly built Krasnaya Zvyezda Factory living quarters were at the time. It was mentioned at the 16th Congress of the Central

Committee of the Communist Party (Bolsheviks) on 25–28 January 1949, praising the lightning speed at which the homes were built: in just 154 days!

S. T. Redka, the deputy secretary of the factory Communist Party committee, constantly bragged about the new housing, proud as a peacock of this unprecedented achievement. At the same time, he forgot that for each of the 36 workers and their families now living in decent conditions there were thousands of others, like Olya, crowded into barrack-like dormitories. But Olya knew, no matter how many seeders she welded, with her past history, she would never even be put on the waiting list for factory housing, let alone be given a home.

But at least she had somewhere to live. Yes, the roof leaked when it rained; the windows were so warped from the humidity, at one point they were closed and from then on, nobody hazarded trying to open them; the door, deformed for the same reason, required using both your knee and shoulder at the same time to close it. And the faulty furnace was more likely to poison the tenants with carbon monoxide than heat the cramped, kennel-like 12sq m rooms.

On every floor of Olya's dormitory, 20 rooms were evenly distributed along each side of a long corridor. Two women were supposed to live per room, but this wasn't always the case. For the nearly 100 residents there were four stovetops for food preparation and 10 sinks with cold water for washing. The only toilet was in an outhouse, and if you wanted to bathe, you had to sign up for a specific day and time at the factory or at a city bathhouse.

"Yes, I have to hurry, Maria Yosypivna," Olya replied to the attractive vakhterka, her voice unexpectedly weak. Attempting to hide her swollen face behind a scarf, she continued: "I must hurry because there is supposed to be a political information briefing before my shift. They're going to tell us about yesterday's 19th Party Congress…"

"Yes, yes, of course!" the vakhterka said in agreement, nodding, her sharp chin moving up and down for greater emphasis, while a group of five other workers passed by. "They were approving the figures for the current five-year plan. It's very important, you mustn't be late." The words coming out of the speaker's mouth did not match what Olya could read in Maria Yosypivna's slightly squinted eyes, implying profound scepticism about what she was saying.

The factory workers call Maria Yosypivna *Muzyka* (Music). It was short for her last name, Muzychenko, and a tribute to her tough character, thanks to which she kept order and discipline in the dormitory, forcing all the residents to dance to her tune.

Like Olya, there were two people coexisting inside Muzyka: one wanting an ordinary, routine pedestrian life without any wild swings from one challenge to another and was ready to toe the official party line for this; and the other who harboured a deep grudge against those who unfairly denied her a life of stability and opportunities. And ironically, both the "official party liners" and the deniers were one and the same — the Soviets.

It was hard to keep a secret in the women's dormitory. The workers gossiped about how before the war Muzyka was a foreman of the mechanical department at one of the Krasnaya Zvyezda workshops, and in 1938 was even a candidate to join the Communist Party. She had excellent career prospects and her personal life was set. But the war changed everything. Her husband was mobilised on 23 June 1941. A little more than a month later, she was holding the certificate of death indicating her Oleksandr died heroically in battle while defending Kirovograd, in the *Zelena Brama* (Green Gate) forest.

Nobody knows for sure what the woman did during the war years, but in spring 1945, she was arrested and accused of collaborating with the Nazis. The NKVD's suspicions obviously didn't pan out, because by the end of the year the case was closed and she was released from custody. The short-term imprisonment and charges cost her dearly, though; she was asked to resign as foreman and her candidacy to join the Communist Party went up in smoke. Hence, she ended up at the dormitory, and being assigned guard duty every other day was all she managed to finagle from the former Krasnaya Zvyezda director Mykola Nykanorovych Shynkarevych.

As much as Olya tried to shield herself from her colleagues, Muzyka had managed to slightly penetrate her armour. Although, in the beginning, their relationship could hardly have been called a friendship. It actually began with a scandal. About three years earlier, the vakhterka was making her rounds in the dormitory when she caught Olya cooking dinner on a camp stove on the floor of her room. Muzyka started shouting, confiscated the forbidden kerosene appliance, and wrote Olya up for the violation.

After keeping a close eye on Olya for several months, Muzyka noticed she wore rather fashionable dresses. Asking around, Muzyka discovered not only was Olya a skilled welder, she was also adept at sewing using the Singer machine her roommate had inherited from her late grandmother. Knowing full well she couldn't turn her down, the vakhterka asked Olya to tailor, hem, or decorate with white collars the formless clothing she occasionally managed to buy at the Central Department Store on Karl Marx Street.

Muzyka was right: Olya humbly tailored her clothes and didn't take any payment. During their time together, the vakhterka picked up on the unbounded sadness shadowing the worker, resulting in her gaze constantly being cast down at her feet, rarely raising her head to look at someone straight in the eyes. *"She's an orphan just like me,"* she guessed one day. Once her suspicion was confirmed through the gossip brigade, her seemingly insensitive heart shuddered, and her attitude towards Olya changed. With small gestures, like returning the kerosene stove, or giving Olya a leftover (not really) scrap of fabric, she gradually quelled the bad aftertaste of their first encounter. This isn't to say Olya trusted her completely, but over time Maria Yosypivna became the person closest to her.

For Muzyka, becoming friends with Olya was also a kind of release. A childless widow branded with the suspicion of having collaborated with the Nazis, she often felt used and unjustly neglected. For no reason at all. Maria Yosypivna never took her pain out on others, every day putting on the impenetrable mask of a person faithful to the Communist Party. But even the strongest mask sometimes cracks.

"Yes, the numbers...it's very interesting and exciting," Olya mumbled unenthusiastically to the vakhterka, forgetting she had to control her intonation when they weren't alone. Such carelessness wasn't typical of her. Waving off her older friend's concerned look, Olya pushed open the dormitory door and stepped out into the morning twilight.

THE ROAD TO THE WORKSHOPS IN KOVALIVKA WAS VERY FAMILIAR. SHE had taken the same route for six years and nine days, and it was unlikely to ever change. Moving from the factory to another job was forbidden by law, and breaking the law was not in Olya's best interests.

The young woman, barely paying attention, took Syvaska Street, past Pavlik Morozov Square and the only remaining cemetery, towards Kolhospna Street. There she usually waited for the number 4 bus and for 30 kopecks rode three stops to get off at the Krasnaya Zvyezda Factory. From there it was only a few dozen steps to the entrance.

That day, while waiting at the bus stop, Olya was in such deep thought she only heard the bus when the doors slammed shut with a screech and it drove off. Now she'd have to walk, even though her legs felt like a ton of bricks.

She'd been feeling unwell for several days. She was very tired, her body ached, and she was feeling nauseous in the morning. And yesterday she fainted, right in the workshop. It's a good thing she wasn't holding an electrode at the time.

The diagnosis by the nurse at the factory clinic caught her by surprise.

"Married? Well, no big deal. It's not shameful to be a single mother these days. The state will help you," she said in Russian, as she pointed to the poster on the wall behind her showing a smiling young cafeteria worker holding a red-cheeked, toothless plump baby boy. "In the country of the Soviets, a woman who is a mother is steeped in honour, respect, and all-embracing care," the poster announced in Russian under the idyllic image.

Olya cried in her pillow throughout the night. By morning her face was so swollen she looked like she had been stung by wasps. You could barely see her eyes from behind her red bulging eyelids.

Maybe if she was living in a different part of the world, she would have taken the pregnancy news better. She didn't believe the fairy tale about "honour, respect, and care." Her mother certainly didn't experience it that way. And there were many other disheartening examples. The stories from the maternity wards where expectant mothers were treated like prisoners sufficed. You couldn't bring personal items with you. Your husband couldn't visit you. You were forced to wash the floors when there wasn't enough cleaning staff. The baby was taken away immediately after birth and brought to you only for feeding. You could forget about painkillers. "Tolerate it, woman," "work harder," and "it's not advanced math, you can figure it out yourself" — that's what the unsympathetic and sullen nurses threw back at you in Russian, when you requested pain relief for contractions or to be shown the proper way to express breast milk or swaddle your baby. It wasn't talked about openly, but Olya heard women with families whisper in the workshop about similar experiences.

On the way to work she imagined all the possible scenarios in her head.

Have an abortion? Officially they had been banned 15 or more years ago. Of course, nobody asked the woman what she wanted. To have a baby, or better yet three, was just one more plan she had to fulfil — the "honourable duty" for the "Motherland." The state needs more workers and soldiers to build socialism and spread the revolution around the world. They even introduced a special tax for bachelors, singles, and small families. Olya heard men in the factory jokingly call it the "tax on balls."

Having a secret abortion was too much of a risk. It wasn't easy to find someone who could do it. Who would go against the law and risk two or three years in prison? Plus, if you started asking around about such brave (or crazy) people, someone was bound to find out. An ordinary woman would be "publicly censured" and have to pay a maximum fine of 300 *karbovantsi* (the Ukrainian equivalent of the rouble). But the

daughter of an "enemy of the people" would probably be sent to prison, following in her parents' footsteps.

Have the baby? It's unlikely the baby's father would marry her. Mykyta was a good man, and he swore he loved her, but would his feelings erode in the wind as soon as he found out about the unplanned child? On top of that, she never had the guts to tell him the truth about her past. And even if he took it well, Olya's "family ties" would forever destroy his potential career.

As a matter of fact, Mykyta was from the working class, a migrant from Voronezh in Russia. He graduated from the Kirovograd Technical School for Agricultural Machine Building with the prestigious specialisation in metallurgy called "cold working." He had also been a front-line soldier in the war and was decommissioned after sustaining a leg injury while liberating Kharkiv in August 1943. An unbelievable combination! Now he was the head of his section in the instrument shop and many more doors would certainly open for him in the future. Granted, the Krasnaya Zvyezda management had long been hinting to him: 30 is too old to still be a bachelor. It's easier to move up the career ladder as a family man — they always receive preference over bachelors. But he could definitely find better options than Olya; there were many women at the plant from which to choose.

Raise a child alone? Where? In the wretched dormitory, in a small damp room with peeling walls which she shared with a roommate? There was no space to move around, let alone fit a crib. There were two metal beds with springs which creaked with every movement and sagged nearly to the floor, two nightstands for personal items, a kitchen table with two chairs — that's all the amenities they had. And even this spartan setup occupied the entire room.

Who would help her? She didn't have any relatives nearby. Other women at least had grandmothers or sisters to lend a hand. Her closest friend was a dormitory vakhterka... Yes, she could get 77 days of paid maternity leave, but then what? Nursery

care? She had to pay and there was a waiting list, because for the state, rebuilding factories and collective farms was always a priority.

"You should give birth!" the Soviets insisted, but Olya knew the truth. "And don't stop at one or two children, have six, eight, 10! We'll hang your photo on the honour board and pin 'hero mother' medals and 'glorious motherhood' orders on your chest... And don't pay attention to the fact there aren't enough nurseries and kindergartens: that is simply nonsense, you can wait. After all, the older children can take care of the younger ones — why support 'dependents' and get nothing in return?"

And even if they found space for her child, Olya heard Svitlana Karpenko from the hardware shop complaining to her friends when she picks up her daughter from the

nursery, her face is red from screaming and crying. The staff either can't handle all the children or simply neglect to do their jobs. They're probably busy with more important matters, such as gossiping about the mothers, especially the single ones. There was no one willing to stand up for them. Or, more likely, the staff was busy flipping through the pages of the latest issue of *Soviet Woman* or *Woman Worker* magazine looking for trendy clothing patterns, recipes, and medical advice.

Knowing this, how could she leave her child there and go back to the workshop for her shift to weld pipes into frames without worrying? Nobody would free her from the responsibility of producing her share of the factory quota.

Leaving the factory wasn't an option. "He who does not work shall not eat" was written in Stalin's Constitution. You couldn't survive on state aid with a child; moreover, they'd kick her out of the dormitory. If it weren't for all these state requests for the endless donations "for brotherly countries of the people's democracy," "to bring cultural enlightenment," and "to help Japanese children who suffered from the earthquake," maybe she could somehow make ends meet. The income tax and singles tax combined ate up one-fifth of her salary...

She could, of course, give the baby up to an orphanage. But she wouldn't wish that on her worst enemy.

Relying on the state to raise a child was risky. She could end up with her very own Pavlik Morozov, who would turn her in to the authorities and denounce her without blinking an eye. This was exactly the "new type" of person all these Pioneer (children's communist scouting organisation) and Komsomol units were nurturing. She remembered how these "new" people — loyal Leninists and Stalinists — later wrote in the press: "I, Nikolai Ivanov, renounce my father..." and "I, Lyuba Sydorenko, condemn my mother..." This newspaper column was regularly read to them at the orphanage, which had accumulated a large and impressive archive of news clippings dedicated to this topic.

Then what, have an abortion? What if you can't get pregnant again, or even worse?

"It's a choice without a choice," Olya sighed, despondently. She was snapped out of her daze by the protracted whistle of the steam train leaving the station just as she ducked into the archway between Novomykolaivska and Kovalivka streets.

The factory was just a stone's throw away. There, 200 metres away, among the poplars, already having shed about half their yellowed leaves, and alongside the green acacias, towered the four- and six-storey buildings of the Krasnaya Zvyezda Factory. If the locomotive hadn't veered off its daily schedule, this meant the clock read 6.00am. And despite her best efforts, this meant she was already late for the damn political information briefing.

IT WAS SOME 20 STEPS TO THE DREARY CROWD OF WORKERS WHO HAD gathered on the square in front of the factory. They blended into a grey mud-coloured mass, the workers indistinguishable in their old, ragged *kufaikas* (wool-padded cotton jackets) and their battle-worn *himnastyorkas* (military pull-over smocks with belts but with the epaulettes removed).

As the young woman passed the main gate, she felt a strong gaze directed at her from above. Raising her head as minimally as possible, Olya furtively looked up, squinting her eyes to look to the right, where a semi-circular glass enclosure stuck out like a balcony from the second floor of the factory management office. Standing in the window was the stern figure of Director Merkulov, hands on his hips, frowning in displeasure at those breaking labour discipline.

The Krasnaya Zvyezda management department was located in a large, 800sq m sky-blue building with a green roof. It was built by the Elworthy brothers in the late 1800s as a family home. The decision to build their own residence on the factory grounds surprised many people at the time, but made it easier for the English businessmen to oversee production. The first floor was for the servants, and the family lived on the second floor. Today, 50 years later, the former owners' dining room served as the Krasnaya Zvyezda director's office, and the bay window of the music room, once echoing with Enrico Caruso's arias playing on the gramophone, was turned into the director's observation post.

"You're late, Comrade Kukharenko. The meeting started 10 minutes ago," said Ms Berestova, head of the factory women's council, whispering her displeasure in Olya's ear. Olya walked past without paying her any attention. She stopped a little further on and got on her tiptoes to scan the crowd for her Mykyta.

Wearing a mud-coloured suit and burgundy tie with grey stripes, a Lenin cap tucked under his left arm, the Deputy Secretary of the Communist Party Committee Redka was standing on a short staircase serving as a stage. He was holding the morning edition of *Pravda Ukrainy* (the Communist Party newspaper in Ukraine) in his right hand, reading aloud in a monotone voice the *Gosplan's* Chairman M. Z. Saburov's report titled "Directives of the 19th Party Congress on the Fifth Five-Year-Plan for the Development of the USSR in 1951–1955." The Gosplan was a Russian portmanteau for "government planning committee." Standing next to him in the "presidium," shifting from one foot to the other, were three people: Krasnaya Zvyezda's Chief Engineer Y. P. Kriuchkov; the head of the hardware workshop and part-time People's Deputy of the *Verkhovna Rada,* the Supreme Council of the Ukrainian Soviet Socialist Republic, H. K. Maliy; and the founder of the brigade named after the Georgian Communist Ordzhonikidze and Communist-Stakhanovite K. K. Stoliarenko.

"What a stupid waste of time," Olya thought. *"Even Merkulov realises it and is waiting out this festival of absurdity in the management office..."* She knew the director would only show up at the very end of the meeting, when all that was left to do was vote for the target numbers. Like he always did.

She also knew her Mykyta wouldn't miss this meeting for any reason, even if he was allowed to skip it. On the contrary, he'd be one of the first there, so he could stand as near as possible to the speakers.

Olya was right. There he was, in the first rows, standing in the company of two designers — his friends Yerofeev and Koziakin, and next to Zozulya, the acting editor of the factory newsletter with the unimaginative name *Krasnaya Zvyezda.*

"In the fifth five-year-plan, further rapid growth in machine building is scheduled," Redka grumbled in Russian into the microphone attached to a stand. From there, wires ran to four amplifiers and loudspeakers placed at various corners of the square. Although meant to increase the volume, the speakers screeched, drowning out any clarity, forcing people to guess what was being said and what to expect in the near future.

"In the next five years, machine production and metalworking will approximately double," the party secretary continued, as Olya slowly moved through the crowd. "There will also be significant growth in production... new types of agricultural machinery..."

"We need to talk," Olya said as she gently pulled at Mykyta's work smock. "Let's meet tonight, at 9.00pm, at our usual spot," she added when he turned around. After he nodded in approval, she slowly made her way to the opposite end of the crowd so as not to draw attention to herself.

She felt completely out of place at this gathering. So much so, she found it hard to breathe.

THE SUN HAD ALMOST DISAPPEARED BEHIND THE HORIZON WHEN OLYA arrived, sitting down on a bench along one of the quieter foot paths in the park on Novomykolaivska Street. From there she could see the fountain on the central, and only illuminated, alley, the one Mykyta would take.

He was late, even though the spot where they were meeting was closer for him than for her. They could have met at Pavlik Morozov Square, only a two-minute walk from her dormitory, but she hated that place.

As Olya waited, the entire history of their seven-month-long relationship flashed before her eyes. They met at one of the *subotnyky,* what the Soviets called volunteering but was really forced unpaid public labour the authorities would use to clean up parks. They were usually scheduled on Saturdays or other non-workdays, but this one was held before the annual celebration of the anniversary of Lenin's birthday. She was whitewashing trees and curbs by the workers' theatre. It, too, was inherited by the factory from the Elworthy brothers. Now it was used for all sorts of Communist Party gatherings and meetings with VIPs like Petrovsky, the former Deputy Chairman of the Presidium of the Supreme Soviet of the USSR, or Marshall of the Soviet Union Budyonny.

When Olya's whitewashing bucket was empty, a tall stranger came to her aid. He had broad shoulders, dark brown hair, brown eyes like hers, and a long scar stretching from his right temple, across his ear, and down to his jaw. But the scar didn't spoil the young man's looks, it just made his face look a bit mean. He rolled up his sleeves, and instead of pouring water into the lime, he poured water into the bucket and then mixed in the lime. The reaction was instantaneous. The contents of the bucket hissed and then exploded like a volcano, white "lava" covering him from head to toe. Olya unexpectedly burst out laughing. True, it wasn't funny, the mix could have easily burnt his skin. The stranger had seemed so sure of himself, radiating confidence, but this was such an epic failure, she couldn't hold back her laughter. At first he was startled, but after a second or two he also exploded in laughter. Olya took the scarf off her head and offered it to him to wipe off his exposed skin. He accepted the scarf...

The two of them were cut from a different cloth. Olya understood this after dating for a few weeks, but continued to let him flirt. After all, she was a young woman, and deep inside she wanted a man's attention, although until now she had reined in her desire.

The biggest negatives she saw in Mykyta was his unbridled ambition and undisguised careerism. Beyond that, she considered him to be a good and honest person. At least he didn't keep any secrets from her. The same couldn't be said about Olya.

She heard a familiar rustle. A shadowed figure approached her on the path. It was Mykyta, limping slightly on his left leg. This was another mark the war had left on him. A fragment of artillery broke the bones in his lower leg and, unfortunately, the doctors couldn't put them back together properly.

"Hi, sweetheart!" he said, as he approached the bench.

Olya immediately jumped up and blurted out the news she could no longer keep to herself.

"Mykyta, I'm pregnant..."

He was reaching out to hug her but froze halfway through the motion, stunned by what he had heard.

"I understand you're in shock. But while you come to... there is something more which may influence your decision in this situation... It's something you must know. I told you in the beginning I'm an orphan. And most likely that's the case now, but it's not the complete truth..."

ENOUGH! STOP YOUR CRYING! CALM DOWN, MY LITTLE MYSHKA!" Muzyka had left her assigned post at the entrance to the dormitory and led her sobbing young friend to the room for the vakhterkas, where she hugged the crying woman. In despair, Olya told the vakhterka about her parents, her relationship with Mykyta, and her pregnancy.

"Well, did you really think Nikita, your Mykyta, would make a different choice? You know his type, it's written all over his face!" the vakhterka burst out, and very quickly regretted what she had said, because it only made Olya wail even louder.

Muzyka sat Olya on a chair by the door and handed her a striped handkerchief she pulled from her coat pocket. She took a yellow enamel can decorated with poppies off the windowsill, poured water into it from a metal mug, and inserted an immersion heater to boil the water.

"I'll make you some mint and lemon balm tea. You'll feel better right away," she promised, sitting down on the wooden bedstand looking for dried tea leaves. Three minutes later, the tiny room was filled with the scent of herbal tea.

"Did you decide what you're going to do?" Myzuka asked after Olya took a few sips and her crying died down. The vakhterka turned towards the window to heat herself some water.

"I heard about an herbal remedy using tansy," Olya said after taking a deep breath.

"Who told you that? Don't listen to the local gossipmongers. Nothing good will come of it!" the vakhterka cautioned.

She put her tea on the windowsill to cool and sat on the other stool next to Olya.

"Don't you dare! You hear me?" she said, squeezing Olya's hand.

Olya, still sniffling, sat without looking up, afraid to admit to her friend she had already purchased the herbs at the pharmacy kiosk.

"Don't even think about it!" Muzyka continued. "You'll regret it for the rest of your life! Just like I do…" she blurted out, her words taking both of them by surprise.

That night would be filled with great revelations for Olya as well. In response to Olya's confession, Maria Yosypivna opened her soul and told a story even the biggest gossiper in the dormitory couldn't have imagined.

As soon as the Hitlerites occupied Kirovograd, she fled to Sentove, the village where she was born, located 30km to the north of the city. Although her parents were already dead, a great-aunt still lived there and took her in. When the occupiers set up their administration in the city, they invited Krasnaya Zvyezda Factory workers who hadn't evacuated to come work at the renamed plant, now called the Kirovograd Plow and Foundry Factory. Without even thinking, Maria rejected their invitation. The pain from losing her husband at the hands of these bastards was still too fresh. Not for a second did she believe the supposedly heartfelt intentions of the "friends of the people" and "liberators from Soviet terror" to build a "new order in Europe." Although some locals did fall for it…

"Can you imagine, they even took photos with the invaders in front of the toppled Kirov monument? How stupid!" Muzyka said, covering her eyes with her hand. "What were they thinking? That the enemy would become their best friends? Or that the Soviets wouldn't find out?"

She and her aunt lived under occupation for a year and a half, surviving on what they grew in the garden, trying not to draw too much attention to themselves. But then, around the autumn of 1942, a decree was issued to export blond-haired, blue-eyed women aged 15–35 to Germany to be domestic servants for Nazi families. This time around, nobody asked Maria whether she wanted the job or not. In May 1943, she was forcibly relocated and placed with a large family in Munich to help an overworked German *frau* raise her five offspring. The head of the family was an SS *Obersturmführer* (the highest lieutenant officer rank in the German SS) and frequently disappeared on official trips. But when he came home, he would often and with sadistic pleasure rape his children's nanny. She became pregnant about a year later. Once her problematic condition was apparent, without bothering to ask her, they immediately performed an abortion, so as not to contaminate the superior German race with half-breeds. Such was the official policy of their insane *Führer*.

Now it was Muzyka's turn to cry and Olya's to console her.

After the war, having fallen for the Soviet propaganda posters showing *Ostarbeiters,* the Nazi designation for foreign slave labourers, being greeted joyfully at train stations, the woman headed home. But nobody welcomed her "return from

German captivity to the Motherland" with flowers and open arms as promised. Instead, she ended up in the Volkovysk filtration camp in the Belarusian SSR. She spent several months in prison, but the NKVD didn't find any evidence she had collaborated with the Nazis and the prosecutor's office of the Kyiv Military District closed the case.

"You know, back then I consoled myself with the idea I didn't need this child. I almost convinced myself I would have always hated it because of how it was conceived. But now, when I have nothing in life..." she rose, took a few steps towards the window, picked up the mug, and sipped her tea, which had gone cold long ago.

"I'll be at your side, I promise. I'll help you with the child. Just don't do anything stupid."

"**O**NE FORCES YOU TO HAVE ABORTIONS, THE OTHER COMPLETELY FORBIDS *them,*" Olya thought to herself the following day as she welded another frame to a seeder. *"When will you all croak, you leaders who so lovingly and eagerly dictate your will to everyone..."*

"Kukharenko!" The section manager called out her name, distracting her from ruminating over the story she had heard yesterday. "Turn off your machine and go straight to the workshop manager. You've been summoned."

She didn't have to be told twice. Olya put down the electrode, pulled the cord out of the socket, and trotted off to the other end of the factory floor. The production space was separated from the third mechanical assembly shop manager's office by an opaque, half-glass partition. As she passed it, she saw he wasn't alone, but couldn't identify the silhouette of the person standing next to him.

Olya knocked on the door, and an annoyed male voice shouted for her to wait. She had no idea why she had been called to the boss' office, but it was probably serious. The people behind the glass were waving their arms like they were arguing over something, but she couldn't hear what they were saying over the workshop noise.

"Come in, Kukharenko!" her boss opened the door, let her in, and went back to his chair behind the desk. To the right of him stood Roza Eduardovna, the Krasnaya Zvyezda Factory employee manager, holding a stack of personnel files.

"I'm not going to beat around the bush. I'll say it like it is, Olya Andreevna," the man said in Russian, in a monotonous, seemingly bored voice, pretending to be indifferent, but his gaze darted back and forth, giving away his discomfort.

"There was an inspection at the factory which revealed a large percentage of defective products... It's very unfortunate, but our workshop was at the top of the list of the offenders. We can't turn a blind eye to something like this because then we'd all be accused of sabotage..." Olya noticed her file was open on the manager's desk. "And you have nothing to lose..."

At last, Olya understood what was going on. Without waiting for him to finish, she turned around and walked out of the room, heading straight for the locker room. She took off her work coveralls and put on her coat. From there she started towards the factory exit. As she was leaving, she looked up and saw Director Merkulov standing by the window with his arms crossed on his chest. Their eyes met for a brief moment.

OLYA WOKE UP THE NEXT MORNING IN THE HOSPITAL WHERE SHE HAD been taken after being found unconscious in a pool of her own blood in the dormitory washroom.

"What an idiot!" the nurse who was changing her IV couldn't resist commenting. "Why is the child to blame?"

Weak and in pain, Olya found the strength to lift herself up and rest on her elbows. Looking curiously at the woman her own age standing there in a white coat, Olya smiled. Then she started haltingly singing the words to a popular Russian lullaby, her voice slightly off-key:

"...Sleep, my little boy, sleep,
Sleep, my dear eaglet,
There is a bright path for you —
Gather your strength..."

The nurse, making a circular motion with her finger at her temple, ran out of the hospital room, as Olya, leaning back on the bed, continued to sing alone, barely moving her lips:

"In the sky, full of light,
The stars shine bright,
The serene sleep of children,
Is protected by Stalin..."

She got lucky. At least there's something in her life she can control.

A LITTLE LESS THAN FIVE MONTHS AFTER this story, the great Soviet leader — the "father of the nations" and "friend of the children" — Stalin, died. Unfortunately, his death didn't mean the end of the Soviet Union. But there were some shifts in the totalitarian regime.

For example, the mid-1950s saw the beginning of a mass review of cases of repressed Soviet citizens. Many of those who had been unjustly convicted in 1937–1938 were rehabilitated and recognised as victims of political repression. In 1958, the Fundamental Principles of Criminal Legislation of the USSR and the Union Republics abolishing the concepts of "enemy of the people" and "family member of an enemy of the people" was passed, removing the restrictions related to this legal status. But in practice, it was a different story...

In 1956, workers were given the right to change their place of work as they chose. Criminal liability was abolished for moving to another factory and for absenteeism without a valid reason. As the number

of able-bodied men increased, women were gradually transferred to easier and less dangerous types of work.

In 1955, the ban on abortions was lifted. According to estimates, in the prior year, at least four million illegal abortions were performed in the Soviet Union. Due to the Soviet totalitarian system's deliberate disregard for basic sex education and limited access to other methods of birth control, abortions would remain the number one method of contraception in the USSR for decades to come. Having deprived women of any alternative, even after decriminalising abortions, state propaganda continued to scare them with possible infertility and loss of sex drive which could lead to broken marriages and loneliness.

Who knows if these changes meant things could have turned out differently for Olya Kukharenko, daughter of an "enemy of the people," orphan at the Kominterna Orphanage, and electric welder at the Krasnaya Zvyezda Factory. Perhaps, at least, her choice would have been a little easier if these changes had happened several years earlier. **W**

UACOMIX

UA Comix is the publishing home for Ukrainian comics.

"For us, the synthesis of drawing and text in each story is the perfect way to speak out on any, even the most complex topics, to tell our own stories and share them with the world. The comics we publish, regardless of the genre, tell something important about us, about our identity and values. We believe the ninth art form is the future, and Ukrainian comics are an integral part of the global industry."

UA Comix is more than just comics.

UAComix.com

TEXTY.ORG.UA

Texty.org.ua is a Ukrainian independent publication specialising in data journalism projects. Our team turns volumes of incomprehensible sets of numbers and letters into profound analytical materials to explain how the world works. Our research covers a variety of topics including history, economics, culture, ecology, war, and Russian disinformation.

Texty.org.ua has been nominated for and won numerous international and domestic journalism awards: Europe Press Prize, Information is Beautiful, Honour of the Profession, Sigma Award, SND Digital, Prix Europa, and the Data Journalism Award.

Please consider supporting the team here:

Texty.org.ua

#VISIONS

Deus ex Ucraina.
The Lost Ones

Story by Viktoriia Antonenko
Illustrated by Mykhailo Aleksandrov

"**G**OOD MOR-NING, TEA-CHER!"
The students stood at attention next to their desks, chanting in near unison with only a few of them off-tempo. Their greeting was directed at the obese woman wearing a brown-coloured wrap dress and a neat bun on her head held together by bamboo hairpins, who had entered the classroom just as the bell rang.

"Sit down," Mrs Mao replied coldly. Leaning on her cane, she limped over to the teacher's desk and stopped to stand next to it. Her intense gaze swept across the six parallel rows of single desks, where her class of second graders was waiting for her, fresh from recess.

"I certainly hope everyone has turned off their electronic devices and put them away?" she asked after a five-second pause. Her tone was closer to giving an order rather than making a request, all the while patting down the black strands of hair near her left temple, trying to conceal the annoying grey roots peeking through her dyed black hair.

"You know very well smartphones, tablets, smartwatches, and other digital toys aren't allowed in my classroom..."

Mao hadn't finished her sentence when seven absent-minded eight-year-olds jumped up from their chairs located in different corners of the spacious classroom and rushed to the cabinet next to the wooden chalkboard. The lower three of its four drawers were already overflowing with all sorts of "digital toys." The bottom one couldn't be closed and the girl who reached the cabinet last had no choice but to leave it half-open.

Disgusted with the students, Mao drew in a deep breath and exhaled loudly enough to be heard in the furthest reaches of the classroom. She turned away and walked over to the chalkboard. Standing with her back to the students, the woman switched her cane from her right hand to her left, opened the top drawer of the cabinet to take out a piece of white chalk and began writing numbers on the dark green board. In one column, she wrote equations: $41 + 18$; $48 \div 3$; $93 - 46$; $37 + 38$; $29 + 54$; 14×4; $78 - 69$... and in the other column opposite the first she wrote the solutions in random order so the student she called on would have to draw an arrow pairing the equation with the solution.

A deadly silence fell over the second graders, one nobody would ever dare break, especially in Mrs Mao's class. Other teachers would occasionally turn a blind eye to the children's innocent pranks, but Mao was steadfastly intolerant of childish mischief of any kind. With a deep frown creasing the space between her eyebrows and not a hint of a smile, her scowl had warned the students of her nature during their first encounter. But not every kid was equally adept at reading non-verbal signals. It took only a few lessons at the start of the 2024 school year for most of them to realise simply sniffling in Mrs Mao's class was a gross violation of discipline and an egregious display of disrespect. Now, nearing the end of the second semester, she had trained the schoolchildren to behave like angels. Having learnt from the bitter experience of pieces of chalk targeting their heads with surgical precision, the students sat as quietly as mice, obediently waiting for the teacher to finish writing the equations. The silence was broken only by the unpleasant screeching of the chalk on the board from the pressure of her heavy hand.

Mao wasn't supposed to be teaching. As the director of Model Boarding School No.1 and head of the Association of Boarding Schools, which opened one after another in the Chinese Occupation Zone of Moscow in autumn 2023, Li Mao had enough responsibilities on her shoulders. Managing an institution in which 2,647 students live and study isn't easy. Not to mention coordinating an additional six schools. The students under her daily care were not orphans without families. The children were those of high-ranking military officers, analysts, economists, finance experts, engineers, construction company owners, doctors, food industry specialists, and others. The specialists had flown from Beijing to the former capital of the Russian Federation to take control of and organise services in the Chinese occupation zone on 9 May 2023, the day after the decision was announced at the Smolensk Conference. Although it wasn't sufficient compensation for the annexation of Taiwan by the Americans, the newly acquired Russian territory did provide a valuable opportunity to protect the interests of Chinese workers.

Mao only wrote on the top half of the chalkboard. Unlike most people who become hunched with age, her back was so stiff she could barely bend over. This would seem like enough of a reason to decrease her workload — after all, she was 76 years old. But Li Mao refused to stop teaching and simply be an administrator. At least not now, when she's reached the peak of her career. She couldn't show weakness at any cost. She wouldn't let anything undermine the authority she worked so long and hard to build. That's why all the elementary school classrooms where Mao taught had step stools, three stairs high, so the children, most of them no taller than her waist, had a fighting chance to reach the equations on the chalkboard.

Mao's hand froze in place when the sound of rustling paper coming from the first row of desks broke the silence. One of the students had torn sheets of paper from their notebook and was now obviously making something out of the paper. A few of the children giggled quietly.

"Stop your racket!" Mao commanded in a deceptively calm but inflexible tone. The students immediately piped down after this first warning, and she continued with her lesson.

Yet, the children were barely able to contain themselves for more than 30 seconds. She heard a creaking behind her back, as if someone had stood on their chair. Without turning around, Mao knew who it was. Only Hector would have the guts to continue fooling around after her warning. The other students instantly capitulated and usually didn't move or let out a peep for the rest of the lesson.

Paper rustled again nearby and someone in the back of the classroom, unable to hold back, burst out with laughter. Then another child's voice giggled, then another, and another — and soon the laughter had infected almost everyone. *"I shouldn't have cut him any slack before. Now he thinks he can walk all over me. I'll have to increase his dose today! I can't stand these shenanigans any longer. Nobody else dares to behave this way with teachers...Or with me!"* she thought to herself as the wave of restless commotion from the students' desks reached her shore.

The contagious merriment was cut short by an unexpected loud thwack. Mao had banged her cane on the hollow step stool next to her.

"You uncultured brats!" she shouted at the top of her lungs, turning to face the second graders. "How dare you show such disrespect? Your bad behaviour will be reflected in your final grades in two weeks! And believe me, every minute we lost at the beginning of the lesson because of your inability to follow instructions and are now losing because of your giggling, will be taken away from you during recess!"

Sixty-three pairs of children's eyes stared silently at her. Some of the kids were scared, covering their faces with their hands, and peeking through the gaps between their fingers; others scratched their heads in puzzlement, while still others froze in place with their mouths gaping open in confusion.

"And you, you little scoundrel," she said, waving her index finger menacingly and taking a few steps towards Hector, who was still standing on top of the second desk by the window. "You'll be sorry!"

Standing in the hot embrace of the afternoon sun stood a small, bewildered boy. Although he looked about the same size as the rest of his classmates, he was in fact two years older. He was crumpling a mock-up of a panda dressed in a brown robe he had made from the torn-out sheets of paper. The panda oddly resembled his fat, and at first glance, cloddish maths teacher, Mrs Mao.

"So that's why you're all sniggering! No more clowning around. Just you wait, I'll teach you how to respect your elders!" The boy didn't even try to duck when Mao swung her cane at him. He simply went stone-still, as if he had been caught in Medusa's gaze.

"*Finally, he's scared,"* Mao thought. The woman was about to unleash all her anger on this violator of discipline when everything went dark, and she felt the classroom spinning like a whirlwind. Her grip slackened and Mao dropped her cane and, shortly thereafter, she collapsed alongside it on the floor.

She was right. Hector was genuinely scared and so were the rest of his classmates. Not because the righteously furious teacher nearly hit him, but because her scribbles on the chalkboard were indecipherable, she was moaning incoherently, and there was a skewed appearance to her face, the right side of which was drooping. When she hit the floor, Mao's prosthetic finger, which she used to hide the absence of two bones on her left pinkie, fell off. Not knowing it was a prosthesis, the wide-eyed boy watched in horror as the teacher's finger slowly rolled across the floor towards the radiator. And with that, the terrified boy fainted, landing on the floor next to Mao.

The woman regained consciousness as four men — a paramedic and male nurse who had responded to the emergency call and two teachers from the boarding school — were lifting her onto a stretcher. Standing next to them was the school doctor Tsai Ai holding Tan Meiling's hand. She was the student who had kept her wits about her and pressed the alarm button, located under the teacher's desk in every classroom.

"*That ungrateful boy gave me a heart attack! And after all I did for him..."* Li Mao was thinking clearly in her mind, but the sounds coming out of her mouth bore no resemblance to actual words. "Th.. un...ful b.. ..ave m... a...art ...ack!..d af... I...did f...im," is what the ambulance crew heard instead while wheeling the woman through the hallways towards the exit where the ambulance was parked.

"Don't try to talk. You've probably had a stroke. It caused motor aphasia. Stay calm, we're here to help you. By the way, the boy is on his way to the hospital. Another ambulance took him away a minute ago." The male nurse's attempts to calm Mao had the opposite effect. She continued jerking from side to side, struggling, without success, to ask "What? What happened to Hector? Why did they take him to the hospital?" She gave up trying to get an answer when she developed a sudden onset of double vision, her mouth filled with bitter, salty saliva, and she felt like she was getting sucked into a whirlpool again.

As the ambulance drove to the stroke centre, announcing itself with a blaring siren, the woman's vision would clear and then go dark again erratically, though all the while she remained conscious. Mao had never felt so helpless in her life. During those moments when she emerged from the dark abyss, she felt like the sole passenger on a boat which had lost its sails and oars in a storm and was drifting in a boundless expanse of water with no hope of being rescued. In desperation, she convulsively grabbed at her absent cane — her only protection, her saving grace. But her efforts were in vain; her body refused to cooperate. Mao stared in doom at the white ceiling of the ambulance, where a light directly above her flashed bright red every second or two.

LEANING TOWARDS THE MICROPHONE ON THE TABLE IN FRONT OF HIM next to a nameplate with the word "Germany," a balding man wearing a black suit with a blue and white tie pressed the button on the microphone stand and, confirming the red LED light was on, began speaking:

"Colleagues, we have gathered in Smolensk to make an historic decision. After six days of long and at times heated debate, we have, unfortunately, failed to reach an agreement on the origin of the current situation in the Russian Federation, which cannot be labelled as anything other than chaos…"

"I hope this is not another attempt by our Western European colleagues to unjustly lay all the blame on Ukraine," interrupted one of the other 12 participants of the conference gathered in the meeting room — the only one clad in a khaki T-shirt and pants. "Because let me repeat, once again, in case my previous statements weren't explicit enough: we, unlike Russia, do not engage in terrorism! Everything we do is dictated by our national security interests." He turned off his microphone as abruptly as he had turned it on and forcefully leaned back in his chair. Two of his neighbours to the right with nameplates "Estonia" and "Latvia" nodded their heads in agreement, while the one to his left, representing Lithuania, reached out and gently squeezed his shoulder.

"Be that as it may," the speaker continued after a brief pause, "we have to conclude, there is no force within the Russian Federation which could stabilise the situation at this time." The man took a white handkerchief from his inside pocket and wiped a few drops of sweat from his forehead. The air conditioning in the large conference room, which for security reasons didn't have windows, had not been working since the morning. Some of the participants had loosened their ties and unbuttoned their collars. Two had taken off their suit jackets and hung them on the backs of their chairs. But the representative from Germany maintained protocol to the very end. "We all witnessed what can happen when there is a government power vacuum. The consequences of the Winter Crisis affected every one of us in one way or another…"

"So, perhaps we should move on to the vote?" asked another one of the participants at the negotiations politely, though insistently, interrupting the speaker for a second time. "How much time can we waste? We've already agreed on the preliminary division of responsibilities." The man smiled and feigned a relaxed confidence to conceal his actual internal tension. Then he scanned the room with a questioning look. The nameplate in front of him read "China."

There was a reason Xi Jinping was pushing for a quick resolution to the negotiations. He didn't want to wait any longer. What if suddenly the participants of the Smolensk Conference changed their minds and refused to award the People's Republic of China a piece of the delicious and long-desired pie that was the Russian Federation?

Xi Jinping had lucked out. As of this meeting, neither Ukraine and the Baltic states nor any of the other Europeans had found glaring evidence of Sino-Russian cooperation during the war in Ukraine in 2022–2023. There was only a suspicion "someone, somewhere, somehow" supposedly helped Putin and his short-lived successor to circumvent Western sanctions. But it was just idle chatter. Their word against

Xi Jinping's. Everyone knew it, and therefore was forced to agree to China's occupation of the Far East and the former northern, north-eastern, eastern, south-eastern, and southern districts of Moscow. The proposal regarding the New Silk Road also played a key role. "Just imagine how much shorter the route will be and how much faster Chinese goods will reach Europe once we no longer have to bypass Russian territory," the president of China slyly whispered to the presidents of France, Germany, and Italy behind the scenes of the negotiations. And they eagerly took the bait.

"These Europeans are so predictable," Xi Jinping said to his assistant, raising a glass of white wine on his private plane as it left Smolensk for Beijing late in the evening of 8 May 2023. He was extremely pleased to be returning home triumphant, having acquired vast expanses with valuable natural resources for China. It was much more than the territory the Qing Dynasty had ceded under the Treaties of Aigun and Beijing.

MAO STOPPED AT THE CROSSWALK AND WAITED FOR THE LIGHT TO turn green. In the one and a half minutes she stood there, some 30 people had gathered around her. They were mostly young people, dressed in business attire and carrying briefcases. A few danced in place to their favourite music in their headphones. Others were finishing their morning coffee while reading something on their smartphones. A girl, skinny as a pole and with an acid-blue streak in her brown hair, was standing next to Mao. She took a mirror and comb from the side pocket of her briefcase and started straightening her bob haircut. Most of the pedestrians, however, simply shifted nervously from foot to foot, checking the time on their smartwatches and fitness bracelets.

As soon as the light turned yellow, the crowd around the woman with the cane rushed to cross the street, nearly dragging her along with them.

"Damn children! What is wrong with you?" Mao thought angrily as she trailed after them, using her left hand to try in vain to smooth her blue blouse, which had been perfectly ironed before the jostling at the crosswalk. Cursing the white-collar workers running late for the office in the morning, willing to take down anyone in their path, the woman hobbled the final 15 metres to her destination: a nine-storey building covered in light grey tiles with large panoramic windows.

Mao went through the revolving glass doors into the lobby, got a pass from the security desk, and took the elevator up to the second floor.

"Li Mao to see the minister," she announced to the young man at the reception desk directly across from the elevator, skipping the formalities. "We have a meeting at 9.15," she said before he could open his mouth. Holding her chin up, it was obvious from the tone of her voice the woman thought highly of herself.

"Good morning! Please come in. They're waiting for you," the young man pointed to a door to Mao's left and sprang up from behind his desk. He rushed forward, two steps ahead of the woman with the cane, to open the door.

As she limped toward the minister's office, from the corner of her eye, Mao saw something move on her right. In the waiting area by the window, four upholstered chairs with high backs stood in a semicircle around an oval glass table. There was someone sitting in one of the chairs, but she couldn't tell who it was because they were facing the window. She only caught a glimpse of something blue. Just then the door opened wide, and she had no time to look more closely to satisfy her curiosity.

"Hello, Mr Minister!" Putting on a sweet, fake smile, Mao bowed slightly to the 50-year-old man, who didn't bother to rise from his chair to greet his guest.

"Please, take a seat," he motioned to one of the two chairs next to his desk. "You have an impressive résumé, Mrs Mao." While she settled into a chair and placed her cane next to her seat, he took a dozen or so sheets of typed paper from a folder and fanned them out in front of him. "Higher education. Almost 40 years of teaching experience. Never failed a teacher's qualification exam. In the past decade, your name was never absent from the national list of exemplary teachers selected from among tens of thousands of educators across the country. Correct?"

"Yes, Mr Minister." Mao sat straight in the chair with her hands folded in her lap like a model student.

"And the loss of a child didn't hold you back," the man said tactlessly, staring her straight in the eye.

"Or the loss of my husband," the woman added coldly, holding his gaze. She didn't flinch. Her entire demeanour indicated his provocation had failed.

For a moment there was an awkward pause. The minister was the first to lower his gaze, acknowledging the mild rebuke. He picked up one of the sheets of paper and scanned it as though he was looking for something.

"For two years in the early 1990s, you interned at the Patrice Lumumba Peoples' Friendship University of Russia, *gdye izuchili russkiy yazyk* (where you studied to

speak Russian)…" His eyebrows arched questionably as he looked directly at the woman.

"That is correct, Mr Minister," she said in Russian, following his cue.

"As you see, your efforts weren't in vain. The time has come to use the knowledge. Of course, many Russians fled. But not all, unfortunately." The minister paused briefly. He let the paper drop out of his hands to float onto his desk, speeding the paper's descent by slamming it down with a heavy outstretched palm. "And we can't afford to delay, like the others are doing. We need to incorporate ourselves into the new territories. Thousands of our experts were relocated to Moscow and have been working there since 9 May. Recognising this process won't be completed in a day, the president has allowed the experts to bring their families with them. Your institution will be closed to visitors and the children will stay there 24 hours a day Monday through Saturday, so their parents won't be distracted from their duties. Construction will start in June and the school will open on 1 September. You will fly out in a week, on 30 May, to monitor the process, starting with the first laid brick. Are you sure you can handle it?"

"This is a great honour for me, Mr Minister," Mao said. She raised herself part way from where she was sitting and slightly bowed to him again. "I will make every effort, possible and impossible, to ensure my service benefits the Party and the Republic."

"I appreciate your enthusiasm. I don't think we could have found a better candidate… The only thing I'm a bit concerned about," the man leaned back in the chair, placed his elbows on the armrests and focused his eyes intently on her, "is your connection to Taiwan."

"There's nothing to worry about. I assure you, Mr Minister, there are no connections. They broke off before they formed, back in 1949," Mao replied slowly, emphasising each word. A chill came over her. The most important promotion of her career could be in jeopardy. The unnatural smile still on her face transformed into a grimace.

"I was hoping to hear you say so, madam director. But we'll keep our fingers on the pulse, just in case," the man commented as he stood up from his chair and gathered the pages of her biography to put back into the folder. Having tucked the folder under his left arm, the minister rounded the desk to approach Mao, who had also risen from her chair. The minister extended his hand in a handshake. "We shouldn't waste the opportunities opening for China. We have been planning this since 2014, when nobody imagined Russia could collapse because of their war with Ukraine…"

The Chinese Minister of Education said the last two sentences while escorting Mao to the door.

"Let's stay in touch," he suggested to her receding figure, having halted at the door to his office. Mao was halfway to the reception desk when she heard his voice behind her: "Yanfen! Take this, it will come in handy."

Mao turned her head slightly to the right to watch in the window's reflection how the minister handed a folder to a young woman in a white blouse and black pantsuit who had jumped up from her chair as soon as she heard her name. She looked young enough to be his granddaughter. The only thing that didn't fit the woman's otherwise business-like appearance was the blue streak in her hair.

S EVERAL MONTHS HAD PASSED BEFORE SHE GOT AROUND TO UNPACKING her personal belongings. Carol of the Bells and other Christmas melodies could be heard floating in from the adjacent UN Occupation Zone in Moscow when Mao asked not to be disturbed for at least a half hour so she could unpack and rearrange her office. Two equal-sized oil portraits were already hanging in the centre of the wall to the right of her desk, one depicting the first president of the People's Republic of China and the other — the current president and general secretary of the Chinese Community Party. Both were in massive mahogany frames at least a metre tall, though only the second one was lovingly wrapped in a transparent white scarf with tassels hanging off the ends.

The woman hung her diplomas closer to the corner of the room, at a respectful distance from the portrait of Xi Dada, or "Uncle Xi." One was her degree in mathematics from Nanjing University and the other in education management from the South China Pedagogical University in Guangdong province. On the table in front of her, waiting their turn to be hung on the wall, were her awards from the Chinese Teachers Development Fund.

Mao was choosing a spot on the wall for her "National Advanced Education Worker" certificate when the telephone rang in the reception area on the other side of the wall.

"Model Boarding School No.1. My name is Wu Yanfen, how may I help you?" her secretary answered the call with her standard greeting before pausing to let the caller speak.

"Wait, please, let me check," the young girl responded to the muffled male voice on the other end of the line. "Yes, we can," she said a second later, after clicking a few keys on her computer keyboard and opening an Excel spreadsheet with endless rows of numbers in different coloured cells.

"Ok, I'm starting." Yanfen pressed a round green button on a black rectangle on her keyboard.

Mao could only guess what this was all about, but from the loud clattering in the neighbouring room, the director surmised her secretary was receiving a fax. The antediluvian apparatus groaned in pain as if its arms and legs were being stretched apart on a medieval rack. It began spitting out a sheet of paper with a black-and-white image at the pace of several millimetres per second.

Two minutes later there was a polite knock on Mao's door before she nudged the door open.

"I'm very sorry, madam director," Yanfen said hesitantly from behind the door, "but there is an urgent matter..."

"Come in," Mao acquiesced. Seeing the cardboard folder in which her subordinate usually gave her documents to be signed, the woman put the framed certificate down on the table in front of her and extended her right hand expectantly.

As soon as the director took the folder, the secretary seemed to evaporate into thin air. Inside was a sheet of paper with the blurred outlines of a child's photo. The brief text under the picture described how during an inspection of abandoned buildings in the former South-Eastern District of Moscow, patrol officers found a six- or seven-year-old Caucasian boy. He was hungry, dehydrated, and had started developing frostbite on his extremities. The militarised police couldn't get him to talk. When they searched the boy, the officers found a handwritten note on a sheet of paper, folded in four, in the inside pocket of his ragged jacket. The note contained columns of numbers and a few words written next to each of the numbers. The writing was probably Russian, but they couldn't be certain, because the paper was accidentally misplaced. The child had no identifying marks other than a tattoo in the shape of a cross on his right wrist.

Annoyed, Mao flung the fax on the table and determinedly pulled the phone towards her. She grabbed the receiver and, without hesitating, began rapidly poking at the buttons to dial a number. Her short, chubby index finger pressed them mercilessly until she heard the call connecting on the other end.

"My institution is not for strays!" The woman went into battle mode as soon as she heard the voice on the other end greet her. "Only children of respectable people who are useful to society study here! You know my position about this is categorical, yet you still try throwing me your random trash from the street..." A vein on her neck throbbed in righteous anger and an unhealthy flush suffused her cheeks.

"Mrs Mao, I understand your anger, but right now there really is no other option. The August assassination of Patriarch Kirill, the head of the Russian Church, provoked a new wave of migration of Russians into Zone 5. We're talking about tens of thousands of people who rushed across the Urals. And so far, it has been impossible to control this process. All the Moscow shelters under our jurisdiction are overcrowded by 50 per cent or more, because in addition to the war orphans there are now lost or abandoned children — how could those Russians do such a thing?" Unmoved by Mao's tirade, the man who had sent the fax two minutes earlier stated matter-of-factly. "This time I will not accept your refusal. Moreover, your secretary confirmed there is space in your boarding school. But if you insist, I will be forced to speak to..."

"But this boy isn't Chinese," Mao interrupted. "Why spend so much effort on him?" The boarding school director retorted with less enthusiasm, realising she may have gone too far. You never know how this may come back to haunt you in the future. Sometimes you must control your temper and be flexible. Mao took this to heart during the Cultural Revolution; otherwise, she would never have reached her current status.

"Yes, he's not Chinese," the man agreed, and Mao had a flash of hope she had hit the right excuse to get rid of the unwanted burden. However, her hope vanished as soon as she heard him continue with steely resolve in his voice. "Then make him Chinese! Isn't that what your boarding school does? Judging by the company in which he was caught, he's already gone through some preliminary training. The rest is up to you. And if your experiment is successful, we'll discuss the introduction of a re-education programme in all newly acquired territories. This is a very opportune time — it's unlikely anyone will make a fuss, like with the Uyghurs and Tibetans. Don't miss out on this opportunity!"

The man hung up without waiting for Mao's reply. Shocked, she stood at her desk for another 20 seconds listening to the short intermittent beeps emanating from the phone. The call had ended and only the beeping sound disrupted the silence of her office. She finally put the receiver back in its place, slowly sank into her chair, and reached for her purse, where she kept a small medicine box.

She popped a pill out of its packaging and pressed the button for the reception desk.

"Listening, madam director," the secretary answered.

"Bring me water. Hurry!" Mao ordered. A minute later, raising the glass of water brought to her by Yanfen, she paused for a second and, not able to contain her rage, railed, "You had to run off at the mouth and blurt out we had free spots? Now you deal with it. This feral boy is your problem. Do what you want with him... Now get out of my sight, you idiot!"

⚏━━━━━━━━━━⚏

WU YANFEN WAS STOMPING HER FEET AT THE TOP OF THE BRIGHTLY illuminated stairs leading to the main entrance of Model Boarding School No.1. She was wearing a cream-coloured, eco-leather coat, black, knee-high boots, blue furry earmuffs, and matching gloves.

"Oh, dear, what a crappy assignment. No one's going to envy me, that's for sure," the young girl complained to herself, blowing into her clenched hands to warm them up. She may have continued had her thoughts not been interrupted by the muffled hum of a motor growing louder as it swiftly approached her.

An instant later, a police car emerged from the dimness of the evening twilight obscuring the view beyond the building's edge, the vehicle's tyres screeching as they crushed the ice-covered snow. As soon as it stopped, the driver's door flung open. A man in his mid-thirties wearing a dark green uniform emerged, placing a cap of the same colour on his head. Without uttering a sound, he took a step towards the back door, jerked the handle sharply, opened it wide, leaned in, and forcibly dragged out the diminutive passenger.

"Good evening, miss! Will you take custody of the juvenile delinquent?" the man quipped as he straightened his posture. Above the visor, his police cap was adorned with a badge of the Chinese People's Armed Militia, composed of a shield decorated with rice and wheat inside of which was the coat of arms of China, towering above the Great Wall. To the man's left, a freckled, brown-eyed boy shifted nervously from foot to foot, casting glances at his guard, who was tightly clutching his shoulder at the base of his neck.

"Good evening," Yanfen muttered, not appreciating the policeman's humour. "If I were you, I'd refrain from immediately labelling the child, especially in his presence," the girl lectured him. She was interrupted by the explosion of fireworks rising rhythmically into the nearby sky and painting the darkness with thousands of shades of red, blue, and green.

As soon as he heard the first detonation, Hector tensed up and cast a wary glance in the direction of the sound. Realising its origin, the boy immediately lost interest. Meanwhile, both adults turned away from the subject of their conversation and stared mesmerised by the multi-coloured bursts. The young girl descended a few steps so she could get a better view. The man turned halfway to watch and slightly loosened his grip on the boy. Right then, the young detainee jerked, trying to break free of the policeman's grip. But his effort was in vain.

"You see what a trickster he is," the man said to Yanfen. "He keeps trying to run away. Maybe it would be better to cuff him..."

"Are you serious?" the girl fumed. Her expression switched from anger to sympathy when her gaze moved from the smug policeman to the sulking boy. The lad was wearing a dirty tattered jacket with sleeves that were too short, torn pants a few sizes too big, and shoes which had already seen countless days.

"Absolutely," the man barked back rudely, giving up his attempt to start a pleasant, unofficial conversation with an attractive young lady. "Considering the neighbourhood where we found him with his friends, covered in tattoos from head to toe, it wouldn't hurt," the policeman said, placing the boy in front of him like a shield and holding him firmly by both shoulders. "Look closer, it's written all over him!" he shook the child, who was already shivering from the cold.

"Enough!" the girl cut him off, raising her voice. Quickly she ran to the bottom of the stairs and crouched in front of the boy. "Hi, little guy," she said in Russian.

"I'm Yanfen. What's your name?" Up close, she saw he had a small scar above his left eyebrow, yellowish bruises on his right cheekbone and chin, battered fingers with dirt under the nails, and the cross on his right wrist mentioned in the fax.

"He also understands Chinese. He just pretends he doesn't," the policeman said, hearing the girl had switched to Russian. "I'm willing to bet he's picked up a bunch of useful skills on those streets. Otherwise, he wouldn't have survived out there."

"Thank you, comrade know-in-all!" Yanfen seethed silently, looking up at the policeman from below. She stood, unruffled, and extended her left hand to the boy. "Come with me. It's late. You should have been in bed a long time ago." The boy, who had been gazing down at the snow while listening to the man, raised his eyes to first look timidly at the girl, then at the guard, then back at the girl again. After hesitating for a few seconds, he finally took a step forward, freeing himself from the policeman's clutches, and gave his right hand to Yanfen.

The girl was almost at the top of the stairs when she turned around and shouted to the man about to get into the car:

"Hey! Did you try to call those numbers?"

"What numbers?" the policeman answered, pretending to be surprised.

"On the sheet of paper you found when you searched him," Yanfen replied.

"There was nothing there. It was junk!" the man snapped, got into the car, and slammed the door.

"Got it..." the girl mumbled to herself. She gently squeezed the boy's hand and walked towards the main entrance of the boarding school.

Yanfen opened the door and let the boy in first. He stopped, looked her in the eyes, and whispered softly to his new guardian, "Hector," as he squeezed her hand back. "Hector Kharabets."

Leading the boy through the labyrinths of the school to the room in the dormitory wing where Yanfen had prepared a place for him, they bumped into Mao, who was limping to her quarters.

"Madam director, here is our newest child," the girl gently nudged the boy forward, so he would step out of her shadow. But Mao refused to acknowledge Yanfen's words and didn't turn her head in their direction.

"I have to ask the other girls about Mao," Yanfen thought to herself that evening lying in bed waiting to fall asleep. She kept trying to put pieces of the puzzle together, but they didn't fit. Why choose an occupation that constantly reminds you of your loss? Does she get some strange sense of pleasure from pain, or does she simply feel nothing?

"L-L-LEEY, S-S-IA-O-B-B-BO, T-T-T-TIN-F-FENG..." YANFEN'S LITTLE CHARGE sobbed on her shoulder as the Chinese New Year fireworks went off over Moscow. Having tightly embraced the girl's neck with both arms and leaned his trembling body firmly against hers, the little boy was listing the names of his abusers.

Half an hour ago, around midnight, unable to sleep because of the loud festivities outside, Yanfen decided to check the room Hector shared with nine other children. She did this occasionally out of concern over how he was adapting to his new home. But tonight the boy's bed was empty. Alarmed by his absence, the girl searched along the length of the corridor, illuminating her path with the flashlight on her smartphone. She stopped next to each bedroom and put her ear to the door to listen for any suspicious noises inside.

Suddenly her ear caught a dull, monotonous thumping. The girl followed the sound, which led her to the boys' bathroom. She wondered for a second whether she should enter, but the desperate sobbing she heard from inside convinced her she should. Yanfen firmly pushed the door open and passed the row of mirrors and sinks in three strides. She rushed into a room with urinals lined up on one side and toilet stalls on the other. The crying was coming from one of the latter, barricaded from the outside by a mop and several stacked chairs.

"Is that you, Hector?" Yanfen whispered. She turned off the flashlight, put the phone in her pocket, and started dismantling the barricade. Regardless of who was trapped inside, they had to be freed.

The noise in the stall hushed for a moment.

"*Da...* Yes!" came a tearful reply, followed by the scuffling of slippers on the tiles. The boy was trying to get some blood flowing back to his feet, which had gone numb while he was sitting on the floor. "Yanfen!" the bathroom captive yelled out when the door opened and then threw himself tearfully at her neck.

The girl hugged him with one arm and stroked his back consolingly with the other. She noticed he was wearing the panda pyjamas she had given him as a holiday present.

"Let's get some cold water on you, it'll make you feel better," she suggested when he calmed down a little. She led him to the sinks and rinsed his teary eyes and cheeks, having to repeatedly place her right hand under the faucet to set off the motion sensor. Finally, Yanfen asked him who had done this.

"Is it because of your canted Chinese?" the girl asked. They were now sitting side by side on the floor, leaning their backs against the wall across from the row of sinks.

"Nooo. Th-they dec-cidd-ed I'm a convict and so I should be behind bars..."

"Your cross?" Yanfen, careful not to startle Hector, took his right hand and gently stroked the ill-fated mark with her thumb. The boy nodded "yes" and yanked his hand away from her. "How did you get it? Will you tell me?" she gently pleaded in Russian.

Hector quieted. The girl thought he wouldn't trust her with the truth, when suddenly he whispered, "M-mom and I were at...the camps. W-we w-waited for many, many d-days, because there was a s-sea of people..."

"Where was this camp?"

"B-by the school."

"By the school in what city?"

"I d-don't remember... Somewhere not far from Mari-u-pol," the boy replied, rubbing his right wrist the whole time he was speaking.

"And that's where they tattooed this cross?"

Hector hid his hand in the pocket of his pyjama pants.

"And where was your dad?"

"They load-loaded everyone into the bus-busses and we left. I saw a sea through the window the whole time..." The boy's voice levelled off and he stopped sobbing. "And then we got on a train."

"And where did it go?" the girl continued to carefully untangle the web. "Where did it take you?"

Hector frowned.

"To Tver!" he cried out after a brief pause, proud
of himself for remembering the name this time. But
then he became sad again. "Mama went to Tver, and
I stayed here…"

"How did that happen?"

"I was sleeping in my mother's arms when
out of nowhere someone grabbed me. I woke up.
My mother was screaming and wouldn't let go,"
the boy remembered bitterly. With each
word his voice became softer. "Then
the… bastard punched her in the face."
Tears welled up in the corner of his
eyes again, so Yanfen decided to let

his curse slide. "He turned around and carried me out of the train car… I tried to break free, but I couldn't," he whispered guiltily and wiped the tears running down his cheeks with his pyjama sleeves.

"It's not your fault," the girl stroked Hector's head. "Do you hear me, little panda? It's not your fault… Your dad wasn't with you?"

"Nyet." To Yanfen's bewilderment the little boy responded with a resentful grunt and turned away sharply when she tried to touch his hair again. After a minute of silence, he added: "The bastard said I now have a new family. He said I was lucky because I had been adopted by Muscovites… But they didn't have any use for me," his voice was tinged with anger.

"Those people were mean to you? They beat you?"

Hector shook his head and began to scratch his wrist, around the cross tattoo.

"They locked me in the pantry. With no light."

"Is that why you ran away?" Yanfen asked. With every word the boy said, the girl felt the lump in her throat grow, fighting back the urge to also start crying.

"No. They fled, and I…" Yanfen and Hector had been sitting on the floor shoulder-to-shoulder but at this point Hector moved away from her and stuck his hands between his knees.

Looking at the gap between them, the girl could no longer hold back her tears.

"I'll be here. I won't leave you," she whispered, trying to build a bridge between them, but the boy didn't react to her words. "Maybe you remember the phone number of one of your relatives? Your mother's?" Hector abruptly stood up.

"Everything was on a piece of paper," Hector said excitedly, looking down at Yanfen. "Mum wrote them all down while we waited our turn in the camp. She told me, 'Be careful and don't lose it!'"

"Well then, let's call your mother!" the girl jumped to her feet too. Wiping away the tears, she started rummaging through the pockets of her dress for her smartphone. The boy took another step back. "What's wrong? You don't want to?"

"They also promised they would let me call her…"

"I'm not lying to you," Yanfen interrupted the boy. "Look, here." She pulled the smartphone out of her left pocket and offered it to Hector, but he didn't move.

"…but the police arrested us," he tried to finish his thought.

"Little panda, we can call your mum right away, this very minute," the girl interrupted, wasting no time, not bothering to listen to what the boy had to say. "It's late, but she'll definitely be happy to hear from you!"

"Yes, she will!" the boy said as he kicked the trash can under the paper towel holder by the sinks with all his might. "But the policeman who brought me here crumpled up the sheet of paper with the numbers and threw it away!" The trash can wobbled with a dull thudding but didn't fall over.

Yanfen froze. Her hand holding the phone dropped to her side. Filled with pity for the boy and shocked by her own heartlessness, she didn't know how to continue the conversation.

"Did your mother manage to tell you anything else?" she dared to ask, breaking the silence between them.

"Yes. She said she loves me. And I should only speak Russian…"

"Only Russian?" the girl asked, confused. "You know another language?"

"Grandma taught me…"

"*H*E'S NOT LIKE THE OTHERS," MAO THOUGHT, LEANING AGAINST HER cane in front of the panoramic window in the brightly lit wide corridor encircling the boarding school's spacious inner courtyard. The woman watched the crowd of first graders playing during recess. Some of the kids were swinging on the swings, climbing ropes, trying to conquer the climbing walls; others tirelessly jumped on the trampolines or slid down the slides; and still others kicked balls or simply chased one another. They were all wearing white short-sleeved shirts, identical red handkerchiefs tied around their collars, and black and grey chequered skirts or shorts. The boarding school director firmly believed uniforms were an effective tool for disciplining children and introduced them from the very beginning, right when the school opened.

Mao noticed Hector out of the corner of her eye. He was building a tower out of Jenga wooden blocks under one of the slides, hiding from the commotion around him.

More than five months had passed since the stray boy was placed in her boarding school, but both the staff and children were having a very hard time establishing a rapport with him. The only person he let get close to him was her secretary. "*The spy Yanfen,*" Mao thought, her lips curling in contempt.

The director made a half turn, extended her tenacious claw, and grabbed a random student by the arm, just above the elbow. The boy, who looked like a fifth grader, had been walking by, joking with his friends.

"Get Yanfen for me from the reception desk. Now!" Mao ordered the boy, who looked at her in shock.

Once he nodded, signalling he had heard and understood the director, she released her iron grip, leaving pale marks in the shape of her fingers imprinted on his shoulder. The fifth grader immediately rushed to carry out the order, while the woman turned to stare intently out the window again.

"I don't see any significant progress in Hector," director Mao told the young girl who had appeared next to her after a short wait. "You seem to be having trouble with the duties you were assigned."

"I'm very sorry, honourable Mrs Mao, but the boy is making some headway," Yanfen proposed in her own defence, her voice trembling. "He can't speak Chinese fluently yet, but he understands enough when people talk to him." The secretary locked her hands behind her back, trying to somehow support herself in a moment of weakness. They both looked at Hector, who had stopped stacking the blocks to scratch his right wrist. "Hector just needs more time. To be honest, I'm a little worried about him. He seems to have had a deeply traumatic experience..."

"Hm," Mao grimaced sceptically, causing the already prominent lines on her face to become as deep as ravines. "*Like the channels of Dujiangyan,*" Yanfen thought.

"Is he the only one who is so 'unique'?" The director's caustic tone suggested to the girl this was a rhetorical question she shouldn't try to answer.

Silence fell between them. Yanfen watched as one of Hector's classmates, Xiaobo, standing in the centre of a group of boys on the other side of the courtyard from the slide, pointed to the boy playing on his own, clearly inciting his classmates to pick on the loner.

"*What can your generation, born in the 21st century, know about traumatic experiences?!*" Mao thought indignantly.

From the distant corners of her memory, a place the woman preferred never to look, recollections of the past flashed before her eyes like a kaleidoscope. The wretched orphanage in Yancheng District where her father abandoned her as an infant in 1949 when he fled from Chiang Kai-shek's army to Taiwan. The endless taunts from the

other children because of her congenital physical defect were only interrupted when they wanted to copy maths assignments from her. Just as she seemed to be getting on her feet, the Cultural Revolution broke out. *"The price of a person is 28 yuan,"* Mao moved her lips silently, remembering a popular saying from those times. She knew it well, because she was one of those who had stood in a long line at the Nanjing Funeral Service to pay for the cremation of her husband, who had been beaten to death by the *Hongweibin* red guards. But the hardest blow was yet to come. She still curses the day when she allowed her seven-year-old son to go on the class trip...

"Maybe Hector would progress more quickly if he had some friends," Yanfen's cautious reply snapped Mao back to reality. "But the other schoolchildren... They see he's different and doesn't know the language well... I rescue him from being locked in the restroom almost every week. The last time he was stuck there nearly half the night."

While the secretary carefully weighed every word she spoke to the director, Hector's classmates went from discussing pranks to executing them. They surrounded the slide and, in an instant, destroyed the tower he had so diligently been building for the past 15 minutes.

"Poor little panda," Yanfen thought, and instantly moved toward the door to the inner courtyard. She was going to stop her ward's abusers, but Mao blocked the girl's path with her cane.

"Hector will not bring any benefit to the Republic and the Chinese people if you continue to keep him under the umbrella of your protection! Let him learn to solve his own problems. Otherwise, as an adult he'll break at the first obstacle; and we have enough weaklings already. Have you forgotten the main purpose of our institution?" the director hissed through her teeth. The secretary, who had felt Mao's displeasure from her first day on the job, didn't dare to openly disobey her, and froze in her tracks.

Through the panoramic window, the two of them watched as Hector, barely holding back his tears, began gathering the wreckage of his tower. But the little brats around him showed no mercy and started throwing the wooden blocks all around the playground. The leader of the group, Xiaobo, was the last to join in. As soon as he approached, Hector wiped the veil of tears from his eyes, clenched his hands into fists, and spoke a few words to him. Mao and Yanfen couldn't hear what he said, but they watched as the other boys turned pale, their mocking smiles disappearing from their faces, and slowly, together with Xiaobo, backed away.

"Hm," the director chuckled in satisfaction. "Maybe the stray isn't a lost cause after all..."

"STOP FOOLING AROUND!" YANFEN SCOLDED HECTOR.

They were sitting on a black and white striped picnic blanket on the freshly mowed lawn in the shadow of an old ash tree. The girl, in a blue viscose jumpsuit with a square neckline, thin straps and buttons on the chest, leaned her back against the tree trunk. In her hands, she held a set of flashcards with illustrations, words, and phrases she was using to help Hector improve his Chinese during the month-and-a-half long summer break. The boarding school was almost completely empty because most of the parents took their kids home for the holiday. Yanfen's workload eased as well, and she was able to devote more time to the boy.

Her charge, in a baseball cap, white polo shirt, and shorts, sat cross-legged across from her and was goofing off. The girl opposite showed him a card with a picture of a teacup and jug of milk, then said a phrase in Russian he was supposed to repeat in Chinese. "Please add some beer to my tea!" Hector translated and burst out laughing, proud of his comedic quip.

"You can't remember the word for 'milk,' but cussing and swearing come easy," Yanfen reprimanded him, recalling the incident in the playground when Hector scared away all the bullies with one phrase. She had asked the other schoolchildren about the incident and learnt what phrase he had used. He had told them to *pu jie* — an extremely vulgar way of telling someone "I will send you to hell."

Hector's good spirits disappeared like the wind. He lowered his eyes, shrugged his shoulders, and folded his arms across his chest. "What happened, happened. There's nothing you can do about it," the boy's body language spoke volumes.

"You should scowl less and try harder. Next spring, all the second graders will go to China for the 'In the Footsteps of Xi Jinping' tour, and you won't understand anything because the tour will be in literary Chinese, not your street talk!" Yanfen put the cards down and continued to gently pressure the child. *"And director Mao will skin me alive,"* she thought, keeping her fear to herself. "After all, soon there won't be anyone left here who speaks Russian. Try harder if you don't want to end up in Zone 5 with your Muscovites…"

The girl's tirade was interrupted by the sound of a xylophone coming from her bag an arm's length away. Yanfen reached for it, took out her smartphone, swiped the screen to unlock it, and pressed the green WeChat icon. "What's new?" the message from an unknown number asked. "I'm doing the work Mao assigned for me," she replied after a two-second pause, and then immediately deleted the chat.

"It's raining!" Hector cried out suddenly, startling Yanfen. Springing to his feet, he turned around and realised there was nothing to worry about: the cool drops of water he felt on his back were from the automatic sprinklers. "May I?" he pleaded. Yanfen smiled gently in response and the boy began snaking around the lawn between the sprinklers shooting up like fountains from the ground…

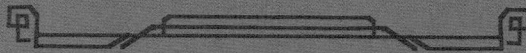

"**M**ATHEMATICS IS THE QUEEN OF ALL SCIENCES," MAO CONSTANTLY told her students. And out of habit added to herself, *"And I am the queen of mathematics."* She wasn't exaggerating. In elementary school, the small, fragile little girl in the orphanage named in honour of Mao Tse-tung, the victor of the civil war — the "red star" and "wise head" of the multi-million strong Chinese people — won various maths student-Olympics and contests in Yancheng District and Jiangsu province. The extraordinary mathematical skills her old, long deceased teacher Zhang Lim laboured to develop in her became the superpower which helped Mao build her own defence and successfully fight off the mean and cruel children she grew up with and who never missed an opportunity to bully her over her shorter left pinkie finger. Many years later, already a grown woman, she would reflexively hide her finger in her pocket every time she was out in public so she wouldn't have to deal with people's stares, and worse, strangers' inappropriate questions about what happened.

"Did an alligator bite off your finger? Or did a panda chew it off? Ohhh, you were born with it... Poor thing! Don't worry, it doesn't look too bad!"

Mathematics is based on understandable algorithms and clear logic, which, when adhering to these principles, invariably leads one to an end goal, a concrete result. Solving equations gave the former orphan a sense of control over her own life, built her confidence, and provided some stability. This was the reason Mao loved maths the way she never loved another living soul... except for her little Wei, of course. Her love for maths was the deciding factor why the boarding school director hadn't completely stopped teaching, but instead kept a minimum number of hours to maintain her status. However, Mao also had a more practical reason to stay in the classroom. Teaching gave her a clear picture of the level her pupils were on, what she could expect from them, and on whom she could depend.

"Teacher, why did I only get a 'satisfactory' on the last exam?" Hector asked after waiting his turn to have a one-on-one meeting with the teacher after class.

Mao, wearing a blue Sun Yat-sen suit with a turned-down collar and four pockets, her sizable frame barely squeezed into the chair, was checking the students' homework at her desk. The boy, with his hair now trimmed in a bowl cut and wearing the mandatory school uniform, was sitting on a chair too tall for his height and was impatiently dangling his feet to and fro. His Chinese had improved significantly and with it his social skills, which was a positive sign for the boarding school director. Perhaps it was possible to mould him into a Chinese — him and the rest of the Russian children — which would allow the People's Republic of China to strengthen its influence in its zone of occupied Moscow.

During the first year Model Boarding School No.1 was open in the Chinese Occupation Zone of Moscow, there were four second-grade classes; now there were seven. Each one of them had an average of 60 students, one or two of which weren't Chinese. Starting on 1 September 2024, the director chose two classes to teach and gave the rest to other educators. Like her, today the other maths teachers were doing mandatory extracurricular work: preparing lesson plans, providing certain students with extra help to complete difficult assignments, writing feedback about their colleagues' lessons — each at their own assigned desk.

When Hector spoke out, Mao was mercilessly crossing out the wrong answers in one of his classmate's notebooks. Keeping her eyes on the childish scribbles in front of her, the woman pointed her pen at the wall. Hector followed her movement and ended up staring at... nothing. There was nothing in front of him at eye level, but higher, when the boy tilted his head back, he saw seven male portraits hung in a row.

The display started with two bearded men. One had completely white dishevelled hair, while the other was balding with the remaining grey hair neatly combed over the bald spots. They were both wearing European style suits. Another one was almost completely bald, egg-headed, with a goatee and red tie. Next to him was a moustached brown-haired man in a military uniform, who for some reason reminded the boy of an ugly black cockroach, so much so, Hector shuddered in disgust. He remembered seeing many of them in the basement where he and his mother hid from Russian shelling. Three Chinese men smiled at him slyly from the next portraits. Two of them were in clothes similar to director Mao's, and the only one he recognised from the group — Xi Dada — was wearing a European suit.

Higher up, above the portraits, hanging from nails looking like they were about to fall off the wall, was a red banner with white writing: "Learning without thinking is useless. Thinking without learning is dangerous." Hector finally realised this was what his teacher was pointing to.

"But I *was* thinking... and learning," the boy protested timidly. He was so worried he didn't realise he was rubbing the cross on his right wrist in a circular motion with his thumb. "And I didn't make any mistakes!"

"And obviously you're very proud of yourself?" Mao said in a sarcastic tone, pushing the notebook off to the side, where the others were evenly stacked in perfect order. *"Yanfen's excessive attention to him has spoiled the boy,"* she thought to herself. *"Or the snitch is deliberately turning him against me..."* The woman clumsily turned in her chair to look straight at the child and reached for her cane as if she was going to stand up. "Do you think the grade I gave you was too low?"

"Yes!" Hector exclaimed nervously and leaned forward, grabbing the edge of the teacher's desk with both hands. "It's not fair! I'm better at maths than anyone else in the class!"

"Nobody in this class is better at maths than me!" Mao thundered and, not holding back, whacked the child's small fingers with her cane full force. *"These children know absolutely nothing about modesty and humility,"* she raged inside. Towering over the boy, she gave no consideration to where her blows were landing. "Oh, I will teach you to respect a teacher!" Hector huddled in a ball, covered his head with his arms, and toppled off the chair. "You feral swine! How many times do I have to repeat it? You should be grateful for and appreciate what you have!" The woman circled above him like a hawk and continued to have at him, despite the boy's cries and tears.

Nobody else in the room tried to stick up for him. The teachers had witnessed director Mao's tantrums on many occasions and concluded the best tactic was to grin and bear it. Her outbursts usually died down as suddenly as they started.

Moreover, it wasn't just anyone — it was Hector. Mao's subordinates noticed a long time ago her attitude towards this child was unique, different. She picked on him more than any other student. It resembled a "beat your own so the others will be afraid" tactic. And it worked very well.

But one had to admit, this stray wasn't like the rest. The teachers had to show the Chinese children only once or twice the wooden paddle on each teacher's desk used to punish those who disobeyed, and the kids behaved. But this boy could never seem to learn the lesson. Sometimes the teachers whispered to each other, trying to find the proper description for Hector. He's too... freedom-loving? Rebellious? Fearless? Or maybe he's just naïve? Or, despite being gifted in maths, he's actually slow-witted?

Be that as it may, he was the one who most often spoke self-critically in front of his classmates, stayed after class to clean the room, and was punished with blows from the wooden paddle on his palms. Although corporal punishment and verbal abuse had been banned in schools in the People's Republic of China back in 2021, Mao ignored the decision. After all, the *Regulations on the Work of Elementary and Secondary School Teachers* stated the director has the right to criticise and educate students in any manner deemed appropriate. And she was educating them. In most cases, by cracking the whip. And very seldomly, by giving them positive reinforcement.

"HELLO! WELCOME TO LIANGJIAHE, THE VILLAGE WHERE XI JINPING, our people's leader, moved in the late 1960s and worked hard and conscientiously for seven years in his youth. My name is Tang Yunhua. I will be your guide today," a delicate girl in her twenties, with a thick woollen skirt, oversized suit jacket, high-heeled sandals, and holding an umbrella to protect her from the sun, stood before the 100 second graders from Moscow and their five chaperones.

"You are visiting here during very hot weather. Let's move a little to the side," the young guide took five steps back from the narrow sidewalk onto the well-trodden ground to let other visitors pass. The group of obedient schoolchildren followed her. "Every year during celebrations commemorating the Day of the Creation of the People's Republic of China, the birthday of Xi Dada, or Labour Day, like today, we have a huge influx of visitors. But we don't complain!" Nailed to the stone wall behind Yunhua was a large panel no less than four metres long and 1.5 metres wide depicting a young Xi Jinping surrounded by fellow members of the Communist Party of the People's Republic of China. "It's so great the young generation is interested in their own history and culture," the girl's lips stretched into a wide, friendly smile. She reached forward and kind-heartedly ruffled the neat bowl-cut hair of the boy closest to her. "And where did you come from?" the girl asked the children, trying to make a connection before the tour.

"From far away," Mao cut her off rudely, not giving the schoolchildren a chance to make friends with the random acquaintance. "And, by the way, we didn't fly 13 hours and then drive by bus over the mountains for who knows how many hours more to admire your crooked teeth! Get to the point!" Sitting in one position during the long trip hadn't helped the woman's mood, pain riddling her lower back the whole time, and now she was lashing out at anyone and everyone.

As soon as Mao started spewing her venom, the girl's smile disappeared off her face and she straightened up, as if she had been reprimanded for slouching during the singing of the national anthem.

"During interviews, when asked about the origin of his views and ideas, Xi Jinping often says, 'I am forever a son of the yellow earth. I left my heart in Liangjiahe. This village made me'," the guide said. Her face and voice were now devoid of any hint of friendliness or excitement.

For the remainder of the tour, Yunhua, the tour guide, seemed more like a robot. The children furtively threw her confused looks while Mao nodded approvingly with both of her chins.

"An authentic relic found in our village is the *yaodong* or house cave in which Xi Jinping lived during the Cultural Revolution. We consider it our greatest treasure. It's a bit tight inside, so not everyone will be able to enter at once. Please break into groups of 15 and take turns going inside," Yunhua said. She folded her umbrella and slipped through the open wooden door into the vaulted room. The schoolchildren who were closest rushed in after her, as if they hadn't heard her instructions.

"Don't embarrass me!" Mao shouted, worrying her students were about to destroy the Great Leader's sacred abode. "And you, get your heads out of the clouds!" the woman waved her cane at Yanfen and the other three teacher-chaperones. "Enough dawdling, time to organise these dimwits!"

One of the teachers to whom Mao was directing her ire moved to the door of the cave, grabbed a few of the second graders by their ears, and began dragging the extra ones out of the cave. The other three went to different spots and called the students over to them. The children didn't follow the teachers' instructions and just ran from one to the other, preventing them from forming groups.

Meanwhile, the children who ran inside first looked around the semi-darkness, bewildered. They had imagined the yaodong to contain spacious, bright rooms. Instead, they ended up in a long narrow room with an arched ceiling looking like a tunnel. Despite the two lightbulbs hanging from the ceiling, the only sources of light were the windows by the door, which for some reason were covered from sill to ceiling in sheets of newspaper. The wall opposite the door and the floor were made of dirt. The other two walls, plastered in clay, flowed together to form an arch on the ceiling. White streaks hinted the walls may have been whitewashed with lime sometime in the past.

The children's faces showed their disappointment. *"We should have gone to an amusement park instead,"* Hector thought, bored with the tour. *"It would have been way more fun."*

A solid raised platform made of a single rectangular slab of stone and clay extended along the right wall, taking up about half the room, waist height for adults but shoulder height for the second graders. The five layers of thin woven cloth spread on its flat surface probably served as mattresses. At the head of these "beds" near the wall lay neatly folded blankets and cylindrical pillows. The wall the platform was attached to was also covered in yellowed Chinese newspaper clippings, same as the windows. The only spot of colour among the clippings was a poster of Mao Zedong dressed in a military uniform. The late leader of the People's Republic of China, standing in the crimson rays of the dawn, directed his crowd of followers holding red flags to work diligently in the people's communes.

"The second bedspace on the left belonged to our great Xi Jinping," the story being told by Yunhua was falling on deaf ears, because the schoolchildren had already stopped listening. "Mao Zedong sent him here from Beijing so as a young man he could experience the difficulties of the lives of poor farmers. Mao himself lived in similar caves in Yan'an in the late 1930s and early 1940s, when the city was the centre of the Chinese Communist Revolution."

"Stop!" the guide suddenly shouted, interrupting her story. She was addressing Hector, who had hopped up to grab the mattress and was trying to crawl onto the raised platform. "It is forbidden to touch anything here! What were you thinking?" Yunhua flew over to the boy, grabbed his T-shirt, and pulled him off the platform. He fell onto the floor, landing on his knees. "Get out of here!" the guide said to the boy, pointing to the door.

"This is total bullshit," Hector mumbled to himself while leaving the house cave and brushing the dust off his knees. He hadn't expected anyone to hear his comment, but Mao just happened to be nearby right when he said it.

"Nothing is sacred to you, is it?!" the woman snapped at him. "Your tongue should be cut off for that!" She reached for the boy with her left hand, intending to grab his shoulder and shake the nonsense out of him. Without warning, he broke free and ran away.

"I'll go after him and calm him down," Yanfen suggested. She was standing three metres from the entrance to the cave, surrounded by schoolchildren who were waiting their turn to go inside.

"I'll go myself! You've already done enough," the director barked at the secretary and jogged after Hector as fast as her aching back allowed. "Keep an eye on the rest of them!"

MAO FOUND THE RUNAWAY NEARBY, JUST AROUND THE CORNER. MORE precisely she only saw half the boy, the part below the waist. Hector was standing on his tiptoes and leaning over a round concrete ledge, peering into a well. There were 70–80 metres between him and the woman. If the child suddenly lost his balance and fell over the edge, she wouldn't have time to reach the well to save him.

Mao went cold inside. A chill ran through the old woman's body, and she felt bile rise in her throat. *"I won't survive something like this again,"* she thought, her heart pounding wildly in her chest. She stopped where she stood and tried to control her frantic heartbeat by inhaling and exhaling deeply. But it didn't help. It made things worse. Her legs turned to mush, and she could barely keep her large frame upright. Mao had convinced herself she had sufficiently released her angst over her son's death and could control her emotions. But her body's instinctive behaviour said otherwise.

"Maybe I shouldn't have reacted so rashly," Mao thought, trying unsuccessfully to swallow the lump in her throat. The woman didn't notice her eyes had filled with tears. But, in the end, not a single drop rolled down her cheek. *"There's no reason to fret,"* she told herself. *"It's his fault. He provoked me. Otherwise, I wouldn't have shouted..."*

She threw her cane aside so she wouldn't frighten Hector and slowly walked up to the well drilled through the dense rock. Some idiot had neglected to shut the cover closing the opening into the well. *"Oh, I'll make sure to write a whole bunch of 'pleasantries' about this in their guest book!"* Mao thought, trying to block the image from the far distant past before her eyes when her little Wei slipped on a wet rock during a class trip and fell headfirst into a waterfall. *"No school will ever come here again after what I write!"*

"Stop what you're doing!" The director walked up to Hector noiselessly, roughly grabbed him by the shoulder, and turned him around to face her. Gnashing her teeth, she crouched down in front of him. "You should listen to me!" For the first time, the woman looked the boy straight in the eyes instead of towering over him. But it wasn't Hector's face she saw in front of her. "If they had been watching you carefully, you'd be alive today." Mao squeezed the small palms in her sweaty, cold hands with uncharacteristic gentleness. Nobody could have imagined she was capable of a gesture like that.

"Madam director, this isn't Wei — it's Hector," Yanfen's sympathetic soft voice behind Mao brought her back to reality.

The woman abruptly let go of Hector's hands. The boy was staring at her confused. She put her hand on her lower back and slowly stood up.

"I don't need you to tell me," the director sadly observed, sighing loudly, not turning to look at her secretary. Instead, she confronted Hector, "If you don't listen and obey, I'll have to send you to Zone 5, to the other Russians. And nothing good awaits you there." As usual, she didn't have anything positive to say, but at least this time her tone wasn't malicious. "It's an endless proving ground for testing nuclear weapons," Mao mumbled, more as a reminder to herself than to Hector.

Still breathing heavily, she slammed shut the well's wooden cover, checked the latch was securely in place, and shuffled over to the spot where she had dropped her cane. The woman could feel her entire body trembling from the stress — from the neat bun atop her head held together by two intersecting bamboo hairpins, down to her black, square-toed, low-heeled, thin strapped slippers.

"Are you coming?" she looked back and asked the boy. Her face was so flushed it could probably have lit a match. Hector was frozen in place, wondering why Mao hadn't hit him. But as soon as she started talking, he trailed after her. "Hand me my

cane so I don't have to bend over," the director asked. The boy picked up the cane and gave it to her, still not fully recovered from her unexpected behaviour.

Yanfen followed in their wake, deliberately staying a few metres behind. Struck by what she had just seen, the girl wondered what this would mean for her. It's unlikely Mao would forgive her for witnessing this moment of weakness.

When all three returned to the group, Yunhua the tour guide was telling the second graders about how Xi Jinping was awarded a motorcycle for his hard work, but turned it down.

"He put the public interest ahead of his personal interest. Instead, they bought two corn threshers for the Liangjiahe commune," the young guide continued, her stories mimicking the official propaganda.

"Hector should see a psychiatrist. He needs some kind of tranquilizers, because he's a not a child, he's a typhoon," Mao thought, resting the cane on her bulbous stomach and massaging her right hand, which had suddenly gone numb.

"LET GO! I WAS FIRST!"

"No, I was first!"

Hector could hear the yelling and jostling by the entrance to the school cafeteria before he got there. When he finally turned the corner of the corridor leading to the anteroom with sinks and mirrors on both sides, he saw a large crowd had already gathered. The children, hungry after a long night's sleep, were ready to storm the doors behind which breakfast was waiting.

As soon as the clock showed 8.00am, the lock clicked and a woman in a black and red uniform and tall chef's hat flung open the doors and jumped aside to avoid being knocked over by the horde of invading second graders.

Hector didn't rush into the cafeteria with everyone else. He waited while the crowd eased up a bit. His thoughts were all about maths class at noon. Today was their yearly final exam, and when the boy was nervous, like now, he would rub the cross on his wrist.

"Your pill, Hector," Dr Tsai Ai snapped him out of his daydream. In one hand he held a small clear plastic cup with an oval blue pill and in the other a larger cup with water. Hector obediently took the smaller cup, brought it to his mouth, and tilted it back, then washed the pill down with the water in the other cup. This was now a daily ritual since their trip to Liangjiahe.

Director Mao convinced him the pills would be good for him and would make him more alert and focused, helping him do maths faster and with less mistakes. After a few weeks, the boy did feel different, but not in a good way. His natural energy and curiosity were gone and replaced by lethargy, sleepiness, and indifference. Mao assured him this was temporary and would soon pass. But Yanfen had more cunning advice, suggesting he pretend to swallow the pills by hiding them under his tongue or in his cheek and then spit them out. "The main thing is to be quieter and not argue with the school staff. Especially during Mao's lessons," the young girl advised the boy. And today he listened to her for the first time.

"Don't take my food!" Hector heard some kids arguing at the other end of the table where he had sat down to have breakfast. The boy recognised the voice of his chief bully, Xiaobo, and leaned forward a little to check if it was him. It was.

"Then share your bread! You took five pieces, and I didn't get any!" one of the members of Xiaobo's gang insisted, rebelling against their leader.

"Here! Choke on it!" Xiaobo threw the bread followed by the scrambled eggs on his plate at the student who had asked him to share. A fight broke out between the boys at the table and soon other kids joined in. Within two minutes, half of Hector's class was having a food fight. The boy quietly moved to the edge of the table, ate his breakfast, and pretended not to care who was pulling whose hair and smearing egg yolk on whose school uniform a few metres away.

DR MO FENG TOOK OFF HIS SURGICAL GLOVES, GOWN, AND CAP, THROWing them into the trash. Exhausted, he pushed open the door to the pre-op unit and went into the hallway. Telling loved ones about a patient's death was nothing new for him, but it was still difficult. People in despair react in various ways.

Some throw themselves around the neck of the person delivering the news in tears. Others faint. Sometimes they go into shock. And the only consolation he as a doctor can offer relatives of the deceased is, "We did everything we could."

The man stopped for a second before entering the waiting room, took a deep breath, then pushed the door handle down and crossed the threshold.

"Who's waiting for news about Li Mao?" he asked the people scattered about the room, nervously squeezing their hands. As soon as the doors opened, they looked up at him in anticipation. "Any relatives of Li Mao?" the doctor asked again, his gaze sweeping the faces in the room. "Li Mao was hospitalised today with a stroke…" Mo Feng reminded them, but nobody responded.

The doctor left, sighed in fatigue, and walked over to the stairs leading to the admissions department on the first floor.

"…Yes, H-e-c-t-o-r Kh-a-r-a-b-e-t-s. No, not with an H, with a Kh. That is correct. And Li Mao…" the man overheard snippets of the conversation from the registration desk. Having heard his patient's name, he hurried to the desk despite being tired. As he approached, Mo Feng saw a thin plain-looking young woman with no distinguishing features other than a blue streak in her hair holding a wooden cane. "They were both brought here today, around noon. Who can I speak to about their condition?" Yanfen asked the woman in a blue lab coat, just as someone touched her shoulder lightly.

"Good evening. My name is Mo Feng," the doctor introduced himself, clasping his hands behind his back. "I accidentally overheard you asking about Li Mao. She is my patient. What is your relationship to her?"

"I'm a colleague. I'm her secretary, to be more precise…" the girl turned around and took a step towards the man. "But you won't find any closer relatives," Yanfen blurted out, understanding where the doctor was going with this. "How is she doing?"

"I'm sorry to inform you Li Mao didn't survive the operation."

"And what about Hector?" Yanfen paled, leaning on the cane, and holding her breath, fearing more bad news.

"The boy is OK. He's in room 227. You can go visit him," the woman from the admissions department said as she leaned over the desk. Yanfen exhaled in relief and a slight smile lit her face.

"I can show you where it is. I'm going that way," Mo Feng said, waving his hand in the general direction of Hector's room. The girl accepted his offer without hesitation. They took the elevator to the second floor and entered the hospital wing on the opposite side of the waiting room. "If you want to say goodbye to Li Mao," the man said to Yanfen outside the boy's room, "you can do so in half an hour." He took a watch out of his pocket and squinted as if counting something in his head. "Or perhaps a little later. They'll wheel her out on a gurney into a room through those doors," the doctor nodded towards the end of the corridor.

Thirty minutes later, Yanfen and Hector were waiting in the designated spot.

"How are you?" the girl asked the boy in the wheelchair.

"I don't know."

"Are you sure you'll be OK?"

"Yes, probably…" Just then the doors to the freight elevator opened and two orderlies rolled out a gurney with a body covered in a light blue disposable sheet.

"You have one minute," one of the men said to Yanfen and the boy. "Do you want to see the face?" he asked. Hector shook his head, "No." The man shrugged his shoulders and walked over to the windowsill to wait with his colleague.

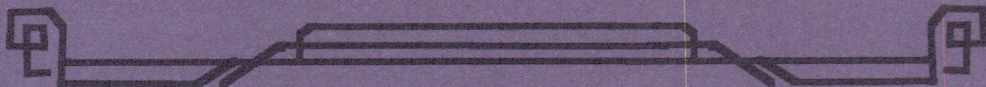

The four of them remained silent and nobody moved. Finally, realising their minute was almost up, the girl took a step towards the gurney. Just then the smartphone in her left pocket vibrated. It was a call from a number she didn't recognise, the third missed call from the same number. Annoyed, she rejected the call and put Mao's cane next to her on the gurney — the director had dropped it during the incident in the school.

"Don't forget your talisman, madam director," the girl whispered her parting words.

The orderlies were about to wheel the body away when Hector jumped up from the wheelchair, grabbed the cane off the gurney, and handed it to Yanfen. 𝖂

THE BLACK SEA WHALE CONTRIBUTORS

Oleksii Dubrov is a historian and recipient of the prestigious Gaude Polonia scholarship program in 2019. He has over eight years of experience working in the field of culture, and seventeen years of experience living in one of Ukraine's toughest cities, Kryviy Rih. A student of the humanities who loves numbers and statistics, Oleksii has been known to occasionally go over to the Dark Side (they have tasty cookies). He is currently serving in the Armed Forces of Ukraine.

Cadmus (pen name): A humble Doctor of Philosophy in History, Cadmus loves to go fishing. Sometimes he spends so much time on the riverbank waiting for a bite, the fish start telling him their stories. This may be related to his Greek roots. Cadmus is currently serving in Ukraine's Armed Forces.

Marichka Melnyk (pen name): Marichka is adept at inviting her readers to become an integral part of the story she is telling, as if they are involved in the action alongside the characters, rather than remaining bystanders, watching the story unfold from afar. The experience is always thought-provoking: she delves into complex themes which may be shocking at times, but nevertheless are begging to be explored.

Oleh Mahdych is a humble PhD in history and was a researcher in the Taras Shevchenko National Museum. Oleh can easily lecture on any historical subject taking place in any time period, making you feel as though he had lived through the events himself and saw them with his own eyes.

THE BLACK SEA WHALE CONTRIBUTORS

Sergej Sumlenny is a German political analyst, founder of the European Resilience Initiative Center in Berlin, and former Director at the Heinrich Böll Foundation Bureau in Kyiv (2015–2021). He prides himself on being a "recovering" Russian.

Nazar Tokar is an investigative reporter. Following 14 years in programming, Nazar remembered how journalism had been his first calling. Today, he writes long form non-fiction investigations alongside hosting the news site Tokar.ua & a blog on YouTube and remains committed to exploring the changing nature of digital security.

Viktoriia Antonenko often reads straight through the night, and when asked what she wanted to be when she grew up, she'd answer "a librarian." But she let her dreams grow, and began to study the story form to craft her own creations. After completing her doctorate in history, Viktoriia took on a new challenge as the Executive Editor of the Ukrainian language journal The Arc. She was born and grew up in a "bandit's" village and categorically refuses to move anywhere else.

ILLUSTRATORS

Mykhailo Aleksandrov
behance.net/mishaaleks

Oleksandr Terez
behance.net/alexterez
instagram.com/alex.terez

Beata Kurkul
instagram.com/beata_kurkul
artstation.com/noldofinve
facebook.com/beata.kurkul

Antonina Semenova
instagram.com/chagooch
facebook.com/Chagooch

Oleh Smal
facebook.com/olegsmalart

Olenka Zahorodnyk
instagram.com/alekon_zahorodnyk
behance.net/olenkazaho9602

Asta Legios
instagram.com/asta_ateralba_legios
behance.net/ateralba

Uliana Balan
facebook.com/UlyanaBalan
instagram.com/uliana.balan

DESIGNERS

Zakhar Kryvoshyya
instagram.com/zakharkryvoshyya
behance.net/zakharkryvoshyya
zakznak.com

Written, Illustrated & Designed in Ukraine
Printed in the United Kingdom